$8

GW01085759

Simon Brown was born
first nine years travellin
settled in Canberra. He
wife and young daughter.

Simon's first profession
Since then he has sold several stories to science fiction
magazines.

PRIVATEER

SIMON BROWN

HarperCollins*Publishers*

HarperCollins_Publishers_

First published in Australia in 1996
by HarperCollins_Publishers_ Pty Limited
ACN 009 913 517
A member of the HarperCollins_Publishers_ (Australia) Pty Limited Group

Copyright © Simon Brown 1996

This book is copyright.
Apart from any fair dealing for the purposes of private study,
research, criticism or review, as permitted under the Copyright Act,
no part may be reproduced by any process without written
permission. Inquiries should be addressed to the publishers.

HarperCollins_Publishers_
25 Ryde Road, Pymble, Sydney NSW 2073, Australia
31 View Road, Glenfield, Auckland 10, New Zealand
77–85 Fulham Palace Road, London W6 8JB, United Kingdom
Hazelton Lanes, 55 Avenue Road, Suite 2900, Toronto, Ontario M5R 3L2
and 1995 Markham Road, Scarborough, Ontario M1B 5M8, Canada
10 East 53rd Street, New York NY 10032, USA

National Library of Australia Cataloguing-in-publication data:

Brown, Simon, 1956- .
  Privateer.
  ISBN 0 7322 5637 2.
  I. Title.
A823.3

Cover illustration by Greg Bridges
Cover design by Darian Causby

Printed in Australia by Griffin Paperbacks, Adelaide

7 6 5 4 3 2 1
99 98 97 96

To Alison, for all her love, support and encouragement, and to my parents for all their love and patience.

Also to Edlyn, for being . . . well . . . Edlyn.

Acknowledgement

The advice, support and encouragement of Louise Thurtell, Phillip Knowles, Fiona Daniels and Terry Dowling have been invaluable. Without them, this book would have been a much inferior work.

Beginnings

The only occasions Aruzel Kidron regretted being a spacer were when his ship *Magpie* slipped between normal space and hyperspace. The transition between the two states of existence was outside of space and time. The disorientation he felt caused by his own momentary loss of existence was something he would never get used to. It was something no spacer ever got used to.

And yet . . .

And yet when it was over, when the ship was surrounded again by the stars of normal space or by the swirling tachyon tides of hyperspace, he always felt elated, as though he had touched what lay beyond death, beyond the universe, and returned to tell the tale.

This time, however, the elation was tempered by trepidation for what lay ahead.

"Do you remember the first time we crossed that hump?"

Kidron turned to meet the gaze of his executive officer, Commander Michael Kazin. He was standing by the captain's gravity couch, talking low so none of the other bridge crew could overhear.

"Thirty years ago on the tramp freighter *Lazy Heidi*," Kidron replied. "It scared the hell out of me."

"Still scares the hell out of me, Aruzel," Kazin confided. "But that's not what's worrying you."

Kidron blinked. "I didn't think it was that obvious."

"Only to me. I know you too well."

"No one has ever done this before, Michael."

"It's not too late to pull out. Our main engines are still powered up – you only have to give the word."

For a moment Kidron considered it, but then his gaze fell on the bridge's main screen. The magnified image of the planet Tunius floated there, looking like a piece of ripe fruit. A Calethar planet. An Uzdar planet.

"It has been too late ever since Jimmy Tolstoi raided the human colony on Allah's Garden."

"Tolstoi's one of us," Kazin said.

"Human he may be, but the Uzdar are his backers."

"Can you see the end of it, Aruzel? Once we hit the Uzdar, where will it lead?"

Kidron's face became impassive. He sat more erect in his couch. "It's time for you to get your team on the cutter."

Kazin was not offended by the brush-off. Kidron was both his captain and oldest friend. "On my way," he said, and made to leave.

"Michael –"

Kazin turned back.

"– at least this way we make our own future, instead of letting the Calethar make it for us."

Kazin nodded and left the bridge.

The Mendart built their freighters with nothing but function in mind, and with no allowance for beauty. The

Harmen was no exception to the rule, looking like nothing more than a series of boxes connected by a central tube for housing the crew and engines.

The freighter's captain, cut from the same practical and unimaginative cloth as the shipwright who built *Harmen*, was occupied with organising the cargo manifest and gave no second thought when informed by his duty officer that a ship had just appeared in local space. After all, he was in orbit around Tunius, home to a colony of Uzdar, the strongest of all the Calethar clans inhabiting the frontier worlds. Who would ever attack the Uzdar or their guests?

Much the same complacency affected the traffic controller on the colony itself, and even though no further visitors had been expected the appearance of a new ship aroused more curiosity than suspicion.

Both the duty officer and the traffic controller waited, unconcerned, to see what the visitor would do next.

Kidron tapped on his couch's armrest while waiting for the first reports on Tunius from his weapons officer. Lieutenant Commander Freyr Danui, well aware of the captain's impatience, refused to be hurried. She carefully rechecked the ship's sensor readings of the planet, a small desert world circling a nondescript F-class dwarf sun in the frontier sector, a huge and only barely explored section of space where dozens of alien species, humans included, were establishing new colonies and profitable trading routes.

"A moment longer," she told Kidron.

He did not answer. Danui was performing her duties scrupulously. Any mistake now could prove fatal to *Magpie* and her crew.

"Sensors confirm only one satellite, in equatorial orbit, designed for communication and weather observation; two ground-based defence installations armed with old anti-ship missiles. Also a small freighter in parking orbit, predicted 30,000-tonne mass, typical Mendart construction."

"Good! A bonus if we can catch her. Line up a beam shot on the satellite." Kidron thumbed the intercom switch by his left hand. "Commander Kazin, it's all clear. Your people ready?"

Kazin glanced at Lieutenant Toma Robinson in the pilot's seat of the cutter *Swallow*. She nodded. "We're ready to go."

Kidron turned to Danui. "That satellite targeted yet?"

"Locked on, Captain."

"Alright, Commander, you're clear to launch."

Magpie shuddered briefly as *Swallow* blasted from her berth in the privateer's belly. Kidron watched her progress directly before tracking her on the small battle screen attached to his couch.

"Any moment now . . ." he said to no one in particular.

"Captain, Friend-or-Foe signal in Calethar coming from the colony." *Magpie*'s signals officer, Lieutenant Kenza Obe, put the request over the bridge speaker. A second later the request was repeated in Interlingua, the trading language of the frontier. The speaker sounded almost bored.

"Give them our reply, Danui," Kidron ordered.

The colony's traffic controller was about to transmit the FoF signal for a third time when his control board flashed red. He looked at it, mystified at first, then horrified. He fumbled for the alert switch and flicked it. Klaxons sounded throughout the colony and blast doors slid out from recesses to seal off rooms from each other.

The traffic controller opened a line to the colony leader. She had been expecting his call.

"What is going on, Arkel?" she demanded.

"Our satellite's been destroyed. Readings indicate a beam shot from a ship that just entered real space five planetary diameters from Tunius."

"Can you identify the ship?"

"Not yet, but it has launched a smaller vessel which is heading directly for this colony."

The leader asked if *Harmen* could intercept the approaching vessel. The traffic controller referred to his screens.

"*Harmen* is not under power, Leader . . ." His words trailed off as the screens blurted new information.

"What is it? What's happening now?"

"*Harmen* is under attack. The enemy ship has fired torpedoes at her."

Harmen's captain had just completed his manifest review when the duty officer contacted him urgently.

"What's that you said about the satellite?"

"Destroyed, sir. There was a flash and then . . . nothing. The satellite's not there any more."

The captain swore under his breath.

"I'm coming to the bridge. Tell the pilot to get us out of here."

"The engines are dead cold, sir –"

The captain had already left his cabin and was now recklessly pushing himself along the central corridor towards the bridge.

"Tell him to use manoeuvring jets!" he shouted into his personal transmitter. "It doesn't matter how he does it, but get us out of this orbit!"

"Yes, sir!"

The captain guessed a beam weapon must have destroyed the satellite: short of sabotage there was no other way he knew that something could be attacked without forewarning. That meant the new ship was not only hostile, but also very well armed: certainly too well armed for *Harmen* to take on with her pitifully weak lasers.

He was halfway to the bridge when the duty officer hailed him again.

"Torpedoes, sir! The new ship's fired torpedoes at *us*!"

The captain halted his rush. He could not get to the bridge in time to do anything to rescue his command.

"Tell the crew to abandon ship," he ordered, his voice heavy. "Immediate evacuation."

Even before the duty officer could reply the captain was heading for the nearest escape pod.

Lieutenant Toma Robinson took *Swallow* through one shallow orbit around Tunius, dropping two pods of guided missiles at the start point directly over the colony. Each pod was programmed to hit one of the Calethar ground defence installations. As *Swallow* came round again to the start point the cutter's sensors showed the missiles had done their job.

"We're clear for descent," she told Kazin.

"Take us down," he ordered.

As Robinson lined up her final approach, Kazin signalled *Magpie* the raid was about to begin.

Lieutenant Obe relayed the information to Kidron. He nodded, returning his attention to the battle screen. Two red tracks showed *Magpie*'s torpedoes heading straight for the Mendart freighter.

Danui reported escape pods ejecting from the freighter. Even as she spoke the salvo of torpedoes hit the target's stern, blowing away its engines.

Kidron smiled grimly. "Good shooting there, Danui. Order Ensign Denton to take a boarding party in *Lark* to secure their prize."

A short while later *Magpie*'s second cutter launched, making for the crippled Mendart ship as quickly as her twin chemical engines could push her.

Kidron turned his attention to the escape pods. He counted seventeen of them, about right for a ship that size. For a moment he felt some sympathy for the freighter's captain, remembering briefly his own years as a merchant.

But no longer, he reminded himself. *Now I am one of the hunters.*

Without the satellite the colony leader had precious little data to work with, but she knew they were in trouble when the ground defence installations each disappeared under waves of small, powerful explosions. She ordered the militia to offer what resistance they could.

The raiders themselves arrived in a sleek cutter, sweeping low over the colony, a small laser in its belly selecting and destroying hard points and the colony's power generators. The leader gathered a handful of subordinates and hurried to the main warehouse. She barely had time to organise the warehouse's defences when the cutter landed on the colony's own spaceport, disgorging a full company of heavily armed soldiers.

"Humans!" she hissed. Through a narrow window, she watched them split into sections and spread out, each section attacking a separate building. She was impressed by their efficiency and professionalism. If only the Uzdar had given her half as many Calethar regulars she might have been able to beat them off.

A female colonist drew the leader's attention to the device on the cutter's hull.

"I can't make it out from here. My eyes aren't what they used to be."

The female clacked her jaws apologetically. "It is a Terran flying creature, Leader, black and white. I think this is the sign of *Magpie*."

Of course! The *Magpie*! Only the humans would openly attack an Uzdar colony, and only the human pirate Kidron would carry out such an attack with any hope of success.

"Here they come!" her companion shouted. She raised a hunting rifle, aimed and fired.

The leader saw two sections of human troops advancing towards the warehouse. At least she would die honourably in combat.

She raised her own weapon and started firing.

Even before *Swallow* had touched down the human troopers were leaping to the ground. Without waiting for orders they started off for their pre-assigned targets.

At first resistance was light and they were able to make cover without any casualties. The last to disembark was Kazin and his escort, five troopers under the command of Santa, one of *Magpie*'s best NCOs.

Kazin waited a few seconds to ensure the attack was going to plan then led his own team in the opposite direction. In a few minutes they were in sight of their own target, the colony's education centre. The building was a round structure surrounded by paved open ground.

"This is the bit I don't like," Santa said. She scanned other, close-by buildings for any sign of the enemy.

Kazin gave the signal to move out, taking the first step himself. Two of the troopers stayed behind in case covering fire was needed. The four humans had gone only a few metres when they heard the crack of a blaster shot. Automatically they all dropped to the ground. Kazin turned his head sideways, saw that Pasquale had caught the shot in his side. The young trooper's blood was pumping onto the paving.

Kazin heard return fire, then silence. For a moment he thought the attacker must have been killed, then a second blaster shot bit into the paving less than a metre from his face. Bits of flying stone lacerated his cheeks and forehead. He knew if they stayed here they would be killed off one by one.

"Let's move!" he cried, jumping to his feet. He focused on the round building in front and ran as fast as he could. The entrance was sealed with a glass panel, and he burst through it with his arms over his head, somersaulting as he did so. He landed on his back, the breath knocked out of him. Santa landed next to him, then another trooper. He recognised Jorge. He looked outside, saw Yu's body spread-eagled on the ground near the entrance. He stood up, splinters of glass falling from him like crystal leaves.

Santa ran into him, pushing him against one wall. A blaster shot missed them by centimetres.

"I see the bastard," Santa breathed, pointing to a low stone structure forty metres away. It had a single window, and framed within it was a dark shape. She aimed quickly and fired two rounds. The troopers they had left behind saw where Santa was shooting and fired at the same spot. Kazin could not tell if they hit anything, but he could waste no more time.

"Stay here," he told Jorge and made his way to the hub of the building. Santa followed behind, alert for any ambush.

The hub was a large room with a domed roof pierced by several light wells. The walls were lined with machines Kazin knew were computers but looked nothing like their human equivalents. This was where the colony's main library and database were kept. He headed for the largest of the machines and got to work while Santa kept watch.

He had broken into Calethar libraries before using a tribe of viruses he had devised himself, but he had never attempted it on one owned by the Uzdar. The computer's defences seemed patchy and badly maintained but one persistent code continued shadowing his viruses without actually interfering. He shrugged. If it did not stop him from getting what he wanted he was not going to waste time worrying about it. In the background he heard the fighting continuing throughout the rest of the colony. Calethar and humans were dying out there. He shook his head, struggled to keep his attention on the job at hand. The sooner he finished here the sooner they could be away.

His interrogator emitted a high tone, telling him all his viruses had returned, carrying with them all the data they had been ordered to scavenge. Kazin removed it from the computer. The shadow code had not re-appeared, and he sighed in relief. With luck, the Uzdar would never know their library had been infiltrated.

"Time to get out of here," he said, and signalled Lieutenant Robinson back on *Swallow* that their primary mission had been accomplished.

The leader was blinded by blood splashing in her eyes. For a second she thought she had been hit, but when she wiped her eyes she saw that the blood had come from her companion. She knelt down next to the wounded female, gasping when she saw the injury – most of her left arm was missing. The female was in shock. Her eyelids fluttered and she was panting.

"You'll live," the leader said.

The female nodded, grimacing in pain, then opened her jaws to say something.

"Don't speak."

"The firing . . . it's stopped."

The leader listened for a moment, realised the female was right. She stood up to peep through the window. There were no signs of their attackers. She turned to another of the defenders, a large male.

"Can you see any humans?"

"No, Leader. But the shooting has stopped every-where."

She called the male over to look after her wounded companion, then made for the warehouse entrance. She ran to the next building, the colony's medical centre, and called out before swinging open its door and barging in. Four surprised defenders looked up, ready to shoot despite her warning.

"The humans. Did you see where they went?"

None of them had, but from a small window in the wall opposite the door she saw small groups of Calethar emerging from their defensive positions, as curious as she was.

It's a trap! she thought. *They're luring us out into the open!*

The leader rushed outside, shouting for everyone to return to their posts, when a sudden blast of hot air threw her to the ground. She rolled, felt her arm catch awkwardly underneath her body and snap. She rolled again, and saw the enemy cutter flash low over the colony as it made its escape, the roar of its engines drowning out her cry of pain.

Magpie recovered her cutters and prepared to jump out of the system. As soon as *Swallow* docked, Kazin went to the bridge and gave Kidron a full report on the raid.

"We lost five. Seven others seriously wounded, but they'll live. The *Swallow*'s hold is filled with equipment and weapons, most of them still in their crates and boxes."

"Some of them just delivered by the Mendart freighter," Kidron interrupted. "And in exchange the Mendart were taking artefacts the Uzdar had procured from the natives of Tunius. They will get a good price back home."

"Do you think the Uzdar will believe that's all we were after?"

Kidron shrugged. "As long as you covered your tracks getting the information from their library. We're still deciphering it, but so far most of it concerns ship movements between their colonies."

"And? Did you get the proof we need?"

"It looks promising, but it's still too early to tell," Kidron replied.

Kazin snorted. "You'll need more than *promising* when news of this raid gets out. The Uzdar will be screaming to the Federation to impound *Magpie*."

"True," Kidron agreed, "but they'll have to kill me first."

"That's probably what the Calethar are hoping you'll say," Kazin said without irony.

The leader, her broken arm sealed in healing gel and trussed to her side, was inspecting the damage done to her colony when she got word the generators had been repaired.

"Good. And the transmitter?"

The messenger looked down at his feet. "At least another two days, Leader."

She breathed deeply, fighting off the weariness she felt. Although few of the colony's structures had been seriously damaged, much of its equipment had been destroyed or taken.

And she had lost forty colonists.

"Not good enough," she told the messenger. "I don't care how it's done, or what parts from the rest of the colony have to cannibalised, but I want that transmitter operating by tomorrow morning. I have to let our people on Dramorath know what's happened here."

The messenger nodded and hurried away.

Chapter 1

Magpie entered normal space so smoothly and with so little loose energy she barely registered on Hecabe's long-range sensors, but Hecabe was a border world and its guardians – computer and human – were ever alert. Within seconds of the ship's arrival, the guardians had transmitted a Friend-or-Foe signal and armed the planet's orbiting defences.

Kidron ordered Lieutenant Obe to broadcast *Magpie's* identification signal, though by now Hecabe's defence computers would have recognised the ship by her engine's signature. It always paid to be polite to the authorities, especially when you were returning to your home port.

Lieutenant Awaba Marin, the navigation officer, told Kidron two ships were already in orbit around Hecabe.

"A busy day," Kazin muttered. A border world like Hecabe might be visited by no more than two or three ships in a week; to have that many at one time threatened to overwhelm the planet's traffic control.

"Scratch that, Captain," Marin said, reading from his screen. "One ship's in orbit, registered *Cachalot*, freighter ex-York. Second ship is a customs vessel. *Magpie's* next in line."

Within a few minutes Hecabe traffic control confirmed Marin's readings, and transmitted the co-ordinates for the ship's course to orbit. "Welcome home, *Magpie*."

"Nice to be home, Hecabe," Obe replied as Marin fed the co-ordinates into the ship's computers.

From now until *Magpie* reached her designated orbit there was little Kidron could do, but he stayed on the bridge because its wide screens gave the best picture of the approaching planet and its swirling orange and blue surface. As his ship closed, it would be possible to make out the green circles that marked settlements and cultivation. Eventually, sometime in the far future, all of Hecabe's land masses would be green instead of orange. Kidron, born and raised on a wild and barely populated Hecabe, was glad in a way he would not live to see those days. Hecabe was home, and home was orange deserts, copper-blue seas and wisps of struggling cloud.

But he knew as humans expanded into the frontier sector, the border worlds would become the old wave, settling into a kind of genteel prosperity. It was ironic – no how matter how civilised they became, planets like Hecabe would always be regarded as wild and dangerous by humans living on one of the old worlds such as Earth and Oceania, but humans living on the new colonies already regarded the border worlds as stultified, even reactionary.

Kidron smiled to himself when he remembered that was exactly how he had viewed Hecabe as a youth, and why he had become a spacer in the first place. He had signed on the *Lazy Heidi* the same day as Michael Kazin.

Thirty years ago, he thought ruefully. He and Kazin spent several years working their way up the merchant ranks until they had saved enough to buy a ship of their own, an intrasystem transporter so old most of its mass was taken up with ancient engines and life support systems. But the pair worked hard and long, investing in newer, larger and more powerful ships. Eventually they accrued the credits they needed to fulfil their oldest dream – to place an order with a shipyard for a vessel built from the hull up to their specifications. The result was *Magpie*.

Something on the screen broke his reverie. There was a distortion above the arc of Hecabe. Other eyes on the bridge saw it as well, knowing what it meant but as yet unconcerned.

"Another visitor," Kazin said. A flash of intense blue light heralded the arrival of another ship in normal space, though in a much more spectacular manner, and in a much greater hurry, than *Magpie*.

"That's a good way to lose a lot of energy," Kidron remarked to no one in particular.

"A good way to get killed quickly," Kazin added, checking the readouts on his console. "They weren't far from atmosphere. Their captain's either very cocky or very stupid."

"Captain, the new entry's high-energy signature is hiding its identity," Marin reported.

Cocky, stupid or very canny, Kidron thought, suddenly uncomfortable.

"Course is set straight for us."

Everybody's gaze lifted to the screen.

"Captain, we can't get in touch with the newcomer," Obe said, "and Hecabe reports it refuses to respond to FoF."

Kidron spoke to Danui. "Expect incoming," he ordered, "and power up the beam generator."

Even as he spoke, Kazin was sounding battle stations over the ship intercom. Lights dimmed and the alarm klaxon sounded in the bowels of the ship.

"How are our verniers?" Kidron asked. The small chemically powered engines were usually sealed and cold, but they had been warming up for the final orbit approach.

"Fully operational," Kazin replied.

Kidron let out a sigh of relief. If this was an attack at least his ship would not be an easy target.

"Particle beam energised," Danui reported.

"Maintain our present course," Kidron ordered Marin. "There's no need to let them think they've startled us."

"Look!" cried someone on the bridge. "On the screen!"

Kidron glanced up in time to see two small yellow haloes brighten quickly, then dim and die out.

"Torpedoes!" Kazin shouted.

"Salvo away!"

The report was in Calethar, but Captain Jimmy Tolstoi knew enough of the language to understand what was said.

"We have them!" said Kumla of the Uzdar.

Tolstoi glanced at his executive officer, saw the alien's crest flattened with suppressed excitement.

"We have nothing yet," Tolstoi said angrily. "That's *Magpie* out there, not some dilapidated freighter."

Kumla snorted. "We have caught the humans unaware."

"She is twice our size and better armed," Tolstoi reminded him. "Order a second salvo loaded."

"We won't need it," Kumla said, but relayed the command anyway.

Tolstoi turned to his helm-captain. "Report!"

"Torpedoes are on course."

"Can we manoeuvre?"

"Our velocity is too high for anything fancy."

"I tell you it isn't necessary," Kumla said. "This will be a great victory!"

Tolstoi was getting sick of the Calethar's crowing. "A victory? We shouldn't even be here!"

Kumla regarded him coolly. "We have our orders from Dramorath."

Tolstoi tried to control his anger. *Fedarwa* was *his* ship. *He* was the captain.

Kumla seemed to read his mind. "The Uzdar paid for this vessel."

"That was my first mistake," Tolstoi said bitterly. "My second was to let the Uzdar crew her."

"Captain, noble Kumla," interrupted the helm-captain calmly, "we are in a battle. And *Magpie* has just changed course."

Magpie swung violently as all her port verniers fired. Hecabe lurched from the screen. Despite being strapped into gravity couches most of the crew were left breathless by the emergency procedure. Cameras, now controlled by the battle computer, locked again on the fast-approaching enemy.

"Captain, we've identified the attacking ship," Marin reported. "It's . . . it's *Fedarwa*, sir, Jimmy Tolstoi's ship!"

19

Kazin, wide-eyed, glanced at Kidron. Jimmy Tolstoi was probably the most despised human in known space. He attacked human freighters, not alien, and his vessel, the sleek *Fedarwa*, was Calethar-built.

"He's coming in too fast for his own sensors to work efficiently, or to be able to manoeuvre," Kidron said evenly.

"Another salvo!"

For a second time the screen showed the blazing telltale haloes of torpedoes accelerating to attack speed.

"Get a lock on *Fedarwa*," he ordered Danui.

"Their first salvo is expended," Marin reported. The enemy's first brace of torpedoes had run out of fuel; no longer able to keep up with *Magpie*, they self-destructed.

"I have a lock," Danui reported.

The whole bridge fell silent. Kidron thought he could see light from Sabbath, Hecabe's sun, glint off something long and metallic just this side of the planet.

"Fire," he ordered.

Even as he ordered the second salvo launched, Tolstoi knew it was too late. *Magpie* had the weather-gauge, as his seafaring forebears on Earth would have said, and there was nothing he could do about it.

"What do you think of your victory now?" he asked Kumla.

The Calethar ignored the question.

Tolstoi silently cursed his alien allies, then cursed himself for ever accepting their backing.

"*Magpie*'s particle beam has a lock on us," the helm-captain reported.

I am going to die, Tolstoi thought. *I don't want to die with these –*

"Open the fuel tanks to the chemical engines," Kumla ordered. He looked at his captain. "*Fedarwa* and all on board must be obliterated," he explained. "No one must know there were Calethar serving on this ship."

Before Tolstoi could answer *Magpie*'s beam weapon hit them full on, tearing through the ship, peeling away its hull like the skin of an orange. Then the beam hit the open fuel tanks and *Fedarwa* disappeared behind a huge ball of fire.

It seemed to Tolstoi he had been swallowed by a sun.

Magpie's main screen was engulfed by a burst of light so fierce some of the crew had to raise their arms to shield their eyes. As shape and colour slowly seeped back into the screen, everyone saw what at first seemed to be no more than a smudge over the rim of Hecabe. As they watched, the smudge grew slowly into a cloud of spreading debris. It was all that remained of Jimmy Tolstoi and his ship.

"What the hell did we hit?" Kazin wondered aloud. Before anyone could answer, *Magpie* shuddered violently. The sound of a distant explosion echoed over the intercom and rattled through the hull. She had been struck by *Fedarwa*'s second salvo. Sections were sealed off and damage reports started coming in. Within a few seconds Kidron knew the damage was serious but not fatal.

Kazin looked strangely at his captain. "Too close," he said.

"Too close for *Fedarwa*, at any rate," Kidron replied grimly.

Chapter 2

On the first day of Midmonth on the border world of Hecabe, two events occurred which drastically altered the course of Aaron Lynch's life.

The first involved the destruction of the traitor–pirate Jimmy Tolstoi, who made the greatest and last mistake of his career by attacking *Magpie*. The second involved Lynch's uncle and guardian, Maurice N'Djama, who finally realised that he was a better merchant than parent, and resolved to rectify the situation as soon as possible.

On the day in question, Lynch was in his uncle's warehouse checking on a new consignment of farm machinery recently arrived from Newton, a heavily populated and industrialised planet orbiting a sun some twelve light years from Hecabe's own. There was over 200 tonne of equipment to match against his record of the manifest, and though Lynch had begun just after first light, it was well into the afternoon before he was sure the consignment was intact.

The major delay was his constant daydreaming. He wanted to be anywhere except the warehouse, and preferably off Hecabe. He was convinced there was no duller place in the universe than this planet, and no duller jobs than those his uncle handed to him.

Thinking about his uncle made Lynch short-tempered. N'Djama insisted the youth's destiny was to follow in his footsteps and one day take over his business. But first he had to learn the business from the ground up.

It seemed to Lynch he had been on the *ground* for far too long and he was overdue to be moved *up*. His uncle disagreed.

What really rankled for Lynch was that there was nothing he could do about the situation. N'Djama was his legal guardian and had been for thirteen years, ever since Lynch's parents had died in an aircar accident when he was only four years old.

Lynch knew the arrangement had not been entirely to N'Djama's liking either. His mother's brother had made a virtue of his bachelor lifestyle, assiduously avoiding any family responsibility. Then suddenly he was a father in all but name to a small child old enough to sense he was more burden than blessing to his uncle.

And in those thirteen years they had never really formed a comfortable relationship. Lynch was grateful for everything N'Djama had done for him – the merchant had never shirked his duties as a guardian – but had never grown close to him, never thought of him as a parent. Lynch was intelligent and perceptive enough to realise his uncle respected and even liked him, but also found his lack of interest in the business both confusing and ungrateful.

Even their physical appearances reflected their differences – N'Djama short, powerfully built, as solid and stable as a rock; Lynch long and lean, always looking hungry for something more. The only thing they shared in common was dark olive skin and hair as black as midnight.

N'Djama constantly tried instilling in his nephew a sense of responsibility and an interest in the merchant business. For his part, Lynch constantly daydreamed about a more exciting and challenging life: captain of a Federation cruiser would do nicely, he thought, or a crewmember on one of the human privateers that helped keep the frontier sector safe for human colonisation.

The only concession N'Djama ever made to Lynch's wilder ambitions was to let him learn how to pilot a shuttle, the small intrasystem craft necessary for transporting goods and personnel between large ships and a planet's surface. N'Djama owned a handful of these broad-beamed craft and Lynch often flew one for his uncle's firm. N'Djama had hoped it would be enough for his nephew, that having realised one dream he might settle down and learn the business. Instead, it made Lynch yearn for more; he had touched the fringe of space – the beginning of adventure, as he saw it – and he was impatient to go further, to fly higher, to leave Hecabe far behind.

And here I am counting farm machinery, Lynch thought angrily. He took a deep breath in preparation for comparing his account with the original manifest when Abu Mahmed, a stevedore and one of his closest friends, called him to come and see what was being reported on the videonet news.

In the common room everyone had stopped what they were doing to watch the holographic image of a newsreader. The reader's voice was excited and tense.

". . . and now, an update on today's main news story – the destruction of the Calethar-built raider *Fedarwa* and the death of its captain Jimmy Tolstoi at the hands of Aruzel Kidron's *Magpie* earlier this morning in orbit around Hecabe. We now have holos of the action as recorded and processed by *Magpie*'s own battle computers."

Lynch paid more attention. *Fedarwa*? And *Magpie*? Although bored by any discussion of interstellar politics and economics, like every citizen of the border worlds he knew the names of both ships. *Fedarwa* and its captain were universally feared and despised, while *Magpie* was regarded with awe and Kidron looked on as a hero, especially on Hecabe, his home world.

The reader disappeared. In his place there formed a patch of dark space, a three-dimensional canvas decorated with stars and, near the bottom, the swollen orange belly of Hecabe.

"The point of light closest to Hecabe is not a star but in fact the freighter *Cachalot*," said the reader's voice in the background. "Next to it is a customs vessel." There was a blue flash near the middle of the image. "This is *Fedarwa* now, broaching normal space and approaching *Magpie* at battle speed."

Lynch watched, fascinated, caught up in the replayed drama. At first *Fedarwa* was nothing more than another bright point of light in the heavens, but slowly it grew into a vague, silvery blur. "This is now under great magnification, of course," the reader commented, his voice suddenly subdued, anticipating the action.

The report, condensed and speeded up, went through the whole action until the destruction of *Fedarwa*. Lynch found it hard to accept that all of this had occurred while he was counting farm machinery.

The videonet showed spreading debris where once had been Tolstoi's ship. The main hull, ripped apart from internal explosions, looked like a dissected whale, its ribs open to space. As Lynch watched, the image shuddered violently. "Unfortunately, *Magpie* did not come through unscathed. One torpedo hit the privateer on its starboard wing. At this time we have no casualty reports."

The reader's face returned, looking appropriately serious, and he introduced a report on some local issue. Lynch strode out of the common room, followed by Mahmed.

"Well, Jimmy Tolstoi gone," Mahmed said. "None too soon, most would say –"

"Mahmed, how long ago did the report say this happened?"

Mahmed shrugged. "This morning, I think."

Lynch started muttering to himself. Mahmed looked on, amused, accustomed to his friend becoming absorbed suddenly with one of his daydreams. Then he noticed Lynch was actually mouthing numbers. Lynch *hated* numbers – they smacked too much of accounting for his liking.

"What are you counting, Aaron?" he asked, mystified.

"How long do you think it would take *Magpie* to reach *Fedarwa*'s hull?"

"Ten hours at least. *Magpie* was a good 50,000 klicks from Hecabe. *Fedarwa* was right on top of us. Why do you need to know?"

"Is one of the shuttles ready?"

"You know better than to ask. Your uncle would have my hide if it were otherwise . . ." Mahmed paused, studying Lynch's expression. "Tell me you're not thinking what I think you're thinking."

Lynch smiled. "Why not? *Fedarwa*'s unclaimed."

"It's blown to kingdom come."

"There must be at least a few pieces left, and it's Calethar-built."

"Aaron, I cannot believe even you would take such a risk. *Fedarwa* is not our kill."

"Irrelevant as far as salvage laws go. If we get there first we can claim her."

Mahmed hesitated. His friend was right about that. Then he considered the consequences. "You'll be the most unpopular man on Hecabe," he said flatly.

"I'll also be one of the richest."

Mahmed's eyes opened. He had not considered *that* consequence. "That's an excellent point. You'll be needing a co-pilot."

"Captain, we're reading a small craft, shuttle-size, ascending from Hecabe and heading for *Fedarwa*. The craft is moving like a bat out of hell."

Kidron checked his own screen. Danui, as usual, was one step ahead of everyone else. Kidron told Obe to hail the craft's crew and ask their intentions. As Obe transmitted the request and then listened to the reply, his expression changed from one of boredom to surprise.

"Captain, they say they're going to stake salvage rights on *Fedarwa*'s remains."

Kidron was astounded. No one had ever tried to claim one of his ship's kills before.

"Tell them to bugger off," said Kazin, who had come onto the bridge as Danui was making her report.

Obe glanced at Kazin, then back to Kidron. "Sir?"

Kidron waved his hand. "They're within their rights, Commander." Kazin mumbled something to himself and looked away. "But there's nothing to stop us from getting there first."

"*Magpie*'s a privateer, not a racing yacht," Kazin said.

"I wasn't thinking of *Magpie*. Send Denton with *Lark* –"

"Denton's on the casualty list," Kazin reminded him. "One of those wounded by *Fedarwa*'s parting salvo."

"Then send *Swallow* and Robinson," he said, starting to lose his patience. "Tell her to reach *Fedarwa*'s remains as quickly as possible."

"Captain, the shuttle is no more than forty minutes from *Fedarwa*," Marin said. "*Swallow* will have to burn a lot of fuel to get there first."

"Then *tell* Robinson to burn a lot of fuel."

"We have company," Mahmed told Lynch.

"A cutter," said Lynch, studying the navigation screen above his head, "and moving at a rapid clip."

"*Magpie* doesn't want to lose her prize."

"Can we beat the cutter?"

Mahmed checked the shuttle's fuel cells. "We can't afford to match her velocity, Aaron. You burned a month's supply just getting out of atmosphere. If we lose another gram we won't have enough to re-enter safely."

Lynch cursed and checked the navigation screen a second time. "What's this?" he asked, pointing to an unidentified blip.

Mahmed consulted his computer. "A part of *Fedarwa*, apparently. The engine mounting and starboard –"

"What mass?" Lynch demanded tersely.

"About 300 tonne, but I don't see –"

"Salvage laws allow a claim to be made for a ship on five per cent of its total mass. *Fedarwa*'s predicted mass was 5,500 tonne."

Mahmed, excited now, calculated the distance between the shuttle and the debris. "We can get there well before the cutter reaches *Fedarwa*'s hull."

Lynch grinned at his friend. "Abu, get the salvage beacon ready, and then start dreaming about all the things you're going to do with your prize money."

The first hint of trouble Kidron had was Obe's startled expression. The signals officer turned slowly to face Kidron, still listening to whatever transmission was coming through.

Kidron sighed. "What is it, Kenza?"

"*Fedarwa* has been secured by a citizen of Hecabe, sir. His name is Aaron Lynch –"

"How the hell can he do that?" Kazin demanded, his face turning red. "He hasn't a hope of reaching the hull before *Swallow* –"

"He didn't need to, Commander," Obe said. "He has reached a section of the ship with enough mass to legitimise his claim. The government regrets to inform us that *Fedarwa* is now out of our jurisdiction."

Kazin opened his mouth to say something, but shook his head instead. He was surprised to hear his captain laughing.

"What's so bloody funny?"

"The presumption of this Lynch character." He leaned closer to Kazin and said in a low voice: "Doesn't he remind you of a certain young spacer from thirty years ago, Michael?"

Kazin snorted. "Someone's going to have to tell Robinson on the *Swallow*."

Kidron's laughter evaporated as quickly as water on a hotplate. He looked apologetically at his signals officer. "Kenza, another job for you . . ."

"What?!" Lieutenant Toma Robinson could not believe her ears. Obe had to repeat his message.

"Return to *Magpie*, Toma. We lost the race."

"*Fedarwa* was our kill, Kenza –"

"The Captain's orders, Lieutenant. Return immediately."

"Affirmative, *Magpie*. Robinson out."

It took Robinson seven minutes to reduce the cutter's velocity and get her heading back to her mother ship, and during the whole time the lieutenant's anger simmered just below boiling point; it almost went over when she received a transmission from the interloping shuttle.

"Better luck next time!" came the message.

Robinson considered buzzing the shuttle, but discounted the idea when she thought of how Kidron and the authorities on Hecabe would react. She settled for sending a one-word transmission of her own.

"Bastards."

Chapter 3

Lynch and Mahmed had not expected a hero's welcome, but nor had they expected Maurice N'Djama to be waiting for them at the shuttleport lounge. He stood there like a colossus, legs wide apart, hands on hips, his square head giving the impression it was carved from concrete rather than flesh and bone.

The two friends stopped short, uncertain what to do. Mahmed broke the silence first.

"I just remembered, Aaron, I forgot to complete the shuttle logbook."

Mahmed threw Lynch a sympathetic glance and walked away before the startled Lynch could say anything.

"Hello, Uncle Maurice," Lynch said lightly, approaching the fuming monolith. "I guess you've heard about my claim –"

"*Your* claim!" N'Djama roared. "Where did you get that idea from?"

"Mahmed and I have placed a salvage beacon on *Fedarwa*," said Lynch. "We now own the remains –"

"You own nothing, nephew. You used *my* shuttle, *my* beacon, and did it on *my* time with *my* stevedore as co-pilot."

Lynch spread his arms in appeal. "But Uncle Maurice –"

"Be quiet, Aaron! Your stunt may have cost N'Djama Enterprises a few million credits, not to mention the loss of goodwill from the people of this planet."

"Millions of credits?"

"If you had taken only a modicum of interest in my business you would know I am one of Captain Aruzel Kidron's principal backers. Furthermore, I handle and distribute the booty he brings back to Hecabe. What do you think Kidron's attitude will be when he discovers my own nephew cheated him of his kill, and used my equipment and staff with which to do it?"

"Uncle Maurice –"

N'Djama closed the distance between them in three strides. "The point is, my idiot nephew, you didn't stop to consider the consequences of your actions. You never do! Not only has your jaunt in orbit possibly cost me Captain Kidron's business, it has also delayed distribution of the Newton consignment of farm machinery."

"I completed the manifest, Uncle," Lynch objected.

"Against the original?" N'Djama demanded.

Lynch blinked. He had not. He had left for the shuttleport with Mahmed as soon as he had heard the videonet news report of the battle between *Magpie* and *Fedarwa*. All the elation he had experienced when the authorities recognised his salvage claim now flooded out of him, leaving him empty and weary.

"Well?" N'Djama insisted.

"No, Uncle."

N'Djama took a deep breath, gained control of his temper. "Go home, Aaron," he said evenly. "Wait for me there. I may be a few hours, but under no circumstances are you to leave before I return. Do you understand?"

Lynch nodded and left the lounge, feeling his uncle's gaze boring into the back of his skull.

When *Magpie* entered her assigned parking orbit around Hecabe, Kidron flew *Lark* down to Salem, Hecabe's capital and only large city. He was met at the spaceport by an official aircar that took him to the city's commercial centre, a cluster of low, drab buildings that bordered a wide, slow-flowing river the locals jokingly called the Styx. He was dropped off outside the most prominent of the buildings, a three-storey bunker with few windows and only one entrance. Kidron entered the building, walked straight up to the security desk and asked the guard to let Commodore Uvarov know he had arrived.

The guard recognised Kidron but pretended to be unimpressed. He pressed a switch on his desk's intercom and quietly spoke into it, then glanced up at the visitor and nodded towards a flight of stairs near the entrance.

The staircase was badly in need of repair, and Kidron had to watch his footing. On the second floor he turned right into a dingy corridor decorated with shabby wallpaper and ancient stains; here and there plaster the colour of old bone showed through. Grim glass-panelled doors lined the way like dark, watchful eyes. There was a single, wan light for the whole corridor. Kidron was glad he was a spacer and not an idler, the spacer term for anyone who made their living on a planet instead of on a ship. Not for the first time he wondered how anyone could ever tolerate working in conditions like this.

The last door was lit from the inside, and Kidron entered without knocking. There was a single desk in the room, an odd assortment of chairs, and ancient fibre cables strewn over the floor, all of them connected to computers, screens or videolibraries. Behind the desk sat a woman who appeared to be in her sixties, her grey hair tied behind in a bun. Her face was lined and sallow, and although her eyes were sunk deep in her skull they were lively and alert.

"Marie," Kidron said, dropping into one of the seats.

Commodore Uvarov, local representative of the Federation navy and chief of Hecabe's intelligence services, eyed him coldly.

"Goodness, if it isn't the saviour of human civilisation," she said dryly. "Welcome home, Aruzel."

"Not the warmest welcome I've ever received," he replied.

"Aruzel, what *have* you done?"

"What are you referring to, precisely?"

"The attack on the Uzdar colony on Tunius."

"The Uzdar attacked Allah's Garden."

"Jimmy Tolstoi attacked Allah's Garden, not the Uzdar."

"Tolstoi's sponsors were the Uzdar. The *Fedarwa* was a converted Calethar frigate."

Uvarov closed her eyes, rubbing her temples with the tips of her fingers.

"We have no proof the Uzdar sponsored Tolstoi, Captain, and now you've escalated the tension between the Federation and the Calethar outworlds to a new high, perhaps beyond what is diplomatically tolerable."

"What does that mean?" Kidron asked guardedly.

She opened her eyes, stared at a point somewhere behind Kidron's head. "It means that the frontier sector, up to now occupied by the colonies and trading fleets of a dozen different races, looks like becoming a full-fledged war zone that could spill over to the border worlds."

"The frontier sector has been a war zone for nearly a decade."

"Skirmishing, Aruzel, between pirates, renegades and privateers. The violence was contained. Both the Federation and the chief Calethar outworld clans, including the Uzdar, stayed out of it. That may no longer be possible."

"The Uzdar have always been a part of it," Kidron argued. "Not just behind Tolstoi, but also behind raiders from the minor clans and other races such as the Mendart."

Uvarov leaned forward so her elbows rested on the desk. "It comes back to proof."

Kidron held out a holographic memory cube.

"What's this?"

He smiled, placed the cube in front of her. "Your proof, Commodore. This is what I went to Tunius for. Recorded messages between Uzdar colonies, their clan world Dramorath and the *Fedarwa*, detailing co-ordinates and objectives for raids on nine human colonies in the frontier, including Allah's Garden."

Uvarov did not move. She stared at the cube.

"It's what we've always wanted, Marie," Kidron continued. "Now we know for sure."

"You're an extremely dangerous man, Aruzel." She reached out for the cube, turned it in her hands as she played with it. "You know they sent *Fedarwa* to intercept you because of Tunius, don't you?"

"I figured as much. They want to hit back."

"And now that Tolstoi has failed, how long do you think it will be before they try something else? A series of raids directed against Hecabe, for example?"

"That's a specious argument. It was only a matter of time anyway before the Calethar and their allies decided to raid as far as the border worlds."

"Are you sure you're not saying this simply to justify your own incursions against the Calethar?"

Kidron sat back, not liking the direction the interview was taking.

"Everyone knows you have a grudge against them," she coaxed.

"I have been commissioned by this planet's government and leading citizens, through your office, to carry out my raids in the frontier sector," he said stiffly. "I have brought back booty, enriching Hecabe's coffers, and gained valuable intelligence on the progress and movements of alien races in the region."

Uvarov smiled. "You didn't answer my question."

"The Federation and the Calethar are the only two contenders for position of dominance in the frontier sector because we are the only races with substantial territory on its borders and the only races with significant military strength. We have to hit them hard now, damaging their trade routes and undermining their influence wherever we can."

"You're talking about war between the Federation and the Calethar High Council. We don't want that. The border worlds would be devastated."

"The Calethar are already planning for such a war," Kidron countered.

"Proof," Uvarov said.

Kidron pointed to the memory cube still in her hands. "There's your proof, Marie."

"The most this will do, if it contains what you say it contains, is implicate the Uzdar in Tolstoi's raids." She paused, as if trying to find the right words for what she had to say next.

"Aruzel, I've been instructed by the government of Hecabe not to renew your warrant." Before he could interrupt she held up her hands. "It thinks you've gone too far. Everyone knows the story of how the Calethar ambushed one of your trading parties on a frontier world back in the days when you were still a merchant. Everyone knows you became a privateer to avenge their deaths. But now people are scared of what the Calethar will do next."

Kidron looked at her in disbelief. "You can't be serious. After all *Magpie* and her crew have done for Hecabe!"

"I'm sorry, but it's not me you have to convince. The government feels it is necessary to deny you official recognition; by doing so it hopes to placate the Uzdar, and to deflect any retribution, military or mercantile, away from Hecabe."

"Onto *Magpie* alone," Kidron said bitterly.

"If it's any consolation, it intends to continue its financial support. It will extend you credit on the booty taken during your last voyage so you can resupply *Magpie*, including weapons from the government armoury. All this is unofficial and deniable, of course."

"And if *Magpie* or members of her crew are taken in action?"

"Then as far as Hecabe is concerned, you were working on your own."

"That makes us nothing more than pirates," Kidron scoffed.

"Aruzel, you were nothing more than pirates before. Hecabe's warrant merely recognised your usefulness to its government. That government is now distancing itself from you as fast as it can."

"Because it is afraid of the Calethar."

"And because the Federation is placing great pressure on Hecabe and other border worlds to cut all ties with human privateers."

Kidron was astounded. "Why?"

"The Federation wants the destabilisation in the frontier sector to end."

"The Federation has never interfered before. If they'd shown some interest ten years ago the present situation would never have arisen."

"Be that as it may, they are interested now."

Kidron stood up to leave.

"Where are you going?"

"To see a man about a ship."

When Lynch got home he considered drowning his sorrows with a bottle of his uncle's best imported scotch, but figured he was in enough trouble already. Besides, he would need all his wits about him if he wanted to argue his case convincingly when his uncle confronted him with his misdemeanours and passed judgment and punishment.

N'Djama finally returned home two hours after Lynch. Instead of calling his nephew to his office immediately, N'Djama ignored him. Lynch saw a visitor arrive and be ushered in to see him. The visitor was vaguely familiar but too far away for Lynch to see him properly.

There was nothing he could do but wait.

"I'm glad you could come," N'Djama said, offering his guest a seat and a drink.

Captain Kidron took the seat reluctantly; he felt at a disadvantage sitting down while others remained standing. In this instance, however, he would do everything possible to appease his host.

"I was grateful for your invitation," he replied truthfully.

"How did your meeting go with Commodore Uvarov?"

Kidron blinked. He had assumed those meetings had always been if not secret then at least confidential.

"There is no need to tell me if it upsets you," N'Djama added quickly. "But I want you to know that as a member of the government I bitterly opposed the decision not to renew your official warrant."

"Thank you." *Who is trying to appease who here?* Kidron wondered.

"However, I did not ask you around this afternoon to discuss that matter – it is now strictly an issue between you and Uvarov. Instead, I want to discuss with you the matter of *Fedarwa*. As you have probably discovered by now, the man who claimed the vessel was an employee of mine and used one of my shuttles to do the job."

Kidron nodded.

"But what you may not know," N'Djama continued hurriedly, "is that the employee in question is also my nephew."

Kidron's eyes widened in surprise.

"Legally, there is nothing you can do about the claim. What remains of *Fedarwa* is now my property."

"I assumed that to be the case."

"I am, however, prepared to surrender my claim to you."

Kidron laughed. "For a price."

"There is always a price, Captain, but I think you will find this one fair and reasonable, not to say just."

Lynch was summoned at last to his uncle's office. When he got there he saw that the visitor was still present. He made his apologies and started to leave when N'Djama called him back.

"Aaron, I want you to meet my guest."

Lynch studied the visitor more closely. He saw a tall man, disproportionately thin, as though his frame had been stretched slightly out of shape. He was clean-shaven and pale-skinned, which gave him away as a spacer; his arms long and taut, veins running along the forearms like thin blue cords; his legs were as long as stilts; his short hair grey at the temples.

At that moment Lynch recognised him.

N'Djama said: "Captain Aruzel Kidron, my nephew Aaron Lynch. Aaron, this is the captain of *Magpie*, whose prize you so unceremoniously stole this morning."

Lynch blushed. "Captain." He tried to smile, then nervously extended a hand, relieved when Kidron shook it.

"Your uncle has generously transferred the *Fedarwa*'s remains to my name. I want you to know I am glad to meet the man who plucked it from me in the first place. You showed a great deal of initiative, a virtue I like in members of my crew."

Lynch mumbled his thanks for the compliment, then noticed his uncle grinning at him, never a good sign as far as Lynch was concerned.

"Your crew?" he asked after a moment.

"Meet your new employer, Aaron. You've just been signed on as *Magpie*'s replacement pilot."

Lynch was dumbstruck.

N'Djama's grin doubled in size. "You are part of the asking price."

"You wanted me, sir?" Lynch asked Kidron.

"Not quite, nephew. The captain would only take you on if I returned *Fedarwa* to him and paid him 3,000 credits."

"And the tarmac fees for my cutter while I am in Salem," Kidron reminded him.

"How could I forget?" N'Djama turned to his nephew. "It was too good an opportunity to pass up, Aaron. You know as well as I do that you are not cut out for the life of a merchant, even less cut out than I am to be a father. Your life here on Hecabe is leading you to a dead end. I love you, nephew, you are my only family, but we can barely tolerate each other's company." He turned to Kidron. "It is best he go."

Kidron nodded in agreement. "Mr Lynch, you are now a spacer."

Chapter 4

Nomelet of the Uzdar, largest and most powerful of the Calethar clans among the outworlds, read the report for the third time since it had been delivered to him by an Uzdar intelligence officer five minutes before. He was so absorbed in the reading he did not hear his secretary enter the reading room. The secretary gently brushed the combs of his feet against the timber floor to get his master's attention.

Nomelet glanced up, irritated at the interruption. "Yes?"

"Noble Enilka requests your presence. He is currently in his house, and would welcome you there."

"Thank you. Let Enilka know I am on my way."

The secretary left and Nomelet returned his attention to the report.

Although he had been expecting the information it contained he still found it hard to grasp the document's full import. However, he recognised he had reached a turning point in his life. His actions over the next few hours would determine what path he followed for the rest of his years. The turning point was unavoidable, its consequences irrevocable.

He read the report a fourth time. Intercepted human signals traffic verified the destruction of *Fedarwa* and her entire crew by the privateer *Magpie*. So Tolstoi was dead. Unfortunate. It would be hard to find another human with his talents prepared to betray his own species. A greater loss was the death of Kumla, one of Nomelet's chief supporters in the clan. And a good friend.

And now he must tell Enilka, the clan head. But how best to present the information so it gave him some advantage?

His secretary re-appeared, his combs scraping more urgently.

"Noble Enilka has requested your presence again."

Nomelet grunted, hurried to dress in his ceremonial clothes. A third request would be more of an order, and would hurt his standing in the clan. He studied his form in a mirror. He was proud of his looks. Tall by Calethar standards, well over two metres in height, and in excellent physical condition. His crest was green and healthy, the chitinous skin on his shoulders and arms shone, the combs on his feet were stiff and swept back gracefully to meet behind his heels.

At least I look the part of a future clan head, he thought.

When he arrived at Enilka's house, which was called a house for reasons of modesty, he was greeted by Inglas, his cousin and chief rival as Enilka's successor. They grasped each other's hands, claws held straight in peace, and touched foreheads.

"Welcome, cousin," said Inglas, and signalled for him to precede her. He showed his trust in her by accepting

43

the courtesy and leading the way to their uncle's meeting hall. The entrance was barred by two drones. Nomelet and Inglas detached their short swords from their belts and laid them on the floor. The drones let them through.

The hall was circular in shape, fifty metres in diameter. A transparent, domed roof arched overhead. Above the dome, the washed-out sky of the planet flickered through the tangled, creeping vines native to Dramorath. The system's sun, a small yellow star called Ia, burned almost directly over the dome like the eye of a demon. In the centre of the hall was a circular dais covered with a layer of soil and humus from the Calethar Heartworld. Enilka squatted on the dais, alert and wary. He held his long, shiny arms out straight before him, his hands resting on the wide hilt of the long killing sword that was the symbol of power for every clan head.

Several Calethar, not all clan members, were already in the hall, standing in front of the dais and conferring with Enilka, but they retired a respectful distance when Nomelet and Inglas approached. Nomelet reached the edge of the dais and scraped a greeting with his feet, the fine combs on their sides making a chirruping sound, then stood still. Inglas repeated the procedure. The two cousins kept their heads bowed. Their posture was entirely deferential: their arms folded, their eyes completely naked – not even protected by the first, nictitating eyelid.

Enilka clacked his jaws and nodded to Nomelet, the signal to begin, but Nomelet waved a deferential arm to Inglas. She threw him a suspicious glance, since no one surrendered the right to firstspeak unless they were confident about the importance of the information they held. But she accepted graciously.

"Uncle, a report from the trading captains who have lately returned from the Heartworld." Enilka's jaws clacked a second time, and Inglas continued. "Our latest shipment of human goods brought excellent prices in the central market. They were auctioned for record amounts, and our fame has increased commensurably."

There was a round of appreciative clacks from the rest of the Calethar in the hall. Even Nomelet joined in. Anything that increased the prestige of the Uzdar was to be welcomed. After all, if things went as he planned, he would one day be its head.

"I have more news," Inglas said quietly. Nomelet felt rather than heard the confidence in her words, but he gave no outward sign of his sudden concern.

Enilka clacked his jaws.

"The High Council met ten days ago," she began, speaking more slowly than usual. "It agreed to accept a new clan to its membership. Uncle, it has called upon us, the Uzdar, to join it."

Nomelet felt something squeeze his heart, and almost swayed from his position, a fatal mistake if done in front of Enilka; the old Calethar was very quick with his killing sword, and any suspicious move would be met with a lethal swipe of the double-edged weapon. Nomelet had been present when one of the clan's best ship-captains had swooned from exhaustion. Her head was off her shoulders and rolling across the floor before her body hit the ground.

Enilka spoke: "The High Council does us great honour, indeed. We will be the first clan from the outworlds to become a member. Our fame will increase to levels undreamt of by our ancestors."

Nomelet again joined in the appreciative clacking. With access to the High Council they could enlarge their trading web to cover all the old clan worlds and so get a share of the profits from the central market itself. Inglas had delivered stupendous news, indeed.

Except . . .

Nomelet almost laughed. His first reaction to Inglas's announcement had been a mixture of pride for the clan and depression because her information, at face value, would in comparison make his own appear grimmer than it really was, but now it occurred to him that his own news would suck the breath out of Inglas's lungs.

"Inglas's news is great indeed," Nomelet began. "It will improve our trading position in the Heartworld." He held his breath. By starting his speech with an observation rather than with information he risked a reprimand from the clan head – an action that would damage his claim as a successor to Enilka. But Inglas, always impatient, took the bait and spoke before Enilka could say anything.

"Nomelet does me honour, but he neglects to point out it will also improve our position with the human Federation. We now have a unique opportunity under the Federation–Calethar agreement to –"

"Forgive me, cousin, for interrupting, but my news bears on this."

Inglas snapped her jaws shut. She saw the trap too late, and had fallen in. None of this was lost on Enilka, of course. Things were turning out better than Nomelet had any right to expect. He offered a quick prayer to his mother. *Judge me right, Creator, it is for your glory and the glory of the Uzdar that I do this.* He quickly followed it with a prayer to the Calethar god of commerce. *Bring us wealth, Lord.*

"I have just met with the ship-captains newly arrived from the Federation. Their news was so important I waited for confirmation from our intelligence unit. This is why I was late, Uncle. *Fedarwa* has been destroyed. Destroyed, what's more, by the pirate captain Aruzel Kidron."

Nomelet's words had the desired effect. There was a worried scraping of foot combs on the hall's stone floor. Enilka even blinked. Inglas was obviously devastated. If only she had refused Nomelet's offer of firstspeak she could have won even more prestige by countering his bad news with her good, but as it turned out the opposite had occurred, and such good news as she had delivered would not come the clan's way again in her lifetime.

"Destroyed," said Enilka. His yellowing skin seemed to tighten. "And my grandson?"

"There were no survivors, Uncle. Kumla died serving his clan. All Uzdar join you in sorrow."

Enilka forced his back even straighter. *He is a strong leader, indeed*, thought Nomelet. *When he is gone, I must be like him when I take his place on the dais.*

"Nomelet, what is your appraisal?"

"Politically, the news is not as grim as it first sounds. As far as the Federation is concerned, *Fedarwa* was given to Tolstoi on a commercial basis, and they believe his crew was entirely human. That means the Uzdar will not have to endure reprimands from the Federation or our own High Council. In its life the ship obtained useful intelligence on human colonies and their defences, as well as information about their ships and planetary levels of technology."

Nomelet paused to let his uncle assess the information.

"What do you suggest the clan do next?"

Nomelet hesitated. If his advice was rejected by Enilka he would lose his new-found advantage over Inglas. But he was committed. Enilka had asked for his advice, and it could cost him his life to refuse it now.

"Right now our shipyards are already in the process of constructing a new frigate, its hull almost complete. I myself have contributed the greatest part of the cost. But now we must turn it into something more. We must invest resources into developing a ship capable of carrying out even greater destruction than *Fedarwa* among the human colonies in the frontier sector.

"Like Kidron's *Magpie*, it must be fast and strong and capable of long journeys. Indeed, it must be capable of taking on *Magpie* itself. If successful, it can be used as a prototype for the escorts that will eventually be needed to protect the invasion force the High Council is even now planning to send into human space. It is time the Calethar stood up to the human interlopers. It is time the Uzdar took their rightful place among the Calethar. Our fame in the outworlds is unmatched, but now that we are a member of the High Council itself we must take greater risks to increase our prestige among the old clan worlds.

"Nor must we forget *Magpie*'s attack on Uzdar property. Tunius was only the first victim; there will be others. We must not hesitate in striking back."

There was an astounded silence. No one, not even Inglas, dared point out what it would mean for the clan if they took up Nomelet's astounding proposal and failed. The consequences would be horrifying. The hated human Federation might even be able to force the High Council to extinguish the Uzdar entirely.

For a long time Enilka said nothing. Nomelet and Inglas remained stock-still. The other Calethar shuffled their feet nervously. All realised that Enilka's decision would determine the fate of the clan not just for the next generation or two, but for millennia. It was a decision as momentous as that made by a previous head of the Uzdar, several lifetimes ago, when she had shifted the clan's base of operations from the Heartworld to Dramorath, here among the outworlds on the fringe of Calethar territory.

"Very well," Enilka said finally. He stood up to his full height and looked at Nomelet, his gaze hardened by a terrible resolve. "Let it be done."

Chapter 5

Magpie slipped into Hecabe's only space dock to repair the damage caused by *Fedarwa*'s attack. There was ten weeks' work to be done, and for most of that time Lynch stayed planet-side since he was not needed on the ship. He continued to work for his uncle in the warehouse and flying the shuttle between visiting traders and the spaceport. On all these flights he looked out for *Magpie*, but never got close enough to see more than a glittering, indistinct shape above the rim of Hecabe.

He discovered most of his friends were happy for him to have escaped what had seemed his destiny as a reluctant merchant. Ironically, the one friend he expected to be happiest for him received the news lukewarmly.

Mahmed understood better than most how frustrated Lynch had become with his life, and yet found it difficult to comprehend how Lynch could so dramatically alter course. Mahmed's ambition in life was to be promoted through the ranks from plain stevedore to chief stevedore; to his eyes, what his friend had embarked on was major surgery.

"You had a secure lifestyle," Mahmed said after being told the news. "Sure, working for your uncle could be boring, but at least it was predictable. No warehouse worker I know ever died from decompression or suffocation or falling into a black hole."

"Don't you think you're exaggerating the dangers a little?" Lynch said, feeling uncomfortable despite himself.

"What does privateering offer you, Aaron? Two things. The lure of quick money and the constant threat of immolation. You earn big credits, but don't live long enough to spend them."

A week later the two friends were in a shuttle together delivering cargo to a small freighter recently arrived from a human colony in the frontier. Lynch located *Magpie* in the space dock, and pointed it out to Mahmed. Under full magnification on the screen it appeared nothing more than a glimmering suggestion of a ship.

"Isn't she something?"

Mahmed looked dubious. "I've been doing my research."

"Research?"

"On *Magpie*. Did you know her average casualty rate for each voyage is close to ten per cent? In ten voyages that makes it one hundred per cent, and *Magpie* often makes three voyages a year."

"I'm not sure your mathematics are right on this," Lynch said.

"Don't *you* lecture me on mathematics. A two year old would be ashamed to know as little about it as you."

"Anyway, I've only signed on for one voyage. I'll be back in a few months, healthy and considerably richer than I am now."

Mahmed dropped the argument. He could see he was not going to win. His friend had stars in his eyes, and nothing he said would shake them out.

Six weeks after *Magpie* slipped into dock Lynch received a message from Captain Kidron to report for duty at the spaceport the next morning. The message arrived in an official looking envelope which also contained a paper declaring that Aaron Lynch was enlisted as an ensign, effective from receipt of the certificate, and was subject to all the accepted rules and regulations pertaining to military service in Federation space, as well as a few especially made up for *Magpie*'s crew.

He showed it to his uncle that night.

"I am happy for you," N'Djama said, his voice wistful.

"You don't sound it," Lynch replied. He had never before heard his uncle sound so uncertain.

"I have been thinking about my decision to let you go with Captain Kidron," N'Djama admitted.

Lynch caught his breath. N'Djama saw his reaction and quickly added, "Don't worry, nephew. I have not changed my mind. I am just not sure I have done the right thing. I am your guardian, after all, but letting you go was as much for my benefit as for yours. On reflection it was a selfish act."

"But *I* want to go, uncle," Lynch said, his voice almost pleading. "I am seventeen now, and old enough to have my own life. You know as well as I that I will never make a good merchant."

N'Djama smiled. "Oh, yes. I have at last realised that. But are you cut out to be a privateer?"

Lynch shrugged. "There's only one way to find out."

His uncle nodded and put an arm around Lynch's shoulder. "Maybe I'm getting sentimental in my old age."

"You're thirty-five," Lynch pointed out.

"Then imagine how soppy I'll be when I'm seventy."

Lynch arrived at the spaceport with his few possessions in a kit bag slung over his shoulder. He approached the security guard at the tarmac entrance and handed him his orders. The guard glanced at them before thrusting them back and pointing to a hangar nearly a kilometre away. A sleekly built cutter protruded halfway out of it.

He walked the kilometre at a rapid pace. As he drew closer, he watched as a tractor attached itself to the nose of the cutter and towed it out to a taxi strip. He could not help but admire the ship's graceful lines, a reminder to himself it was designed for combat. Nearly sixty metres long, its stern flared to accommodate powerful chemical engines and wide wings swept up at the tips. Except for the cockpit, it had no viewing bays or portholes. An aerodynamically shaped nacelle under its belly was where Lynch knew it carried its weapon load-out. Just aft of the cockpit was emblazoned the device of its mother ship, a swooping magpie, the Terran butcher bird. Next to it was the cutter's name, *Lark*.

He saw two people underneath the vessel inspecting the vents under its wings – used to assist in take off and which also gave it a VSTOL capacity. He hailed the two but they ignored him until he stood beside them and said: "Excuse me, I'm Aaron Lynch."

The pair, a man and woman, turned to face him.

"I don't care if you're Lord Bloody Muck," the man said. "We're busy here."

"I have orders from Captain Kidron," Lynch persisted. The man held out his hand and Lynch gave him the orders. The man scanned them, handed them back.

"You know anything about a new ensign, Santa?"

The woman, very tall, dark-skinned and solidly built, studied Lynch as if he were a particularly venomous spider. "The Captain said one would turn up today."

"Santa? Is that short for something?" Lynch asked, offering a hand.

"Yeah." Santa gave his hand the briefest of shakes. "This is Balkowski."

Balkowski's handshake was firmer and friendlier.

"What's your specialty?" the man asked.

"I'm your pilot replacement."

"A short life but an exciting one," Santa said with half a smile.

Lynch stiffened. Before he could reply, Balkowski took him by the arm and led him away. "The Captain's on board. I'll take you to him."

Lynch followed the man to the cutter's nose. Balkowski reached up and pressed a panel, then stood aside as a section of the hull slid back and a gangladder unfolded to just above the tarmac. Balkowski climbed the ladder, disappearing into the ship; Lynch took a deep breath and followed.

At the top he found himself in a narrow section with a hatch at either end. There was barely room enough for the two of them. His guide pointed to the stern. "Beyond the hatch is the crew section with gravity slings for up to a hundred fully armed troops, and aft of that the hold." He moved forward and opened the other hatch. "This way to the cockpit," he said, waving Lynch through. "Captain, visitor to see you."

Lynch edged passed him into the cockpit. It was larger than he expected, certainly much larger than any shuttle cockpit he had ever seen. There were four gravity couches, two forward and two behind, and in front of each a bewildering number of controls and screens. Balkowski did not follow, but closed the hatch behind him.

Captain Kidron stood up from the pilot's couch and turned to greet him. His face was impassive. He said brusquely: "Ensign Lynch, welcome aboard the *Lark*." He indicated that Lynch should take the co-pilot's couch, waiting for him to sit down before resuming his own place.

"What do you think of her, Mr Lynch?"

"I've never seen anything quite like her," he admitted.

"Get used to her; *Lark* will be your responsibility eventually."

Lynch looked at Kidron in surprise. "I know how to fly a shuttle, Captain, but this is . . ."

"You'll learn quickly enough," Kidron said dismissively. "I'll fly her up to *Magpie*, but from then on she doesn't leave the ship without you in the pilot's seat. Your teacher will be Lieutenant Toma Robinson. She's the best pilot I've ever known."

Santa's voice came over the intercom: "Captain, everything checks out down here. We're ready to go whenever you are."

"Fine. Get Balkowski and climb aboard."

"Aye aye, sir."

As Kidron started the pre-take-off checklist, Lynch looked on, fascinated. The other two crew members entered and took their places in the couches behind the pilots' positions. Kidron warned Lynch to strap in and then signalled the spaceport's traffic control.

"*Lark* ready for departure, Hecabe."

"Okay, *Lark*. You're cleared for take-off. Good luck for your next voyage, Captain."

"Thank you, Hecabe. See you next time. *Lark* out."

Kidron started the engines, waited for them to reach their operating temperature before resting his right hand on the throttle controls and easing them forward. The cutter edged from the taxi strip to the runway. Kidron took his hand off the controls.

"Mr Lynch, all stops out, please."

Lynch looked startled.

"Mr Lynch, carry out my order," Kidron said sternly.

"Full throttle." Lynch eased the controls to their fullest extent. *Lark* accelerated down the runway so smoothly he had no idea of their speed until the spaceport's control tower flashed by to starboard.

Kidron pulled back on the pistol grip attached to his couch's right armrest, and the cutter's nose lifted into the air. In seconds the spaceport dropped behind them, and a few minutes later the rim of Hecabe came into view, edged by its thin blue envelope of atmosphere. The pressure on Lynch's chest was more than he was used to in a shuttle, but the couch was so well designed he felt no great discomfort.

Kidron eased back on the throttle and switched the controls to automatic. Turning to Lynch, he said:

"Alright, Ensign. We have time for me to give you your first lesson. Under your seat you'll find a helmet. Put it on."

Lynch did as instructed. The helmet was slightly large and awkward, but sliding clasps at the back made the fit more snug. Cables led from above the clasps to a control box by Lynch's couch. Kidron reached across and pulled down a clear, sepia-tinted visor.

"On the control panel in front of you is a toggle marked 'DISPLAY'. Press it once."

Lynch did so, and immediately the visor was illuminated by a green display, numbers and symbols running across its borders. A floating crosshair sight followed the movement of his right eye. The shuttles he had flown had a similar display illuminated on cockpit windows, but this was much more sophisticated . . . and complicated.

"Adjacent to the DISPLAY toggle are a series of switches and buttons that control what you see. Try some of them out."

For the next few minutes Lynch pushed and flicked various controls, experimenting with the different effects. The most startling was a set of controls that created a window within the display, magnifying whatever the crosshair was aimed at, as well as providing different visual information such as infrared signature, energy emissions and others.

"All the information the visor can show you can also be produced on the computer screen in the middle of your control panel," Kidron told Lynch as he experimented with the controls. "Generally, pilots leave the screen showing navigation data and use the visor for most everything else. Press the switch marked 'LOCATE', then push '1' on the number pad beside it."

A flashing red arrow appeared on the visor display, pointing to Hecabe's rim. A series of numbers and letters ran underneath the arrow.

"The arrow is pointing to *Magpie*'s location, currently over the planet's horizon. The alphanumeric gives the ship co-ordinates and its distance from us in kilometres. The last three letters give *Magpie*'s power status. Unless Commander Kazin and the crew have mutinied and flown the coop, it should be reading 'ORB', which means the ship is power down and in orbit."

"You're safe, Captain," Lynch told him. "Your crew is still loyal."

"Good to hear. Keep the helmet on as we approach the ship; watch how the alphanumeric changes. Also try the zoom control and various visual information sets. If you push other numbers on the LOCATE number pad you'll get information about other preset targets: our second cutter *Swallow*, for example, and even Hecabe."

A short while later the Captain told Lynch that *Magpie* was above the horizon. Lynch tried finding it with the visor up but could only see sunlight glinting off the ship's hull. He put the visor down and switched on the zoom window. The privateer suddenly flashed into existence.

What he saw was a ship that looked like a jigsaw puzzle put together by a robot with the IQ of an ant and the dexterity of an ore mover. The main hull was a cylinder a kilometre or so long and a hundred metres wide, beginning with a round, egg-shaped bow and ending in a wedge-shaped stern that housed the main drive. Bisecting the hull at right angles about two-thirds along its length was a second cylinder, 200 metres long and fifty wide, giving the ship a cruciform shape. This spar revolved slowly around the hull. The oddest looking parts of *Magpie*, however, were the various pods and bulges, housing the ship's sensors, attached to the main hull and cross-spar in what seemed a haphazard fashion. They looked like pimples and warts.

Lynch had seen plenty of holographs and holovideos of the ship, but this was real-time and he gasped at its sheer size, the sheer *mass* of the thing.

"Not exactly the most beautiful ship in the galaxy," Kidron said. "But I won't have any other."

"She *is* beautiful," Lynch said.

Kidron smiled with pride. "In combat she can out-turn and out-accelerate any vessel except a frigate, and she has more firepower than one of those."

The cutter was firing its verniers every couple of minutes, fine-tuning its approach to the cutter bay yawning open just forward of the cross-spar.

During the final approach, Kidron gave Lynch a brief summary of the ship's layout. "The core hull is divided into several decks; a main corridor runs its length. Among other things, the hull houses the main bridge, crew accommodation, hydroponics and cargo holds.

"The spar revolves around the hull when we are in normal space, imparting standard gravity within which to work. When in hyperspace or on alert, the spar stops revolving and the whole ship gets about eighty per cent gravity from the inertia drive, which can only run when the main engines are powered up. The spar is where the galley and crew mess, laboratories, guest accommodation and backup stations such as the emergency bridge are located."

Kidron had not touched a single control since leaving Hecabe's atmosphere, and the automatic systems now docked *Lark* as well. The cutter bay swallowed them whole. A lightweight rig attached itself to the *Lark*'s hull and manoeuvred it into its berth next to *Swallow*. There was a metallic clang as the cutter came to a rest. As the bay doors closed behind them and air was pumped in, yellow alert lights flashed. Lynch could see crew in spacesuits watching proceedings from gantries along the wall.

A few moments later the bay was fully pressurised, the alert light changed from yellow to green and the figures outside the cutter removed their suit helmets. Santa and Balkowski left their couches and exited the cockpit to lower the gangladder.

"Welcome aboard *Magpie*, Ensign Lynch," Kidron said.

Chapter 6

The shipyards of the clan Uzdar had always been famous amongst the Calethar for their size and for the sturdy, efficient trading vessels they built. A good part of the clan's income was derived from the manufacture and selling of ships to other, smaller clans. In future, however, the fame of the shipyards would spread even to the human worlds. They now took up enough space, and employed enough Calethar, to be considered a small city in orbit around Dramorath, with Floran, the Uzdar's master shipwright, its chief citizen and mayor.

In the time since the news of the *Fedarwa*'s destruction had reached them, a large portion of the Uzdar's wealth had gone into new research facilities and testing grounds. And with the rapidly growing importance and size of the shipyards had grown the importance and influence of Floran.

"To the extent," the master shipwright told himself proudly, "that Nomelet and Inglas now have a new rival to the succession." Floran grinned at his reflection in the plate-glass window of his office. He was short for an adult Calethar, under two metres, but as broad as most of his species – half again as wide as an adult male human. His long face was covered in greying, leathery skin, welted above the forehead and rising to a small crest that ran down to the nape of his neck like a shark's fin. His powerful arms ended in short, thick claws, his wide legs rested on tough cushions of skin and hardened flesh, a fine comb of bristly hair splayed out from both heels in a semicircle and ended on top of the foot.

He had never before admitted to himself that he had become the clan's fourth most powerful member, and if things continued progressing as they had over the last year, he would soon be its *most* important member. He patted himself on his ribbed chest. "Clan head," he whispered. "Thank the Creator." He made the sign of the heavens. Never before had a shipwright made it to the highest position of the Uzdar. His name would be counted among the most fortunate of Calethar.

His reverie was interrupted by a polite scraping at his office's entrance. He turned to see Nomelet looking at him almost benignly. Floran's spine straightened. *Did he hear my mutterings?* He forced himself to relax. *What of it? He's as aware of my new influence as I am; indeed, he is largely responsible for it.*

"Cousin," Floran said, "you are welcome here. It has been some time since you last graced the shipyards with your presence."

Nomelet entered the office and exchanged formal greetings with the shipwright. "I regret that I have been unable to visit more frequently, but matters of trade keep me tied to my own office, even though business is not as good as we would want it."

Floran nodded understandingly. Though he believed the prospects of the Uzdar were brighter than ever before, he was aware that its current standing in the Heartworld had suffered recently, despite its promotion to membership of the High Council.

Nomelet's prediction about the effects of *Fedarwa*'s destruction had been correct insofar as the reaction of the humans was concerned, but the *Fedarwa* enterprise had not been solely funded by the Uzdar; powerful clans from the Heartworld had also backed the project with moneys as well as with political support, and they were beginning to demand some sort of compensation from the Uzdar, the organisers and main backers of Tolstoi's incursions into human space. Nomelet had been angry at their response; they had reaped a great deal from the profits of Tolstoi's activities and had enjoyed the respite offered by one less privateer preying on Calethar trade, but still they wanted more! He had consoled himself with the thought that their shortsightedness and greed would be their downfall. The future of the Calethar race lay with the outworld clans, and chief among them the Uzdar.

Nomelet sometimes wondered if the humans of the border worlds, their equivalent of the Calethar outworlds, did not also bridle under the capricious demands and expectations of a central authority located far away.

Indeed, it sometimes seemed to him that Calethar and human had more in common with each other than either did with any other alien race: a still active world on which their peoples had evolved – the Heartworld and Earth respectively, a fringe of systems where they first established colonies, the next frontier – the border worlds and outworlds, and now the new frontier, still being settled and fought over.

No wonder we're enemies, he thought. *We're too much alike ever to be allies.*

Both Floran and Nomelet looked out the office window and across to the huge construction bay located three kilometres away. A gleaming vessel was suspended there, Calethar technicians crawling over her hull. She was bigger than any spaceship ever built before by the Calethar, bigger even than the feared *Magpie*.

"*Canar Calethari.* The Curse of the Calethar," said Floran; his voice almost whispered her name, as though it belonged to a god. "See how she swells in the sunlight. Not long now, cousin."

Nomelet found it difficult to look away from the ship. She was a thing of great beauty, a thing to love . . . almost to worship, he admitted to himself, but secretly; there was no point in arousing the jealousy of the gods.

"Latest reports indicate that her range and speed will be even greater than we hoped," said Floran, his face beaming. "She is the clan's greatest daughter."

"Don't let Inglas hear you say that," Nomelet jested.

"When the Heartworld learns of this they will pay more attention to the Uzdar and Dramorath," continued Floran, getting carried away with his own enthusiasm.

Nomelet studied the other Calethar. He understood the pride and joy Floran must feel for *Canar*, and to a certain extent he was happy for the shipwright, but . . .

"This project has greatly increased your standing in the clan," Nomelet began carefully. "In fact, I would go so far as to say you are considered as a rival successor. This, of course, must be gratifying to you and your family."

Floran did not look away from the great ship, but his mind was racing. What was Nomelet up to? Was he building up to a threat? Or was he interested in some kind of pact? "Naturally I'm aware of, and pleased by, my new position within the clan. Does it disturb you?"

"Not yet," Nomelet answered truthfully. "When there are only two recognised successors things can easily get tense, uncomfortable. Everyone seems to feel that they must belong to one faction or the other, there is no middle ground. To a certain extent this polarity must cloud the clan's judgment and acumen. With three successors the situation becomes more fluid, the tension is diffused. This is one side benefit from this project. Believe me, Floran, I am glad you are doing well out of it."

Floran turned to face his cousin and bowed his head in thanks. "I should point out at this stage, though I gratefully accept the mantle of a successor, I have no misconception about my position. I come a very poor third after my two distinguished cousins. I am not forgetful of the part luck and fate have played in my rise; either, just as easily, could bring me disgrace. As such, rest assured that I will walk with due deference and . . . caution. At present, I am not a threat to you or Inglas."

Nomelet clacked his jaws in approval. Floran's little speech was well delivered and phrased. Everything was understood, and for the immediate future at least any rivalry could be put aside while the main business was pursued to satisfaction.

"How long before the *Canar* will be ready for her engine trials?" Nomelet asked.

"Five weeks," answered Floran. "Then another ten to fully equip her. Her maiden flight will be a short run to Veneera and back. Then, cousin, the *Canar* is yours. You have her first mission planned?"

Nomelet chuckled. "I have had her first mission planned now for several years. Most of her crew have been chosen carefully and gathered together for almost as long."

"Is it presumptuous of me to ask, Nomelet, what her first task will be?"

Nomelet put his hand flat against the window, as though by doing so he could actually reach out and touch the ship.

"Why, haven't I told you already? That was unforgivable. We will be hunting down *Magpie*. And after we've destroyed the pirate Kidron we'll hit the human colonies in the frontier sector; we may even raid one or two of the border worlds, doing to them what their raiders for years now have been doing to the Calethar. The Uzdar have stood apart from the conflict for too long. We can no longer be indifferent as our species succumbs to the human invasion."

"The border worlds?" Floran's face showed his surprise. "That is a dangerous beginning indeed." He smiled then, thinking of what the reaction would be from the humans. He almost wished he was going along, but spaceflight itself held no appeal for him.

"A dangerous beginning, yes, and perhaps the most important ever carried out by an Uzdar ship. Our fame will spread beyond the Calethar, Floran."

It was at that precise moment the shipwright suspected just how great Nomelet's ambition really was. He was shocked by its audacity, and at the same time thrilled, caught up by the small glimpse he had been given of his cousin's vision. Nomelet did not simply want to succeed Enilka as head of the outworlds' most successful clan, he wanted to be chief of the most successful clan among the entire Calethar. He wanted to be paramount leader of the species. Floran swallowed, and repressed the shiver climbing up his spine. Compared to Nomelet's ambition, his own was insignificant.

"How do you think the Federation will greet the news that the Calethar are raiding their planets?"

"What can they do? The High Council will claim it is no more responsible for the actions of errant Calethar than the Federation claims it is for the actions of pirates like Kidron." Nomelet smiled. "The Federation will be helpless."

Chapter 7

Lynch lay exhausted on the cot in his cabin. He had never felt so tired in his life. Since joining *Magpie* the week before he had been working two five-hour shifts each day. The first shift was always with Lieutenant Toma Robinson, the privateer's chief pilot, learning how to launch, fly and dock *Lark*, as well as everything there was to know about every aspect of the cutter's construction – mechanical, electrical, structural, chemical . . . there seemed no end to the list.

In the second shift he found himself under the tutelage of Santa. Santa ensured Lynch knew every centimetre of the privateer, from the tip of the bow sensor domes to the stern engine faring. As well, she gave him basic training in weapons use and close combat, neither of which Lynch was keen on, especially the bruises and strains gained from the latter.

He tried to relax but he could not get out of his head the facts and figures, the specifications and dimensions, the procedures and regulations, that seemed to have completely taken over not only his waking life but his dreams and memories as well. He found it hard to remember what his previous life had been like, as though he had been on the privateer for a year instead of a week.

Despite his exhaustion, Lynch had adapted quickly to shipboard routine. While human colonies and outposts measured local time according to the orbits and revolutions of their respective worlds and suns, all interplanetary and interstellar time-keeping was based on the Earth calendar and 24-hour day. On *Magpie*, the day was divided into five shifts. Every member of the crew had two five-hour work shifts, an eight-hour sleeping shift and two three-hour leisure shifts. The word "leisure" was not entirely an accurate description, for the time was taken up with anything that did not fit into the other shifts: eating, personal hygiene, extra study, weapons training, emergency drill and punishment duty. As a new recruit, Lynch's work shifts and leisure time tended to merge together.

For all that, he was happier now than he remembered ever being. If it was too soon for him to say definitely the life of a privateer was for him, at least he was certain he had made the right decision in leaving Hecabe. He had no regrets about the move, only a sense of being on the right course, of having fulfilled some part of his destiny.

Finally the figures stopped whirling around in his head and he fell into a deep sleep. It seemed only an instant later that the intercom by his head beeped and Lieutenant Robinson's voice was reminding him he was due to meet her on board *Lark* in fifteen minutes.

Robinson was waiting for him at the bottom of *Lark*'s gangladder. She was a slim, short woman with blonde hair and almond-shaped eyes. Still in her early twenties she was young for a chief pilot, but was respected by the crew as a natural, someone who seemed to fly largely by instinct.

At their first meeting Lynch was introduced to her as the shuttle pilot who had claimed salvage rites on *Fedarwa*. He had not been able to help his chest puffing slightly.

Robinson had shaken his hand firmly and stared levelly at him until he lowered his gaze.

"I was the cutter pilot you beat to it," she said tightly.

Lynch swallowed, his chest deflating. "I hope that . . . incident . . . won't affect our relationship," he said carefully.

"That depends."

"On what?"

Robinson grinned at him without humour. "On how well you suck eggs."

Lynch blushed at first, but then thought of life with his domineering uncle.

"I can suck 'em with the best of 'em," he said shortly, and Robinson surprised him then by laughing. Lynch liked the sound, and decided there and then he liked her.

"I'm going to teach you how to fly."

"I've flown shuttles for years . . ." he began, his tone defensive, but she cut him off with a wave of a hand.

"The problem, Lynch, is that none of that was really flying."

And indeed, she taught Lynch the basics, counting for little his experience as a pilot.

Robinson never let him use any of the cutter's automatic systems on their flights, and he soon found himself enjoying taking *Lark* out, manually controlling the sixty-metre vessel, slowly developing the same skill for flying that the crew respected in Robinson. Like her, he took to flying like a bird on the wing.

She forced him to spend hours with the cutter's mechanics going over the engines, and with the system engineers going over the cutter's electronics and computers. As time went by he began seeing all the different aspects of his instruction draw together. He understood how a left bank in atmosphere affected the structure of *Lark*, which signals were sent from one computer to another, how air currents and turbulence affected the turn, which laws of physics were being employed to stop it from dipping into an irreversible nose dive . . . the knowledge coalesced in Lynch's mind to perform one smooth manoeuvre.

"You're on time," she said, feigning surprise.

"As usual," he retorted, starting up the gangladder. Robinson followed him.

"What's on today?" he asked over his shoulder.

"Special treat," she said without elaborating.

They settled into their couches and completed the preflight check. Robinson allowed Lynch to use the automatic system to take them out from *Magpie*. "You'll be doing plenty of real flying today," she said. "I want you to remember that flying is more than watching instruments and trusting to your computers. You have the talent to be a great pilot, but you have to learn to trust it more."

"Then why do we do so little flying and spend so much time learning about consoles, displays, switches –"

"Because although instruments will never do the job for you, they allow *you* to do your job. This is a multimillion credit machine you're flying, and its equipment wasn't installed for decoration."

Lynch used one of the visor's displays to watch the privateer shrink behind them. With better knowledge of its function and design, he appreciated its solid appearance even more now. He was beginning to think about it as his home in a way he had never considered his uncle's house to be.

"Enough daydreaming, Ensign," Robinson said, breaking through his reverie.

She flicked off the automatics, told Lynch to prepare a new course and gave him the co-ordinates for their first destination. As he was entering them into the navigation computer he stopped suddenly.

"That's on Hecabe's surface," he said, thinking Robinson had made a mistake.

"It's 300 metres above the Western Ocean," she said calmly. "Not far from your home town, in fact."

"We're landing at the Salem spaceport?"

Robinson shook her head. "We're not landing anywhere, Aaron, just flying. Take her down."

Lynch did as commanded, letting the cutter slip through the planet's atmosphere, its hull easily absorbing the heat generated by friction. At an altitude of thirteen kilometres he extended the cutter's forward canard wings, giving him greater control in the atmosphere. *Lark*'s speed dropped to just under 3,000 kilometres per hour, and he set it on course for the first co-ordinates, reaching it less than fifteen minutes after entry.

"Next?"

"Due east. That will take us a hundred or so klicks north of the city. Keep your radar altitude to 300 metres."

"That area is very mountainous. I don't think 300 metres –"

"Then fly around them," Robinson answered tersely. "I'm not asking you to fly in a straight line. I want you to fly as fast as possible, as low as possible. This is a military cutter, and its main function is to fly into enemy territory to either attack them from the air or to land troops as close as possible to them. Sometimes Captain Kidron will ask us to fly lower than 300 metres. A ship this size, and with its heat signature, is very hard to hide from any sensors. The lower you are, the more chance you have of not being blown out of the sky before you've carried out your assignment."

"And after the assignment?" he asked sarcastically.

"That's ultimately up to you. But we would hate to lose *Lark*. These beauties are expensive to replace," she replied.

"And pilots aren't?"

"Not ones as inexperienced as you, no."

"Well, that puts things into perspective for me."

"If you're reluctant to carry out my orders we can return to *Magpie*," she continued. "I'm sure Captain Kidron can find you other duties. The purser is asking for a new assistant."

Lynch smiled. "Heading due east, Lieutenant, at 300 metres."

They were soon over land, and almost immediately the cutter was being alternately lifted and dropped by shifting air currents and thermals.

"Since we're flying early in the morning, try to keep us over darker ground; although during the day it will absorb a great deal of heat, this early in the morning it actually reflects less, and you'll get less warm air lifting under you. In the afternoon, keep to lighter ground."

Lark responded quickly and gracefully to the controls, and Lynch enjoyed flying the cutter between mountains, their huge flanks towering above them as they sped past at over 2,000 kilometres per hour. After three minutes Robinson said: "This is getting boring. New heading: 360 degrees. Increase speed to 2,500 kilometres per hour."

Lynch banked the cutter so steeply it was almost standing on its port wing. He increased the throttle as the nose started to drop. As he levelled off their speed rose to 2,500. *Lark*'s black nose started glowing cherry red.

On their old course they flew along the grain of the range, slipping from valley to valley, the steeper ground on either flank. Now they were flying against the grain. Lynch found himself using full throttle to lift the cutter over ice-capped peaks, then using airbrakes to slow their descent as they swooped down to cross the narrow width of successive valleys. At first he fought a rising sense of panic: there were too many factors to consider, too many gauges to read, not enough time to make the correct decisions.

And then, quite suddenly, he knew *exactly* what he was doing. It was as if his mind had merged with the machine, his physical senses linking directly with the cutter's instruments and controls. The cutter's skin was his own, its mighty engines his lungs.

He let out a small whoop of joy, the exhilaration of flying so low and at such speeds flooding him with adrenalin.

And then beneath them the landscape changed. The mountains gave way to low hills, and the steep valleys to gentle dales. *Lark* steadied off and picked up speed, accelerating to 3,000 kilometres per hour.

Lynch rested back in his couch, panting as if he had run and not flown across the mountains.

"Seven minutes," Robinson said, checking the ship's chronometer. "Not bad."

Lynch was surprised. It had felt as if he had been cheating death for an hour or more.

"Take up her up to twenty kilometres," she ordered him. "From there we'll boost into orbit."

"Going home?" he asked.

"Not yet. One more task."

Once in space, Robinson gave Lynch a new set of co-ordinates that put *Lark* into a parking orbit above *Magpie* and on the other side of Hecabe. They completed one circuit of the planet, Robinson not speaking, Lynch checking all the cutter's systems. They started their second orbit when a bright yellow message appeared on the main screen. OBJ COURSE INT LARK: ABORT ORBIT. Lynch accessed the navigation computer for more information, but it would only confirm that an object had been detected on a collision course with the cutter.

"Well?" Robinson asked, an edge in her voice. To Lynch, she seemed prepared to take over.

He forced himself to stay calm.

"Do we abort?" Robinson persisted.

"Not yet," Lynch replied firmly. He sent out a warning call on all general communication frequencies to warn off the other object in case it was a spaceship. He then checked the course of the cutter and the incoming object on his navigation screen. The computer told him how much fuel he would have to expend to avoid the interloper if it continued on its path, and how much extra he would need in order to put *Lark* on a course back to *Magpie*.

Robinson was listening to the communication channels, and reported there was no response.

"Abort now," she instructed.

"Not yet," he said. "It's not optimum. If we wait three minutes and fire a four-second burst with the main engines we'll avoid the object and place ourselves on the best return course to *Magpie*."

He half-expected Robinson to overrule him and take the controls, but she nodded and said: "Okay. You're the pilot."

Lynch wished he felt as calm as she sounded. For the next three minutes he constantly checked his sensors. After two minutes they indicated the object consisted of largely iron and silicon. It was not an artefact. There would be no reply to his messages. Thirty seconds later he readied himself to fire the main engines, and counted the time down in his mind as the numbers flashed on the screen.

"Firing," he said as evenly as possible, and was pushed back in his couch as the cutter accelerated out of its present orbit and onto a return course to *Magpie*.

Something moved at the edge of his vision and he looked out of the viewing screen in time to see a dark shadow about the size of a man move across their bow and disappear to port.

"Shit," he whispered.

"What next?" Robinson asked.

"We return to *Magpie* . . ." he started saying, realising at the same time that if the answer was that obvious it must be wrong.

"And leave that rock for someone else to run into?"

"We're not armed," he said.

"Have you checked?"

Lynch swore under his breath. No, he had not checked. He did so, and the display on his visor told him the laser in the nacelle in *Lark*'s belly was connected to the main drive. He had a live weapon on board.

"I can blow it apart," he said firmly, pressing the toggle that lowered the laser beneath the nacelle.

"Great. Instead of one rock intercepting a regular parking orbit, you'll make two or three."

"Then what –" Lynch snapped his mouth shut. One sure way to fail a test was to ask the teacher for the answer. Then the solution came to him. "I use the laser on low power on one side of the rock. I push it out of orbit, send it well away."

"Well away where?"

"Into space . . . no, into the planet's atmosphere! It will burn up!" He almost shouted the answer.

Robinson nodded. "Get to it, Ensign. We'll soon be too far away."

Using the navigation computer, Lynch quickly calculated what strength to set the laser, and from what angle to hit the rock. He double-checked his figures, then fed them into the target computer. It locked the laser onto the rock. Lynch fired. The beam of coherent light was invisible, but the surface of the rock immediately started steaming. Small splinters scattered into space, their size too small and their velocity too low to harm any ship.

"Sensors indicate it's moving in the right direction," Robinson said. "Another burst."

Lynch fired a second time, and again the rock let off a spume of vaporised iron. Robinson checked the sensors a second time. The slightest of smiles flittered across her face.

"It's done," she confirmed. "Get us back to the cutter bay."

"On automatic?"

"You're not on holidays, Lynch."

When *Lark* was secured and the bay pressurised, Lynch made to get up from the couch but was stopped by Robinson.

"I think it's only fair to let you know I'm marking this flight as your first failure," she told him.

Lynch looked at her, confused. "I don't understand. I did everything you ordered me to: I flew nape-of-earth through a bloody mountain range – or as damn near, avoided a maverick rock, and then ensured it wasn't a danger to future shipping."

"In the first place, if I hadn't been there you would not have thought of destroying the rock. You weren't even aware you had a live weapon on board. At no stage, despite all your checking and rechecking of *Lark*'s systems, did you ever think to consider it. In the second place, your first solution to destroy the rock would only have created a greater hazard to navigation. It was my prompting that made you arrive at the correct solution.

"But worst of all was your decision to take the optimum navigational course in avoiding the rock and returning to *Magpie*, instead of the safest course, which would have been to avoid the object altogether as soon as possible and then figure a separate solution for a return course to *Magpie*."

"But then I wouldn't have been able to destroy the bloody thing!" he said angrily.

"Destroying the rock wasn't the test. Making the best decision to protect *Lark* was. You failed."

Chapter 8

"How did he go?" Kidron asked Robinson when, at the captain's request, she reported to the bridge an hour later.

"As expected, sir," Robinson answered.

"Will he shape up?"

"I think so. He certainly has the right feel for piloting a cutter. He got through the mountains section with flying colours."

"You didn't tell him that, I hope."

"Of course not, sir."

"And he was suitably chastised after the encounter with the rock you planted in orbit yesterday?"

"Humbled might be a better word. He was angry, like he'd been asked a trick question in an exam, but he'll get over it."

"Good. We're loading the last shipment of torpedoes now, and I want to get going as soon as possible after everything's secured. I don't want to leave Hecabe with only a make-do pilot in charge of *Lark*."

"Lynch will be fine, sir."

"You think he'll perform well in his first action?"

"Kill or cure, isn't it? Same for all of us, once."

"Cure, Lieutenant. Make sure of it. I don't want to have to report to my biggest backer on Hecabe that I've just topped his nephew."

Robinson nodded. "Aye aye, sir –"

Her words were drowned out by the wailing sound of an emergency klaxon.

Lynch was sleeping fitfully when the klaxon went off near his ear. He stumbled out of his cabin to find spacers rushing to emergency stations. He slipped into his overalls and entered the crowded corridor. Red emergency lights flashed in his eyes. Santa seemed to appear from nowhere and grabbed him by the elbow.

"Do you know where your station is?" she cried.

Lynch shook his head, dazed by the lights and noise.

"Come with me, and stay close!"

Lynch had grown used to weightlessness but still had trouble keeping up with Santa. He tried increasing his pace but lost his rhythm and ended up tumbling head over arse down the corridor. Santa returned, impatiently righted him and from then on kept one of his hands in hers as they continued. Other spacers rushed by them in both directions, silent and grim-faced. Lynch's initial confusion gave way to small stabbings of fear.

Seconds later the pair ran into a billowing curtain of greasy black smoke.

"What the hell's going on?" he shouted.

"It's a bloody fire! What the hell did you think was going on?"

She scanned the bulkhead, found an emergency panel and smashed it in with her fist. Lightweight respirators sprung out, floated in front of them. Santa grabbed two, donning one and giving the other to Lynch, who needed help adjusting the mouth and nose piece.

They continued on their way, pushing through pockets of smoke that collected along the bulkhead between ventilators. They soon came to one of the small loading bays located aft of the cross-spar. Through the respirator's restrictive mask, Lynch could make out orange-suited crew grouped into two teams, the first fighting a raging fire in one corner of the bay, and the second preparing burn victims for evacuation.

As soon as they appeared a suited man approached Santa.

"It was one of the torpedoes we were bringing on board," he said. "It exploded. We don't know why."

"Are there any other torpedoes in the bay?" Santa asked.

"No. It was the last of the batch. We're going to have to open the bay to space. It's the only way we can get the fire out."

"Not until the injured are cleared," Santa said, and gave orders as she clambered into firefighting gear a second spacer handed her.

Lynch stood by, aghast. Streams of foam played against yellow sheets of flame, most of it evaporating into steam. Bubbles of molten metal bobbed around the bay reflecting the fire and smoke, rapidly hardening into perfect ball bearings. The fire was out of control, and the blaze threatened to spread to the main corridor.

Santa shouted to Lynch to remain by the loading bay hatch and rushed off to supervise the firefighting. In the weightless conditions the firefighters had to work in pairs, using foam packs strapped to their backs or carried in one hand. One played foam against the flames, the other held the first steady by keeping a foot or hand locked in a wallgrip.

Something burned Lynch's hand. He pulled back from the hatch, swiped his hand against his leg. The skin was blistered and bleeding. Another drop of metal spat on the floor near his feet. He looked up, saw the fire had reached the bay's ceiling and was running along power and communication lines. The heat was so intense insulation peeled away, exposing wires and cables which then melted. He called out a warning but no one heard.

He searched frantically for a foam pack, found a batch of them lined up against the corridor bulkhead behind him. He grabbed the closest one, pulled out the nozzle pin and squeezed the trigger. Foam spewed out of the nozzle, the force slamming him back into the bulkhead. Without gravity his feet had no grip. He scrambled back to the bay hatch, jammed his foot in to the recess and sprayed foam above him.

Again and again hot licks of metal spat on his clothing and hands. He was crying with pain and frustration. The fire above his head was spreading faster than he could put it out.

His first foam pack ran out and he retreated to the corridor to get a second. By the time he returned some of the first burn victims were being evacuated, gliding like ghosts through pillows of smoke. They were carried out into the corridor where first-aid teams waited to stabilise the most seriously hurt before taking them to the ship's sick bay.

He took up position near the hatch again, but before he could ready the fresh foam pack a length of cable above him slipped free. It writhed as flames ran along its length, and globules of molten matter sprayed throughout the bay.

Lynch saw a globule bump into one of the firefighters. The man screamed as it seeped into his suit through a gap between his glove and sleeve. Lynch could only look on as flames spread inside the suit, making the man twist and spin uncontrollably until his partner hit him over the head and brought him out.

Something in the far corner of the bay exploded. Lynch cringed involuntarily.

The smoke from the fire became lighter in colour, almost yellowish. The heat was so intense the hairs on the back of Lynch's hands curled and crisped. More and more spacers retreated from the bay, and then Santa appeared.

"Is everyone out?" she cried. No one could tell her.

She pushed Lynch out of the way and slammed shut the hatch. She scrambled to a set of controls on the bulkhead and flipped a switch. A panel slid back revealing two red buttons which she pressed simultaneously.

For a second nothing happened, and then there was the sound of gushing air on the other side of the hatch as the bay's external doors opened to the vacuum of space. Lynch was pressed against the hatch porthole, and he saw the fire wither instantly, waving in the miniature storm before being completely extinguished.

Crates banged against each other, against stanchions, against the bay bulkhead, the vibrations clanging through the hatch. Jacks and cables, hoses and lines whipped frantically, disappearing into space. Plastic sheeting flapped like sails as they were sucked out. And amid all the debris were the bodies, tumbling against equipment, other bodies, somersaulting into the vacuum.

Lynch did not see one corpse until it slid past the hatch porthole, smearing blood against the glass. It was so badly burned the head had been reduced to a charred skull, and its skin, puckered on the limbless torso, shone like polished steel. It bumped against the hatch wheel, turned on its axis, spun out into space.

Lynch pushed himself away from the hatch. Suddenly free of the crowd, he floated back down along the corridor, unable to get a handhold. A second later the klaxon ceased its wailing, and the emergency lights along the corridor stopped their staccato flashing. Lynch put one foot out against the bulkhead to stop him tumbling, then pushed himself gently away in the opposite direction to the bay. He had seen enough, and wanted no more of it.

The disaster brought home to him, as nothing else short of combat could have done, that he was living in an environment that no amount of precautions could make as safe as the surface of Hecabe. What might amount to no more than a mishap on the ground could easily destroy a ship in space. For the first time on *Magpie* he felt frightened and alone.

Someone grabbed him by the ankle and tugged him down. It was Santa.

"Lynch?"

"I saw –" he started to say, but couldn't finish. Bile churned up his throat and made him gag.

Santa saw the burn marks on his hands, the singed clothing, the blood on his overalls.

She grasped his face with both hands. "Before this voyage is over, son, you'll see a lot more bodies, some in worse condition than those. It goes with the job."

Lynch nodded, his body sagging. "I'm sorry."

Santa sighed deeply. "You've done alright, Aaron. You'll do for *Magpie*."

The official enquiry discovered the fire had been started by a faulty torpedo brought up from Hecabe's armoury. Fortunately it had not been the warhead itself that was wonky but part of the torpedo's propulsion unit, otherwise *Magpie*'s main hull would have been ripped apart from the inside, causing much greater damage and more casualties.

As far as the enquiry could determine, the weapon was being positioned onto a trolley that would take it to the ship's magazine when it had jarred against the loader's restraining arms. The resulting spark caused a small explosion, instantly incinerating one of the bay workers. Thanks to *Magpie*'s emergency procedures and the experience of her crew only six had died, although several people suffered serious burns.

The accident had other repercussions. *Magpie* was delayed for another week while the damage to the loading bay was repaired and the remaining torpedoes were checked and checked again for any possible defects.

The official service for the dead spacers was short and sombre. Their burnt remains were never recovered, but coffins were ceremoniously ejected into space on a course that would take them through Sabbath's corona.

Santa ensured Lynch attended the wake. "It's the way of it, Aaron. We're giving the poor old sods a proper send-off. We're all here to say goodbye."

The wake went on for several hours. By the end of it Lynch found himself genuinely mourning the victims, and for the first time truly felt a part of the crew.

Chapter 9

Kazin found Kidron in his day cabin behind the bridge. He was reviewing the files on each of the crew members who had died in the fire.

"None of us really expect to go like that," Kidron said.

"No. We all look for the heroic exit: shot through the heart, protecting the flag."

Kidron smiled. "You *are* a romantic, Michael. No death is heroic."

"Deep down I agree. But sometimes just to make it from day to day you have to pretend there's something intrinsically noble about your efforts. Especially true if your efforts involve risking your life. We all want to believe there is such a thing as an heroic death because we think such a death is easier than any other. Nobility brings surcease."

Kidron sighed. "There was nothing noble about how Tbelisi and Hannover and Gordon . . ." His voice trailed off.

"I know it sounds trite, Aruzel, but for god's sake, accidents do happen. This is a warship, not a luxury liner."

"Seven dead, Michael, and we haven't left Hecabe yet. And when we do go it's without a warrant."

"So, pirates at last."

Kidron shook his head. "We never set out on this business for plunder. We're not pirates. We're the vanguard."

"Then not having a warrant shouldn't matter to you."

"I have a feeling things are different in the universe, old friend. We blinked and the rules changed on us. Before we attacked Tunius you asked me if I could see an end to what we were about to start. *Then* I could. *Now* I'm not so sure."

Kazin did not like the way Kidron was talking. It was too fatalistic for the man he had known for thirty years. "What are you getting at?"

"Uvarov told me the Federation is finally getting concerned about the situation in the frontier sector."

"Isn't that what we always wanted?"

"I thought so, but suddenly we are a very small fish swimming in increasingly dangerous waters."

"*Magpie*'s a small fish with large teeth, Aruzel."

Kidron said nothing for a moment and Kazin stood to leave.

"Michael, what do you think the Uzdar will do next?"

Kazin shrugged. "The Calethar are hard to predict at the best of times, and the Uzdar are the most unpredictable of all."

"If you have any sudden insights let me know."

Kazin nodded and left.

Kidron ordered *Magpie* to power up when he got word the official enquiry into the fire was completed. Soon after, the ship slipped out of orbit around Hecabe, smoothly accelerated to her jump point and disappeared from normal space.

Lynch was sleeping at the time. Before retiring he could have viewed Hecabe on any screen; six hours later, when he woke up, the planet showing on the ship's screens was Omega, a small border world nearly seven light years from Hecabe.

The previous day he had contacted his uncle and Mahmed to say his farewells.

The conversation with Mahmed had been awkward, as if Lynch's need to leave Hecabe behind had placed a gulf in their friendship. Mahmed wished him a safe journey, but Lynch got the feeling he was really wishing things did not have to change, that they could have gone on as before.

There was a moment during the conversation when Lynch felt a twinge of doubt for the first time since leaving home. The fire had shaken his confidence in his own personal invulnerability, but not in his decision – or rather his uncle's decision – to come to *Magpie*. But talking to Mahmed achieved that for an instant, reminded him of what he was giving up. Along with the frustration his previous life had also involved good friends, even some good times. And down there, down on Hecabe, his dreams had been pure, untouched by reality. Now, on *Magpie*, those dreams would be put to the test. But doubt disappeared when Mahmed signed off, as if cutting the link finally set Lynch free.

The conversation with his uncle had none of that awkwardness for Lynch, but was harder on him emotionally. Ironically, their separation had healed the rift between them. N'Djama was his family, all that was left, and they talked for a long time about matters neither had ever broached before: about Lynch's parents, about N'Djama's personal plans for the future, about friends they had in common, about a dozen subjects that were once incidental but now suddenly were important because they defined their relationship. They had become friends at last, and it left an ache in Lynch he had not felt before and could not explain.

He realised that of all he was leaving behind on Hecabe, he would miss his uncle the most.

Lynch was kept so busy over the next two days he had no time to dwell on the past. He flew *Lark* between *Magpie* and Omega, dropping off goods and picking up cargo the privateer would deliver to other border worlds on the way to the frontier sector. It was a profitable milk run for *Magpie*, and provided an invaluable service to the smaller settlements infrequently visited by interstellar traffic.

In the following weeks the privateer made several such stops, and for Lynch it was an exciting and eye-opening experience. He discovered completely new lifestyles, new cultures and societies more exotic than he would ever have thought possible.

On Omega he encountered a people whose principal aim in life was to discover the spiritual and moral laws they believed underpinned the universe. The Omegans readily admitted progress over the millennium had been painfully slow, but on the way they had devised a system for communicating ideas that was a mixture of language and music, a new branch of topology and an alternate judicial system based on moral rather than legal rights.

On New Siam he visited temple complexes that incorporated designs and features from every major culture on old Earth – huge domes and spires, peaked roofs, marble and wooden columns, stained glass windows, halls with perfect echoes, stone archways carved with intricate patterns, eternal flames, priest's huts and meeting halls; human history given form and substance.

When *Magpie* reached Burgess, one of the last and most isolated of the border worlds, Lynch was made one of a party assigned to attend the famous Burgess Fair. Together with Kazin, Santa and a middle-aged woman called Aberdeen, one of *Magpie*'s best negotiators, Lynch was taken down to Kanik, the planet's largest city and only spaceport. Robinson and two well-armed troopers stayed behind on *Swallow* to protect the cutter and its cargo.

"Why the precaution?" Lynch asked Santa. On previous planetfalls they had only ever left one guard with the cutter.

"Look around," Santa said. "You'll see more aliens and a greater variety of humans on Burgess than any-where else in known space. Burgess has a well-developed society right on the border with the frontier sector. It is the most accessible such planet for colonists, human and otherwise. Burgess Fair is where they all collide. A lot of rare and valuable goods are traded here for big money, and where there's big money there's often big trouble."

The fair was held in a huge building in the centre of the city. It was the largest building Lynch had ever seen. Inside there were thousands of stalls – small, large and magnificent. Humans and aliens were buying and selling, bickering and laughing, dressed in clothes of every colour and shape and form. Lynch was most startled by the range of smells, from the sweetest perfume to the most vile stench, coming from a hundred kitchens, livestock and the traders themselves. He followed the others from *Magpie* in a daze, constantly distracted by a kaleidoscope of new sights, new sounds and new scents.

His attention was caught by a particularly loud argument at a nearby stall. A collection of Actane and Mendart merchants were haggling over a deal. The Actane – tall, pale and whip-like bipeds – appeared frail next to the Mendart, shorter but much wider bipeds with torsos almost as square as their ships, but they seemed to be holding their own. They frequently took time out from insulting one another to insult any human who came too close. They were both ancient spacefaring species, and resented upstart humans; hell, they even resented the Calethar, who had been in space centuries longer than humans.

Kazin stopped at a large table displaying several bolts of brightly coloured cloth. Lynch touched one of the samples. It was smoother than any silk.

"Wiwaxian spider cloth," Aberdeen said in his ear. "One metre of this material uses the threads of over a million spiders and takes five Earth years to weave."

"How much does it cost?"

"One bolt would cost *Magpie* the profits from a whole voyage."

Lynch turned his attention to the pair of Wiwax merchants behind the table. They looked like Terran tortoises but without heads or legs. Their metre-long green shells, each surmounted by two parallel lines of

93

vicious looking spikes, were propelled by thousands of fine hairs that grew from the soft bodies underneath. Strung between the spikes were crystal sensor nets that let the Wiwax communicate with other species and make sense of worlds that were not hot and humid pressure cookers like their own planet. When talking, their crystal nets vibrated rapidly, making a sound that perfectly imitated the voice of whomever they were in conversation with. Lynch listened in wonder as Kazin talked to one of the Wiwax, Kazin's own voice being used to reply.

They moved on, stopping at a wide stall displaying small tear-shaped bottles made from the most beautiful glass Lynch had ever seen. The bottles were organised in rows, each row a different colour, and each bottle in a row a different hue of that colour. The vendor was a tall creature, its caramel-coloured head and torso almost square in shape. The head had a mouth and a single eye, as well as a pair of arms. The torso had its own eye, another pair of arms and two pairs of legs.

"I've never seen one of those before," Lynch said. "What is it?"

"No idea," Santa admitted. "Every time I come here I see a new species or two. Sometimes I never see them again."

Aberdeen asked the alien a series of questions, none of which elicited a response. Aberdeen gave up after a few minutes of this and shrugged at Kazin. Her action made the alien cry out. The arms on its torso reached up and detached its head, placing it on the table before Aberdeen. The torso then left to hide behind a curtain at the back of the stall while the head started gibbering excitedly at Aberdeen, picking up bottle after bottle and waving them at her furiously.

"I've had enough of this," she declared and led the party away, the detached head shouting at their backs.

They next stopped at a stall that seemed to be one of the busiest in the hall. Potential customers were queuing to look at the wares for sale. Lynch could not see what was being offered, but he could make out the vendor – a large Ediacaran, a flat, segmented worm two metres long and half again as wide. The alien was standing on its head on the table. The top of the head had a flexible sucker that fixed it in place; from its other end extruded frilled tentacles that waved in the air, trapping small flying insect-like creatures that it brought to one of the several mouths circling its midriff. Four sets of three tiny black eyes were set around the torso between midriff and the tentacles.

Occasionally it would utter commands in a high, sing-song voice to one of its two human servants. Whatever it was dealing in, trade was brisk.

"Why start our business here?" Lynch asked Aberdeen, noticing many stalls without any queues.

"I checked the Kanik spaceport log before coming here," she said. "The Ediacaran's shuttle is scheduled to leave in a few hours, which means it will be eager to sell off its stock. We should be able to get a good deal."

Kazin said something to Santa and the big trooper nodded and left, making her way quickly through the crowd before Lynch could ask her where she was going.

A short while later Kazin and Aberdeen had reached the table, Lynch in tow. Laid out on the table in shallow boxes were thousands of gems and precious stones.

Aberdeen gained the attention of one of the human servants and pointed to a box of clear, round gems each with a fiery red centre. The servant talked briefly to the Ediacaran. The alien looked at Aberdeen, then said to her: "You have a good eye for a human. I have many beautiful wares, but none as beautiful as these soul-stones."

"I have seen better examples," Aberdeen said matter-of-factly.

The Ediacaran rocked back on its sucker, its tentacles waving like seaweed in a strong current.

"Indeed! I think, however, you will only have seen better in your dreams! These soulstones were gathered by myself at great personal risk from the heart of a live volcano –"

"I have seen better at markets on Omega and Newton, and even on Calethar worlds where the Ediacaran rarely go. I offer you 1,000 credits for the whole box."

The alien stopped its rocking, the tentacles hung limp. "Only 1,000 credits! They would not buy one. I will accept 7,000 credits for the box and its eight gems, nothing less."

Aberdeen picked up one of the gems and studied it closely. "Outrageous. For the box I offer 2,000."

"I was wrong when I said you had a good eye, human. You have no idea of these gems' true worth. The box will cost you 6,000 credits."

Aberdeen conferred with Kazin, turned back to the alien. "We can afford no more than 2,700 credits."

The Ediacaran said something to its servant and then ignored them completely, turning its attention to another customer. The servant said to Aberdeen: "Agreed. Our shuttle leaves in two hours. Have your agent meet us with the payment at the spaceport gate."

The three companions moved away from the stall.

"Well done, Aberdeen," Kazin said. "We got a good deal. The soulstones will bring a handsome return back on Hecabe."

He retrieved a ceramic credit disk from a jacket pocket and inserted it into one of the credit machines scattered throughout the hall. He punched in a code, then the amount. The machine ejected the disk and Kazin handed it back to Lynch.

"That's now worth 2,700 credits, so look after it. Meet the Ediacaran at the spaceport. When you're given the gems take them to the cutter. We'll meet you there later."

Lynch nodded, hid the disk inside a waist belt and left the hall.

He arrived at the spaceport gate half an hour early. He found a convenient piece of shade, sat down and waited. The Ediacaran and its servants arrived precisely on time in an aircar. Lynch stood up to attract their attention and the aircar hovered to a stop. A door opened and one of the servants leaned out. His master squatted in the back of the aircar, ignoring Lynch entirely.

"The money," the servant said.

Lynch withdrew the credit disk from the waist belt but held onto it. "The box," he said.

The servant reached behind him, brought out a closed box and handed it over. Lynch gave him the disk and opened the box.

"Good to do business with you," the servant said, pulling the door shut.

Lynch's hand shot out, stopped the door from closing.

"There are only five gems here," he said. "There were eight originally."

The servant glanced at his master. The Ediacaran said in a disdainful tone: "Tell the human that 2,700 credits only buys five stones."

"That wasn't the deal," Lynch said.

"It is now," the servant replied, producing a small pistol from a sleeve. He pointed it at Lynch's forehead. "Step back and we'll be on our way."

A new voice came from the other side of the car: "Ensign Lynch wants eight stones, Ensign Lynch gets eight stones."

The servant whipped around, found himself staring into the barrel of a gun much larger than his own. It was held in the right hand of a solidly built black woman. Her left hand held a gun as well, this one aimed at the Ediacaran's midsection.

"Santa!" Lynch cried.

"The one and only!" she boasted, grinning mischievously. "Kazin thought there might be a problem and asked me to leave early so I could tail this mob when they left the hall."

Santa's gaze never wavered from the servant. "Put the toy down, son, or I will kill both you and fishbait here."

The servant dropped the gun. It clattered on the ground by Lynch's feet. He picked it up.

"Fishbait?" the Ediacaran said, its tone puzzled. "What's fishbait?"

"And now those extra three stones."

The servant brought out three soulstones and gave them to Lynch, who put them in the box.

Santa waved them on with her guns. "If you don't hurry you'll miss your flight."

The servant closed the door and the aircar sped off.

"Great timing," Lynch said.

"Had to live up to my name," Santa replied.

Lynch thought about it for a moment. "I don't get it."

"Santa always delivers the goods."

"I still don't get it."

"Old Earth myth," she said without elaborating.

Chapter 10

Two weeks after leaving Burgess, *Magpie* entered the frontier sector. No longer interested in trade, she entered normal space above the Calethar world of Apore, and went to war.

On her first pass in a tight equatorial orbit *Magpie* destroyed the space defences of the only outpost located on a large island some ten degrees south of the equator. Now it was safe for her cutters to enter the planet's atmosphere preparations were made to land a raiding party.

Kidron gathered his officers in the war room, including Lynch, who stood at the back of the group, nervous in their collective presence. The group was circled around a holographic map of the planet suspended in the middle of the room.

Kidron pointed out the exact location of the outpost, and its ground defences.

"The information is very reliable. I bought it off Captain Mursten who obtained it from data libraries on a Calethar supply ship his raider took three days before we met.

"To the north and east there are three laser batteries, two fully operational. To the south and west two batteries, both up and running. They are placed to counter attacks from the natives, typical of Uzdar outposts. Apparently the natives here are even more hostile than usual, and are canny warriors. The reports detail losses they'd suffered in one especially large attack. That means three things for our own assault. First, the cannon will be programmed to counter attacks at surface level, though they will of course be able to manually retarget them; second, they've had loads of combat experience; and third, their combat units are below strength."

Kidron let his words sink in before continuing. "I want our shuttles to drop vertically on the island. This means giving them more warning of the exact timing of the raid, but the usual skimming approach runs the risk of the cutters getting blown out of the sky at low altitudes by their cannon.

"Once down, troops will head for the outpost's communication building. Chances are there is no Calethar ship within hailing distance of Apore, but there's no point in taking any chances. We're already jamming from *Magpie*, but we can't detect all the tight beam messages and one will get through eventually. Second objective is the batteries. Third objective for the first squad is mopping up any resistance, or if it's entrenched to keep up suppressing fire while the second squad loads the cutters with whatever they can lay their hands on. As usual, I want a thorough search done of the outpost's computers and data libraries. Any questions?"

"You've told us about the laser batteries," said Lieutenant Commander Spiez, an old marine who had served with Kidron for more than ten years and who was in charge of *Magpie*'s combat squads, "but what about mobile lasers and surface-to-surface missiles?"

"We can expect them to have a few mobile lasers. Probably broad-beam jobs for mining and excavating. The Calethar reports don't mention them being used in combat against the natives, so I don't expect much trouble from them. They have no missiles."

Spiez nodded; there were no other questions.

"Alright, we launch in thirty minutes. I'll fly with Lynch, Spiez with Robinson. Kazin, you're in command here."

Lark and *Swallow* launched exactly thirty minutes later, their trajectory placing them on a descending track ahead of *Magpie*, in the privateer's fire envelope in case there were ground-to-air batteries Kidron's research had missed. The cutters skipped twice on Apore's atmosphere before beginning their descent, a screaming, plummeting fall that made their hulls glow like miniature suns. They came out of their dive 100 kilometres east of their destination at an altitude of 15,000 metres. They dropped vertically over the island, their engines roaring with the strain.

Lynch saw the ground hurtle up to meet them, and wondered if even the cutter's mighty engines could slow their descent. Relief flooded him when he felt the craft losing speed. It was easier to breathe and once again he could use his fingers and hands freely. He adjusted their trajectory, and less than a minute later *Lark* hit dirt, the landing jarring the breath out of him. Kidron ordered the squad out. Lynch was left by himself in the cockpit, his head still spinning with the speed of their descent.

"Are you alright?" Robinson asked over the intercom.

"Winded, but otherwise OK."

"Hell of a ride, wasn't it?" She sounded elated.

"You can say that again," he replied, the adrenalin still pumping.

Kidron made directly for the communications centre. While he investigated the computers, Spiez organised the destruction of transmitters and signalling equipment.

It did not take Kidron long to discover the computers held no data of any interest. Spiez and he then took a squad each to destroy the ground-based laser batteries, the only threat to the cutters on their ascent.

Magpie's troopers overwhelmed any resistance. Although the colony had a handful of regular Calethar soldiers, the colony leader had decided to split them up to lead small units of militia, diluting their effectiveness so much they had no noticeable influence on the battle. The laser batteries were quickly dealt with by blowing up their power sources.

Kidron then ordered the plundering to begin. The troopers stripped the entire colony from one end to the other. Anything of value or interest was taken back to one of the two cutters. Anything too big to move or not worth anything was blown up, sabotaged or wrecked beyond repair.

The surviving Calethar colonists, disarmed and herded together in the communications centre, could only watch in anger and despair as the humans went about their work. All their years of hard labour were ruined before their eyes.

In turn, Kidron watched them without sympathy. Within fifty metres of where he stood lay several

Calethar corpses; most of them had not being carrying arms when killed. It occurred to him he *should* feel something.

His thoughts were interrupted by Spiez appearing at his side.

"Captain, we've finished loading the cutters. We can go when you're ready."

"The sooner the better, Lieutenant Commander. Give the word."

Lynch listened to the battle's progress on the intercom, but could make little sense of the messages in code being passed between the different units. Occasionally he heard weapons being fired, sometimes nothing more than rude static, sometimes sharp cracks like bones breaking. He checked his watch every few seconds, sure that minutes had gone by.

He tried not to dwell on how vulnerable he was sitting on top of a sixty-metre rocket parked like a metal tree in the middle of a lonely paddock. One shot at the cutter's chemical fuel cells would mean a catastrophic explosion and fire.

This isn't what it's supposed to be like, he thought. *This isn't exciting. This isn't adventure.*

He heard an explosion that made him jump. He frantically checked his sensors to find what had caused it, and discovered it was the enemy's laser batteries being destroyed. He swallowed, ashamed of his fear.

"Stop thinking about what can happen," he told himself. "Concentrate on the job."

He checked all the cutter's systems, was about to recheck them when he heard troopers clambering on board. His intercom sounded and Kidron ordered: "Get ready for launch, Ensign." As Lynch fired the engines Kidron entered the cockpit.

"How did it go, Captain?" Lynch asked.

"Well enough. Lift us out of here."

Lynch checked the loading hatch was sealed and gave the engines maximum power.

The approach to *Magpie* was more casual than their departure. There was no reason to risk damaging their booty, some of which was fragile Calethar equipment. The cutters reached a low orbit around the equator below *Magpie*. An hour later they boosted into a higher orbit and slowly gained on the privateer.

They were fifty minutes from docking when Kazin called Kidron on his personal line. Lynch could not make out more than a few words, but there was no mistaking the increasingly worried expression on the captain's face.

"The outpost's communication centre managed to get off a signal before we took it," he told Lynch after Kazin signed off. "And *Magpie*'s just intercepted a reply. A Calethar frigate is on its way. We haven't much time. A couple of hours at the most."

"Is that enough?"

Kidron shook his head. "No. At least we have a warning."

"Can *Magpie* take on an enemy frigate?"

"When we're powered up and moving, yes. But in orbit we're an easy target. How long before we dock?"

Lynch checked his instruments. "Forty minutes."

"It will take *Magpie* that long to get the thrust needed to break free from Apore's gravity."

Lynch waited for Kidron to make a decision. After a few seconds the captain got in touch with Kazin again and ordered *Magpie* to power up immediately.

The Exec's reply crackled back over the intercom. "But, Captain, the cutters won't be able to dock –"

"I know. We'll take our chances. If you don't defeat the frigate we're all dead, anyway."

"You don't know that, Captain –"

"Commander, you have the bridge."

There was a pause, then: "Aye aye, sir. Good luck."

"And you," Kidron signed off.

Chapter 11

The cutters returned to a lower orbit to get some protection from the planet, putting it between them and the predicted trajectory of the enemy ship. *Magpie* powered up and began edging towards her plotted attack position, a point where the incoming frigate should appear between her and Apore. Thirty minutes later the three human vessels were in position, and all the crew could do was wait for the enemy to appear. Kidron maintained constant contact with Kazin, checking and rechecking their battle plan. Basically, *Magpie* was to hit the frigate with everything she had as soon as it appeared, and then close to finish it off.

The cutters' task was to stay out of the way. Their small lasers could be used against ships in an emergency, but were definitely weapons of last resort. Against a frigate they would be as useful as a knife against an elephant.

"How can the frigate respond so quickly to Apore's signal?" Lynch asked Kidron.

"The outpost knew it was patrolling in the general area, or the frigate was on its way for a visit, or on its way back after a visit. I don't know. What I do know is that it was close enough to answer the outpost's call and that it's coming. Any other questions?"

Lynch shut up.

Minutes later the expected visitor arrived. The first sign was a disruption in normal space. Alarms went off simultaneously in all three human craft and passive sensors immediately locked onto a Calethar-built vessel moving towards the planet at battle speed.

Danui gave Kazin the frigate's vector. He was calm enough, if uncomfortable, perched on the edge of the captain's couch as though Kidron would turn up at any moment demanding Kazin vacate it.

"Coming in just like *Fedarwa* over Hecabe," he said. "Have you a lock?"

"Aye, sir."

"Fire our first salvo."

Magpie thumped gently as the torpedoes were launched.

"Frigate's changing course," Danui reported.

Kazin watched the enemy ship on his own screen. She fired all her port verniers, sending herself into a high, arcing polar orbit. The manoeuvre, tight and dangerous, had the desired effect: *Magpie*'s torpedoes wasted their fuel trying to match their target and lost the lock.

"Bugger me," Kazin said, his tone half surprised, half admiring. "That was beautiful to watch.

"Destroy the first salvo and load up a second."

"The frigate's found us," Danui said. They watched as the enemy performed another tight turn to bring her around and then accelerate towards *Magpie*.

"Keep them trapped between us and Apore," Kazin ordered.

The privateer accelerated, and Danui fired off a series of decoys to confuse the enemy's battle computers.

"*Uzir*!" Kidron shouted. "It's Calethar, alright, a fleet unit. Under the authority of the High Council instead of a clan. Thirty thousand tonne, armed to the hilt and fast. The ship's only a generation old. Kazin's going to have his hands full."

Lynch and Kidron watched the opening moves on their screen. To Lynch, it was like a deadly, slow-motion ballet. Occasionally, fire registration lines twisted and jumped on the screens like cut snakes, indicating a broadside of torpedoes or defensive missiles, but no attack ever came near to its intended target.

"*Uzir*'s captain is good," Kidron admitted grudgingly. "But Kazin should have his measure by now." He was finding it difficult to contain himself. Lynch wondered if he had ever seen *Magpie* go into battle as an observer before.

"It's too fast and agile for us," Danui told Kazin.

It was forty minutes into the battle and the enemy frigate had avoided being sandwiched between *Magpie* and Apore. The two combatants were now equidistant from the planet and from each other, forming an invisible triangle.

Kazin watched the Calethar ship fire torpedoes followed by a cloud of decoy missiles, and then a second salvo of torpedoes on a different course to the first. He swore under his breath. The first salvo would keep *Magpie*'s defences busy, and the decoys would overload her sensors. And the second strike . . .

"Danui! I want defensive missiles against that first salvo, and fire all the dorsal verniers!"

Magpie lurched with the sudden manoeuvre, seats and control panels shaking so violently it felt like they might come loose from their fittings. Kazin watched the screen fill with the enemy's last salvo.

"Prepare for a hit!" he shouted. Seconds later the first Calethar torpedo streaked into *Magpie*'s stern. The ship shuddered and emergency klaxons and lights came on line. The second torpedo hit near the first, and the explosion threw everyone on the bridge off their couches.

Kazin scrambled back to his feet, feeling too light, and saw Danui do likewise. She flicked some switches on her control. Her face was pale.

"Main drive down and inertia control damaged," she reported.

Kazin resumed his couch. They could no longer make major course corrections. *Magpie*'s small verniers were the only motive power left to her. The damage to the inertia drive had also significantly reduced the ship's artificial gravity. He felt about a third his normal weight.

"What's the frigate doing now?" he asked Danui.

"Manoeuvring behind us, sir. She's coming in for the kill."

A red hatch pattern appeared over *Magpie*'s icon on Lynch's screen as one torpedo hit, and then again as the second found its target. The data showed *Magpie* was seriously damaged. They watched, horrified, as the still undamaged *Uzir* positioned herself behind the privateer.

"She's bringing her particle beam generator to bear," Kidron said.

Lynch felt his stomach knot. Magpie's *going to die,* he thought, fighting the panic rising in him like bile.

Kidron took a deep breath. "Get in touch with Robinson. We have to attack. If we can distract the frigate it may give Kazin a chance to catch *Uzir* with a salvo."

Lynch contacted Robinson and they quickly plotted an intercept course. He fired *Lark*'s engines, boosted out of orbit and set up the attack run. He could hear his heart banging away in his chest like a piston. Fear rose with the panic.

Kidron opened all channels between the three human craft. An open flood of messages between them might overload the enemy frigate's battle computer.

Danui looked up from her station in shock.

"The cutters are attacking the enemy ship!"

Impossible! Kazin thought. He checked his own battle screen.

"They'll be wiped out!" Danui exclaimed.

Kazin forced himself to stay calm. "How many torpedoes are remaining?"

"Seven."

"Fire five of them at the frigate," he ordered. "One at a time at thirty-second intervals. That should focus her captain's attention on us."

"And stop them getting a good lock with their beam weapon," Danui added. She fired the first torpedo.

Lynch powered up *Lark*'s laser.

"Hold your fire for as long as possible," Kidron said. "There's no point in letting *Uzir* know how feeble we are. It isn't the cutters that will destroy the frigate, but a salvo from *Magpie*."

Five minutes later the screen whited out for an instant. *Uzir* had fired her beam weapon at *Magpie*. Kidron hailed Kazin.

"It was close, Captain, but no prize," Kazin reported.

Kazin's voice was followed by Robinson's. "Twenty seconds, Aaron. Five-second burn as plotted."

Usero, captain of *Uzir*, could not believe his luck. The most feared human ship in known space drifted uselessly before him.

Magpie! My first victory! he thought. He glared at his helm-captain. *If only we could shoot straight!*

"Make sure we hit her next time," he said testily.

"It's difficult getting a proper target lock," the helm-captain said. "We have to manoeuvre to avoid *Magpie*'s torpedoes."

Even as he spoke *Magpie* fired another one. The helm-captain shouted a course change.

"You see?"

"She has to run out of them eventually," Usero said. "Just get me that lock!"

One of the junior navigators made a choking sound.

"What now?" Usero demanded.

"Two cutters, sir!" the navigator said. "And they're coming straight for us!"

"Show me!" Usero roared.

The navigator magnified the view on her screen. Two new ships showed.

"High velocity trajectory –" the navigator began.

"I can see that for myself! What weapons have they?"

"Lasers, sir. One each."

Just lasers! Usero could not believe it. *Surely the humans would not be that stupid.*

"Are you sure they're carrying nothing else?"

"Unlike lasers, torpedoes have no energy signature until they are fired, and so would not show up on our screens," the helm-captain said.

Usero fell back in his couch. *This can't be happening!*

Lark and *Swallow* completed their last burn. Kidron shouted "Now!" and two invisible laser beams lanced out from the cutters and hit *Uzir*. The lasers fired again, a longer burst this time.

"I got a damage response!" Robinson cried. "Minor, but on one of her starboard verniers."

"I read it, too," Kidron confirmed. "Good shooting, *Swallow*."

Then the screen whited out as *Uzir* fired her beam weapon again.

Magpie groaned like a live thing. Bulkheads shook, small electric fires spat sparks into smoky air. Crew members picked themselves up from the deck, scrambling for their seats; some did not get up at all.

Kazin touched his scalp, felt wet hair. He found it hard to concentrate. Danui was saying something to him, then Kidron's voice spoke to him from somewhere nearby. He glanced around, expecting to see him on the bridge. His gaze fell on the communicator in the arm of the couch.

He shook his head. Pain lanced through his skull, but his senses cleared.

"Aruzel, we're in trouble."

"Do you still have teeth?"

Kazin looked at Danui. She held up four fingers. "Four torpedoes," he told Kidron.

"We're coming in for a second pass against *Uzir*. See what you can do."

"Aye aye, Captain," he signed off. Uzir? *So that's her name. What a bitch.*

"Danui, I want all four torpedoes ready to launch against that ship – as wide a fan as you can make it. We've got to hit her with something or we're dead."

Danui turned to her station.

"*Magpie*'s badly damaged," the helm-captain of *Uzir* reported.

Usero smiled grimly. "One more shot."

"The cutters are returning!" the navigator cried.

Before Usero could stop him the helm-captain ordered a course change.

"We'll get them this time."

"No!" Usero shouted. "They are nothing! Only a diversion! *Magpie*'s our target, you fool! Have you still got the lock?"

The helm master checked his screen. "Almost –"

"Get it back! Forget the cutters! I want *Magpie* destroyed!"

"Lynch," Kidron said, his voice low and calm, "take us in closer. As close as you can."

Lynch nodded, made another five-second burn. *Uzir* swung square onto the screen and grew at an alarming rate. He noted *Swallow* copying *Lark*'s manoeuvre. *Do or die,* he thought to himself, wondering where his bravado was coming from.

The cutters fired their lasers continuously. They started to overheat. After a small course change the frigate had ignored them as though they were gnats. Lynch could see the glowing beam weapon protruding from *Uzir's* belly, getting brighter and brighter as he watched.

Then the screen suddenly lit up with a host of new registration lines. Kazin's voice came over the intercom: "Veer away! Veer away!"

Without thinking Lynch fired the engines. The frigate disappeared from the screen, and then the screen itself went completely blank. A circuit board above his head shorted out. *Lark* was shaken like a leaf, and Lynch struggled to bring it back under control.

"What the hell – !"

"He's done it!" Kidron exclaimed. "The old bastard's done it! Blown *Uzir* to kingdom come!"

Lynch swung the cutter back around. He could not believe he was seeing *Uzir.* The whole forward section of the frigate was gone, only jagged beams and drifting cables like severed ganglions remained; twisted bodies and pools of liquid floated from the gaping wound that remained. Fires coruscated in the stern, greedily eating what was left of the ship's air.

And that could have been Magpie, he thought to himself.

And then Robinson was screaming over the intercom: "Heads up! A second ship! A second ship!"

Lynch dragged his gaze away from the wreck of *Uzir* and back to the screen. He saw another ship floating in space not a thousand klicks from their present position, larger and heavier than *Uzir*. He fell back against the acceleration couch, exhausted and despairing.

Chapter 12

Lynch's despair turned to anger; anger at the odds fate seemed to be throwing at him and anger at his own fear. He pushed it down, kept his mind on the job. If he wanted to survive he had to respond quickly and efficiently.

"It's not a warship!" Robinson shouted over the intercom. "Check your sensors. Forty thousand tonne, pod built . . . it's a freighter."

Lynch felt faint with relief.

Kidron got onto the line to Kazin. "We read a freighter. Have you any more information?"

"Sorry, Captain. Our sensors were blown when *Uzir* went up. It will take hours to repair them."

"Robinson, dock with *Magpie*. We'll take *Lark* and do some investigating."

Lynch put the cutter on a comfortable intercept with the new ship, now drifting sunwards from its point of entry into normal space. As they approached the vessel their sensors relayed more detailed information. The stranger had also recently been in a battle, and had either come off the loser or a very sorry-looking winner. Kidron relayed the information back to Kazin, and then tried to hail the new ship on a broad band, identifying *Lark* as human-controlled but offering no more information.

There was a crackle before some faint and barely distinguishable words returned the signal. The tongue was human, but the wary look in Kidron's eyes told Lynch his captain still was not convinced. He wondered if traitors other than Tolstoi had been employed by the Calethar.

"Could you make any of that gibberish out?" Kidron asked him. Lynch shook his head. "I thought I heard the word 'friend', but that could be my imagination at work. Break off at 200 klicks. That's close enough for us to give each other the once-over."

A message came through from *Magpie*. *Swallow* had docked safely, and teams were working on repairing the sensors and engines. "I don't know about the main drive, Captain," Kazin said, sounding rueful. "The damage is extensive. I reckon we could be in orbit for up to a week before jury-rigging anything."

"We'll have to do better than that," Kidron replied. "If the Calethar don't hear soon from the outpost or the frigate they'll infest this part of space with destroyers and troops. I'd rather be far away when that happens."

"Captain," Lynch interrupted, "we have a clear message coming through."

Kidron listened attentively and Lynch saw a smile crease his face.

"I'll be damned. It's *Toucan*. That bloody pirate!"

"Sir?"

Kidron gave a short laugh. "*Toucan*, a human freighter. Her captain is Israel Zoubek, the nastiest piece of work this side of the border worlds. Also possibly the best spacer I've ever met. He occasionally indulges in a little unofficial privateering – but only when the odds are heavily in his favour." He pressed the transmit button. "Hello, Zoubek. This is Aruzel Kidron. What made you drag your fleabag ship to this part of the universe?"

"Kidron? It can't be!" *Toucan*'s captain replied. "There's no god in the universe. What are you doing out here? Wherever here is!"

"Here is the Hanar system, around which circles the planet Apore, home to an Uzdar colony. I repeat, *Toucan*, what are *you* doing here?"

There was a pause, then: "Looking for sanctuary, Aruzel."

"At a Calethar world?"

"We did not know that, Kidron. We are flying blind."

"What happened?"

"It's a long story, best told face-to-face. Will you come aboard? Or would you prefer I came to *Magpie*?"

"You're welcome to join me on my ship, Captain."

"Our sensors are recording a lot more free energy here than there has any right to be. Not *Magpie*, I assume?"

"No. *Uzir*. A Calethar frigate."

"A frigate? It must have had a brave and skilful captain to take on *Magpie*. What damage have you?"

It was Kidron's turn to pause. "Our engines are damaged," he said at last.

"We may be able to help you. How are your navigation systems?"

"Intact to the best of my knowledge."

"Ah, good. Then you can return the favour, my friend. Maybe there is a god after all."

"I'm sure we can come to a comfortable and mutually rewarding arrangement," Kidron said dryly.

The senior officers of the two ships met in *Magpie*'s war room, gathered around a table. After brief introductions, arrangements were made for essential repairs to be carried out immediately on both vessels. They could not risk hanging around in hostile space in their present condition.

Kidron then asked Zoubek to tell his tale.

The visiting captain sipped on a whisky for a moment, considering his words carefully. Then he told his audience how *Toucan* had teamed up with another privateer from his home planet, the border world of Sumer.

"The other ship was a small, converted surveyor named *Mosquito*," said Zoubek. "Her captain was a she-devil, Balethusa Martyn, better known as Malaria Martyn. She was a real old-fashioned pirate. Well, how I imagine one would have been. Only a metre and a half tall but all spit and fury. She had some information about a gathering of Calethar traders around an artificial satellite in the Mandragora system."

"I thought that system was uninhabited," Kazin interrupted.

"It is," Zoubek said, "except for this satellite the Calethar put into a grade D orbit around the binary there. Ostensibly for scientific research, but more likely for intelligence gathering. That part of space is filled with the colonies of several species, including human."

Kazin nodded, and *Toucan*'s captain poured himself another drink before continuing the story.

"Martyn heard that upwards of four Calethar merchants would be gathering at the satellite to arrange a special mission to a world inhabited by a new and recently contacted species called the Ped. The ships were all from different clans, so the meeting had to be on neutral ground. That's why they chose the satellite. It had a refuelling station and comfortable quarters the merchants could use. The High Council never fails to bend over backwards for merchants.

"Martyn's idea was for us to reappear in normal space as close as possible to the satellite and deliver the Calethar with a *fait accompli* – hand over all their information about the new world or watch their vessels be destroyed. Once the information was handed over we would disable their engines and communications, take their cargoes for ourselves and go on to do business with the Peds."

"Nice idea," conceded Kidron. "But to do that you'd have to arrive in normal space very close to the satellite or you'd give the merchants time to power up and escape."

"Exactly. And the information Martyn had included precise co-ordinates for just such a jump."

"Where did this information come from?" Kidron asked.

Zoubek shrugged. "Martyn wouldn't reveal her sources. Understandably, of course. This was very rich food, indeed, and if she was the only one with access to it then she need never worry about finding partners for her enterprises, no matter how unlikely they might be. In fact . . ." Zoubek's eyes narrowed for a moment as he searched his memory ". . . yes, I seem to remember her saying that she had first tried to get in touch with you, Aruzel. But apparently you'd already left Hecabe. She couldn't wait, so she settled for me instead."

Kidron said nothing. If Zoubek expected some reaction he was disappointed. He shrugged, then continued.

"Accordingly, everything was arranged and we left Sumer brimming with confidence and dreaming of the riches we would be bringing back. We made our jump two days after departure, and arrived exactly where we planned. Our screens were filled by the most beautiful sight I'd ever seen. Four fat Calethar freighters and an unarmed research satellite.

"We signalled the Calethar as agreed, and waited for their answer. Of course, it didn't come immediately. We knew they would be suffering from shock. We didn't try to jam their distress calls, confident we would be well away before any help could arrive. We pictured ourselves among them, the representatives of four clans at each others' throats, accusing one another of treachery and deceit. We waited a decent interval and then fired a warning salvo to remind them of our presence."

Zoubek paused and stared into his drink. Lynch noticed how *Toucan*'s officers avoided the eager glances of *Magpie*'s personnel. Zoubek's hands began to shake.

"Suddenly, from out of nowhere we were hit by a beam weapon. Not from the satellite or any of the freighters, but from behind us, sunwards. Everything was chaos. I ordered our stern verniers to fire, and it saved us; a second shot missed by a fraction. On board there were fires and the hull was losing pressure. Our sensors picked up at least three salvos of torpedoes heading our way. We released our defensive missiles and let off a salvo ourselves in the general direction of the incoming fire. The binary was effectively hiding our attacker, so we weren't able to get a fix or a reading on it.

"Three of the incoming torpedoes hit us. That's when we lost our navigation section and a lot of good people. *Mosquito* wasn't nearly so lucky. One minute she was there, the next nothing but radioactive dust. It was that quick. The beam weapon again, I think. As far as we could tell, the torpedoes had all been directed against us. I thought there must have been at least three Calethar frigates for there to have been that much beam fire, but I couldn't figure out how that many vessels could have hidden from our sensors, binary or no. There would have been too much energy, but we found no traces."

Zoubek stopped for a moment to steady his hands. Kidron quickly poured him another drink. *Toucan*'s captain nodded gratefully and swallowed it in one mouthful.

When he resumed, his voice was ragged. "Fortunately we didn't have to wait for the main drive to power up, and we immediately made a short, random hop. We ended up 10,000 klicks away, sunwards. And then our sensors found her. My God, Aruzel, she was . . . terrifying. Bigger than *Magpie*, and packed with weapons. I think she could have taken on a Federation dreadnought and won. She was beautiful to look at. Not pod-built, like a freighter, nor as cumbersome and balloon-like as most warships, but built like a sword. All power and death. She found our new position with incredible speed, and performed the most frightening manoeuvre. I shudder to think of the Gs she was pulling. Her crew must all be wrapped in webbing, or made out of something other than flesh and bone.

"We jumped out of the system as quickly as we could. That's when we discovered our navigation system was damaged. We programmed the drive computers to jump, via a series of F- and G-class suns we aligned optically, towards what we hoped were the border worlds. As we were gliding up to our next jump, she appeared again. We got away just in time. I don't know how she found us, or how she got there so quickly, but she did.

"She's a monster. And she was waiting for us at Mandragora. We were set up, my friend. I have never before in my life been so scared.

"This ship is death, Aruzel, death for all of us."

Chapter 13

Nomelet reclined in his couch on the bridge of *Canar Calethari*. In front of him stood two Calethar. The shorter of the two wore a haughty demeanour Nomelet found insulting. His name was Raenar, eldest son of Floran the master shipwright. His position as executive officer on *Canar* was ambiguous, the position rare on Calethar ships and almost unheard of on warships, but Nomelet had accepted him as part of the crew as a favour to his father. Raenar assumed the position was no more than his due as heir to the newest claimant to clan leadership. He was overbearing, supercilious and unpopular with the other officers. Nomelet would find a way to teach him some manners, but there was no hurry. It would be a while before *Canar* returned home.

The second Calethar standing before Nomelet was a different creature altogether. She was tall, standing two metres in height. Among all the crew only Nomelet was taller. Her bearing was confident and professional, but not obtrusive. She was a secretor, a Calethar who belonged to a clan too small to have its own ships and therefore too unimportant to have even its clan name recognised by the High Council. Her name was Teonar of the clan Sien, and she was *Canar*'s war-captain. It was common practice on Calethar ships to employ secertor in important positions because their decisions would not be affected by intra-clan rivalries. All her wages and share of profits would go to her clan which, like all secertor, was saving and investing so that at some time it could purchase or build its own starship and gain official recognition.

"You have a report for me, Raenar," said Nomelet.

"Cousin, I have a report from our navigators and communication specialists on the recent battle we fought in the Mandragora system."

Nomelet clacked his jaws, and Raenar continued.

"The destroyed vessel was *Mosquito*, a vessel commanded by a certain Balethusa Martyn." Raenar had trouble with the name. *He is not spending enough time learning the human language,* thought Nomelet. "She was the human given the bait by our accomplice on Sumer. We assumed she would contact Captain Kidron for the mission, but she apparently failed to do so. The other ship has been identified as *Toucan*, a freighter. Her captain is known as Israel Zoubek. I have been advised that *Toucan* probably suffered extensive damage amidships. Whether she will reach sanctuary or not we have no way of telling."

"That is the report?" asked Nomelet.

"It is, cousin."

"And you, Teonar?"

"I have a report from the war section."

Nomelet clacked his jaws.

"It's assumed *Toucan* was making random jumps to throw us off her trail. It is further assumed the jumps were random because the crew did not know where they were going."

"Explain yourself," said Nomelet. He could not help noticing Raenar's expression. Obviously the whelp thought Teonar was in trouble because she offered nothing but theories. *He will be disappointed.*

"The damage *Toucan* received amidships could have destroyed her ability to accurately navigate. Human freighters of that size tend to place the navigation section in that part of the ship. Though it is dangerous to generalise, I lean towards this explanation for *Toucan*'s unexpected jumps, and thus our losing track of her."

"Expand," Nomelet ordered. Raenar was almost sneering now.

"If she was making random jumps with the intention of losing us, then it is reasonable to assume her crew was aware of *Canar*'s ability to track her across a limited distance of hyperspace. Since only a few Calethar know we are fitted with this new device, it would infer the humans have an intelligence service better than anything we've previously suspected. It would also make their initial surprise at the ambush difficult to understand."

Nomelet nodded. What Teonar said made sense. They had come so close to destroying both ships that the victory they achieved seemed almost of no importance compared to the victory they might have had. Ah, well. At least the merchants were grateful, and their gifts of appreciation would do the Uzdar coffers no harm. *Canar* might even manage to pay for herself on her maiden voyage, an unprecedented event in Calethar history. Nomelet smiled at the thought of how pleased that would make Enilka. So much Uzdar wealth had gone into *Canar*'s creation and construction, so much time and research, so much pride. Uzdar agents and spies had scoured the weapons laboratories of every spacefaring species, even those of the humans, to get the most advanced equipment. The result was the first ship built by the Calethar that they were sure could beat *Magpie*.

Raenar and Teonar waited patiently while Nomelet stood deep in thought. This was the privilege of rank, allowed the others only in the privacy of their own cabins. They dared not move until they were dismissed, for although Nomelet did not have a killing sword, to disgrace him in such a way could only result in their losing position and authority.

It is time, Nomelet thought, *to teach Raenar a little humility.* "Your opinion, Raenar, on what we should do next."

"I suggest we hunt down this Kidron. We failed to entice him into our trap at Mandragora. We should cast aside subtlety. Hunt him down, and destroy any human vessel we happen across in the meantime. This is a warship; let it go to war."

"I appreciate your eagerness, but I do not want to start a war. Too precipitous an action on our part could result in the High Council actively condemning us, and that would prove fatal to the cause of the Uzdar." *Not to mention to my own,* he thought.

"Your suggestion, although honourable, is inappropriate. Kidron could be anywhere. What if we appear in a system being visited by a taskforce of the Federation Navy? We believe we could take on one of their dreadnoughts, but a whole fleet of them? No. Our deaths would only serve to add to the glory of the humans, and take away from that of the Calethar."

"Then what do you suggest, cousin?" Raenar asked, unable to disguise his displeasure.

"On the bridge, Raenar, you will refer to me as Captain," Nomelet said calmly, but not so quietly he wasn't heard by all the assembled officers. Raenar sucked in his breath at the public reprimand. Nomelet continued as though nothing untoward had occurred. "We need a challenge of sorts. The humans are not entirely without honour, this Kidron especially."

"They know nothing of honour!" Raenar exclaimed, venting some of his anger.

"Perhaps not as you understand it. But Kidron's pride can be used against him. We will raid several systems in the same sector. Eventually Kidron will come calling, looking for his mysterious rival. Pride or honour, I don't care which, will lead him to us. Then we will destroy him and his ship."

Raenar sat fuming in his cabin. He cleaned the combs on his feet with furious, jerky motions of the brush; his own ineptitude, his own lack of control, merely served to feed his anger. He felt like an embarrassed cub. That witch Teonar had Nomelet under her thumb. Nomelet did not deserve to be ship-captain, Raenar told himself bitterly.

Ever since they had left Dramorath he had fought to secure his position as executive officer. He had served faithfully and loyally. Perhaps he had been overbearing to the crew at times, but they *must* recognise his authority. He had been so proud when his father embraced him for the last time before he boarded the shuttle taking him to *Canar Calethari*, and when he arrived the crew had just glanced at him and turned away. The shame he had felt burned his very soul.

And now Teonar. The secertor witch. Her report had been more thorough and professional than his, her conclusions more reasonable given the evidence. Why had the navigation and communication specialists not realised all that Teonar had? The war-captain was a growing threat to his authority, and she would have to be dealt with.

Something cold ate at his mind, and he chased the thought until he had it pinned down. Destroying Teonar would require destroying Nomelet as well.

The path he must inevitably take began forming in his brain. When *Canar* returned to Dramorath, it would have a different captain. His line would become paramount among the Uzdar.

Raenar shivered at the audacity of his own ambition, his anger transformed into a terrible dream.

Teonar's ambitions and dreams were of a different order altogether. She lay in her cot, her mind's eye surveying the savanna of her home world. She relived the last hunt she had been on, a huge clan gathering that had lasted several days and spanned a whole continent. She was a galenthar, one of the hunters who used only their own body's weapons to kill their prey – the long sharp claws of their hands, and the strong gripping teeth of their jaws. She remembered the hot blood of her prey seeping into her mouth, its last convulsions as she held it down beneath her own weight.

Hers had been the biggest catch, the greatest honour. And her ambition was to end Raenar's life the same way. Not for reasons of pride or honour, but of practicality. She could feel his hatred, and knew it would be the downfall of either him or herself. She must overcome this upstart youngster. Her clan was depending on her. The profits and the reputation she would bring back from this journey would be enough finally to raise their clan above the status of secertor.

She remembered how her aunt, the clan head of the Sien, had summoned her to an audience after the great hunt. When she arrived her aunt was already in discussion with another Calethar. Teonar recognised the garb of the Uzdar, and her pulse had quickened with excitement. Most of the secertor clans in the outworlds had heard rumours and reports of the Uzdar's great project.

Her aunt had turned to her and said: "The Uzdar need a war-captain. I have suggested you."

That was all. The stranger studied her closely but said nothing. He was obviously impressed by her size. But how could she prove her worth? And then, as though the gods themselves had intervened, her drones, carrying her catch, a beast nearly three times her own weight, walked by outside the audience dome. Her sash was wrapped around the beast's bloody muzzle.

The Uzdar laughed. "We have found our war-captain," he had said, and the deal was settled.

I will not fail you, Aunt, Teonar thought to herself, stretching out on the cot, her long claws glistening in the cabin's single, wan light. *I will bring back to you the corpses of our enemies like bound animals. First the human called Kidron, the black pirate. And second the Calethar called Raenar.*

Nomelet enjoyed being on the bridge. In his cabin doubts assailed him, but here he was at the centre of power. He loved his ship, her graceful lines, her hand-picked crew, her very name. Sitting in his captain's couch he never doubted his mission.

Canar Calethari was his ambition given form and substance. She was the sword he would wield to tear out the heart of the Federation.

She is vengeance, he thought, and the thought gave him pleasure.

Chapter 14

Pandami was stronger than she looked. Already she had been in the colony's garden for eight hours, picking fruit, digging up tubers and collecting nuts. Winter was coming and the colony needed all the food it could gather. The planet Lagash had mostly been kind to its human settlers, but its soil was hard and the work was back-breaking. As the sun started to set, she was the only one of the farmers who stayed behind.

Just one hour more, she promised herself, standing erect and stretching out the cricks in her spine. She gazed up at the darkening sky, searched for the group of bright stars that made the pattern of an old man's face. The yellow star that made one of the man's eyes was Newton, her homeworld.

"A lifetime away," she said aloud, although there was no one around to hear.

As she looked there was a burst of white light in the sky. Whatever it was dimmed immediately. Seconds later, in the same part of the sky, there was another flash of brilliant light which lasted longer but still faded away too quickly to be natural. She realised then what she had seen. Her heart went cold.

"Oh, God, no! The colony ship!"
She ran back to town, shouting her warning.
It was already too late.

Teonar was in command of *Canar Calethari*'s first battle car, named *Kudu*, which meant "Talon". It was small for a troop transport, but manoeuvrable, an important asset when it had no weapons to defend itself with.

Teonar flew *Kudu* herself. She found the hurtling descent to the surface of Lagash exhilarating, the perfect preparation for combat.

She levelled *Kudu* out at only a hundred metres from the ground and almost on top of the human colony. The battle car swooped over the settlement. Teonar found the perfect landing site, swung around for the final descent. She saw humans scrambling to meet the invasion, most with weapons. She grinned. This would be a good and bloody fight.

Pandami reached the colony as the Calethar battle car landed. Even though the race from the garden had exhausted her she ran on. She burst into her house, but her husband was already gone, the weapon rack empty.

She rushed outside, saw columns of brown smoke rising from the far side of the settlement. Her legs felt like rubber and her lungs burned for air, but fear for her husband spurred her on.

The first body Pandami came across was that of a young man. He was so badly mangled she could not recognise him. She grabbed the primitive rifle on the ground next to him. It was undamaged and the ammunition clip was full.

Pandami heard shots ahead of her, but smoke obscured her view. She continued on, the rifle held ready. More bodies littered the street, most with terrible wounds. All were human. Tears came to her eyes. She wanted to see if her husband was among them, but knew she was needed to help fight off the invaders.

Suddenly colonists burst from the smoke, fleeing towards her. She heard wild whoops and a group of aliens appeared, chasing them. They were all Actane except their leader, a Calethar in full battle-dress.

Pandami saw one male colonist lose his footing and fall. The Actane jumped onto him with glee, lifted him to his feet. They held him for the Calethar. The man lifted his head. It was her husband.

Before she could do anything the Calethar raised his blaster and fired. A bolt of electric-blue energy tore off her husband's head. The Actane let the jerking body fall to the ground, ignoring the blood that hissed over them.

"Jamie!" she screamed. "Jamie!"

Fleeing colonists grabbed at her as they ran past to pull her along with them. She shrugged them off.

The aliens looked at her, surprised. Here was a lone female standing her ground. The Actane whooped in joy and came for her.

Pandami raised her rifle and aimed at the Calethar. He too stood his ground, aiming his own weapon at her. She fixed his head in the sights, saw him smiling at her. She squeezed the trigger.

The recoil from the ancient firearm kicked her back, but not far enough. A blaster shot struck her in the side, throwing her to the ground. She tried to get to her feet but her legs would not obey her.

She felt no pain, only a great hollowness. All she could think of was her husband. Dead. Her life meant nothing to her any more.

Alien hands pulled at her, stood her up. She saw she had hit her target. The dead Calethar's blood pooled with her husband's.

A second Calethar appeared. A female. She bent over the slain leader, looked up at his killer.

"It was well done," she said in Interlingua, then motioned to the Actane.

They picked Pandami up in their arms and carried her away. She passed out before she had time to wonder why.

Nomelet descended in the second battle car, named *Anma*, meaning "Claw". He had time to marvel at the beauty of the sky, pale blue and gold-rimmed, and then *Anma* dropped through the clouds and reappeared above the human settlement. Below he could see ordered fields and the grey, squat shapes of factories and workshops. Thick plumes of greasy smoke billowed up from the main centre of habitation.

Nomelet met Teonar in the settlement's main building, used for meetings and celebrations. It was one of the few structures that still had a roof, and many of the human wounded had been brought there to be tended by those of their medical personnel who had survived. Nomelet was surveying the pitiful remnants of the defenders when Teonar approached him.

"Congratulations," Nomelet said. "Another victory. Another bonus. You have done well. What are our casualties?"

"Forty-three. Five dead. Seven seriously wounded, and they may not survive. Jarold was killed, the only Calethar."

"He was a drone. The payment for his bones will be small. But he was a good soldier and he will be missed. Human losses?"

"At least 400 dead. We haven't collected all the pieces yet, so we can't be sure. All these wounded that you see here. We suspect many of their old and young ones are hiding in the woods a little distance north of here. Do you want us to flush them out?"

"No. Just get whatever booty you can back up to *Canar*. Do we know who killed Jarold?"

Teonar made a sound to one of the mercenary Actane. He walked over to one of the wounded humans, a young female who had been shot in the flank, pulled her to her feet and dragged her before the Calethar.

"What is your name?" Nomelet asked in Interlingua.

"Pandami," the human answered. She was obviously in some pain. Nomelet nodded and studied her carefully. She was lean and hard from the labour of many years. Suddenly another human had joined them, a middle-aged man with a bandage around one foot. He was supporting himself with a crutch. He faced Nomelet.

"You, Calethar. You are in charge?" he asked, and before anyone could answer, said: "Then you know you cannot mistreat or torture this prisoner in any way. There are conventions signed by all spacefaring species. We were defending our homes . . ."

Nomelet glanced at Teonar, who unsheathed one claw and swiped at the speaker. The man's head leapt from his shoulders. Blood gushed over Nomelet and the wounded prisoner. The body slumped to the ground like a marionette whose strings had been cut. There was an awful silence in the building, broken in the end by Nomelet clapping his claws together.

"Prisoners will only speak when spoken to," he said in a loud voice. "At all times be courteous, and courtesy will be returned."

He returned his attention to Pandami, who was shivering with pain and fear. "You have done a brave thing," he said. "Tell this Calethar –" and he pointed to Teonar "– which house is yours, and it will not be ransacked."

The Actane mercenary took the woman away and Nomelet used his claws to wipe off the blood that had washed over his jerkin and thighs. He then spoke to his war-captain in a voice loud enough for all to hear: "Teonar, leave the old and young ones where they are. We are not butchers. Let the humans know this before we leave, but brook no bad manners. There is never any excuse for bad manners, not even among humans. If they behave, make sure they have enough food to last until assistance comes. Repair their communications for them."

"It will be done," said Teonar.

Chapter 15

Lynch woke, screaming, from a sleep filled with strange dreams, his skin covered in a patina of sweat. He remembered parts of the dream: the burnt corpse sliding by the cargo bay hatch, the destroyed *Uzir* floating in space like a gutted animal, and then the two images superimposing on each other – *Uzir* filled with bodies melted into grotesque, glistening shapes, then the corpse from the cargo bay, its entrails made from cables and its ribs from twisted girders. Shaking, he forced himself into a shower bag, and floated in hot, oiled water until the skin pruned on his fingers.

Later, as he was about to board *Lark* with Robinson for another lesson, she held him back.

"You look like shit," she said. She touched his forehead. "You're not running a temperature."

He brushed her hand aside. "I'm fine. Let's get on with it."

He clambered up the gangladder before she could say anything more.

When she joined him in the cockpit she said lightly: "I guess you can call yourself a privateer now you've survived your first battle."

Lynch nodded absently. "Do you know how many crew *Uzir* carried?"

She shrugged. "A hundred or so. Depends on whether or not she was carrying any extras – a military detachment, a scientific expedition, whatever." She studied him closely. "It was them or us, Aaron. Don't get sentimental about the Calethar. It's not a courtesy they'd afford you."

"I know, but as far as the Calethar are concerned we're pirates. *Uzir* was a military vessel, simply doing its job, right?"

"Doing its job, as you so politely put it, meant destroying *Magpie* and killing us."

"I can't think of them as an enemy, Toma, that's all. They're more like . . . rivals."

"Rivals with guns," Robinson corrected him. "I sometimes think we humans and the Calethar were evolved by the universe to balance each other. We're natural opponents, enemies by nature."

"We were at war with the Mendart once, and now we're at peace."

Robinson snorted. "What exists between us and the Mendart isn't peace. They hate us more than words can describe, but the Mendart will never be as much of a threat as the Calethar. We don't bother with the Mendart, and most of them do their best to avoid us. The Calethar are a different matter. They're a great people, I don't deny it. I respect them. And I'm afraid of them."

"Do *you* think they want to invade human space?"

"Nothing surer. They're only biding their time." She smiled. "*Magpie*'s just getting a few blows in before the main event."

Robinson's tone was calm, as always, but while they were discussing the Calethar, Lynch noticed her face harden and her eyes narrow as if focusing down the sights of a rifle. He realised she was not simply afraid of the aliens. The insight startled him.

"You hate them, don't you," he said.

Robinson turned away, and he wondered if he had gone too far. Then she said: "Have you ever heard of the *Mercury*?" Lynch shook his head. "It was a survey vessel, one of the last human ships to explore the frontier sector. Fifteen years ago while on its way back from an expedition it was destroyed by a Calethar fleet unit." Her voice tightened. "My parents were scientists serving on *Mercury*. The entire crew was lost with the ship."

Lynch looked at her blankly. His own parents died so long ago and when he was so young he had never really grieved for them. Despite N'Djama he felt a gap in his life where he knew his parents should have been, but the feeling was one of incompleteness, not loss.

"The Calethar made excuses and all the right sounds, of course," she continued. "Very apologetic. The Federation responded with all the right sounds, and accepted all the excuses. The Calethar got away with a slap on the wrist when they should've gotten a bloody nose.

"Now they know they can get away with murder, and the Federation will do anything to keep things on an even political keel. The Calethar are building up their strength for a real test, and humanity just sits on its backside waiting for things to happen."

"Not all humanity," Lynch said quietly, suddenly feeling the need to comfort her in some way. He was surprised by the emotion.

"No, not all. There are still a few people with the intelligence and imagination to do something constructive. Pecking at the Calethar, keeping them wary and guessing. It's better than nothing, and *Magpie* and Kidron do more than anybody else.

"For the moment it's still a game, Aaron, but both sides know these are just the opening moves to a war. It's coming, and sooner than you think; sooner than anyone thinks."

Lynch had never heard anyone talk about the possibility of a war so enthusiastically. There was an eagerness in Robinson's voice that chilled him. She calmly accepted – welcomed! – the prospect of war. He wondered if the driving force behind it was hate for the Calethar or grief and self-pity for the loss of her parents. He found himself torn between the desire to comfort her and wanting to keep his distance. He sensed she had sacrificed some essential part of herself to feed her anger.

She glanced at him, read in his eyes some of the conflict he was experiencing. She sighed and looked away.

"Engage the engines, Ensign," she said quietly. "We've got work to do."

Magpie and *Toucan* returned together to Burgess. From there Zoubek took *Toucan* on deeper into human space, first to find a Federation Navy base to make a full report about the encounter with the new Calethar ship and then to return home to Sumer for a complete refit. Kidron suspected Zoubek would also be doing some heavy thinking about his occasional forays into privateering.

The battle he had been through would make anyone reconsider their options.

Magpie's damage, although serious, could be repaired in orbit around Burgess, and Kidron had no intention of withdrawing all the way to Hecabe. The booty they had extracted from the outpost had been significant. Some of the Calethar equipment and native craftworks fetched a good price on Burgess, and the rest he put into storage there to await the eventual return voyage home.

Kidron asked Kazin to come and see him two days after hearing Zoubek's account of the ambush at Mandragora.

"I've been thinking about our encounter with *Uzir* and what Zoubek told us of the new Calethar ship," Kidron said. "The Calethar have become much more aggressive."

"You think they're actively hunting down human privateers?" Kazin asked.

Kidron shook his head. "That, or just us. I can't make up my mind. I knew the attack on Tunius would spark a response, but not this soon and not in this strength."

Kazin shrugged. "Maybe the encounter with *Uzir* was a coincidence."

"Possibly, but remember Zoubek said Balethusa Martyn had first tried to enrol us in her expedition to Mandragora."

"I'm not sure what's troubling you. We wanted a response, remember?"

"Maybe I'm just surprised at how rapid their reaction was. It makes me think much of it was already in place."

Kazin laughed. "You mean they *knew* you were going to attack Tunius? I know the Calethar are very clever, Aruzel, but they're not psychic."

Kidron did not smile. "My concern is that this new ship and their plan to destroy us – perhaps all human privateers – is merely part of a much wider strategy."

Kazin's eyes widened. "You're suggesting it's the first stage of a Calethar invasion of human space?"

Kidron faced Kazin, his expression showing his frustration. "I *don't* know, Michael. My ego is not so big I think the Calethar are going to all this trouble just for my benefit. But what if we're not talking about the actual first stage of an invasion, but a reconnaissance or a trial of strength. By eliminating *Magpie*, the Calethar force the Federation to react to defend human interests in the frontier sector."

"If the reaction is a strong one, the Calethar pull their claws in for a while."

"Exactly. And if the reaction is a weak one . . ." Kidron let the sentence hang.

"In the meantime," Kazin said after a moment, "we have to make a decision about this new Calethar warship. Where has she come from? What are her objectives? What clan built her? Who is her captain?"

"And most importantly, can *Magpie* match her?" Kidron added.

"Why not leave her to the Federation?" Kazin asked.

"She has to be dealt with before the Federation gets off its collective arse or the political and military balance in the frontier sector will swing completely against humanity.

"Besides, Obe says reports have come in of high levels of Calethar activity in the Triangle, a collection of nine human-occupied systems near the middle of the sector. The reports are infrequent, but become more consistent and reliable as they are cross-referenced." He paused for effect. "And we have a name for her. *Canar Calethari*, 'Calethar's Curse'. It hits often and hard. Seven freighters have disappeared in the Triangle in as many weeks, and four have limped away from encounters, damaged and filled with dead crew."

"As Zoubek inferred, *Canar* seems to be equipped with some amazing weapons and devices," said Kazin.

"She obviously carries a particle beam generator that is both quick-targeting and quick-firing," Kidron pointed out. "Not to mention several points for launching torpedoes; defence systems that would do a dreadnought proud; and most dangerous of all, a method of tracking ships through hyperspace."

"The fact that any freighters survived at all suggests the tracking system is effective only over a limited distance," Kazin pointed out.

"Better than no system at all," Kidron muttered darkly. "Another thing the reports indicate is that *Canar Calethari*'s ship-captain and war-captain are both very good at their jobs."

"But *who* are they, and what clan do they come from?" Kazin asked.

"Danui tells me *Canar* makes a habit of hitting the settlements themselves, something the Calethar have done only infrequently and rarely with great success before. The Calethar can put together a great navy, but ground combat is something they're not renowned for. Although tough individually, usually they fight inefficiently as a cohesive military unit."

"Most clans raise small and reputedly very professional units," Kazin said.

"But they are maintained for the defence of their respective homeworlds and to put down serious uprisings among native populations on worlds where they have large and important settlements. The point is, Michael, although reports reveal most of the ground troops employed by *Canar* are mercenaries, many Calethar are also being sighted.

"*Canar*'s captain is throwing us a challenge. The Calethar know reports of their ship will circulate rapidly after they started hitting human settlements, and they know that only one non-naval vessel would dare try to stop them." Kidron smiled. "I'm flattered."

"You're not going to accept it, are you?" Kazin asked.

"Not until we've changed the rules. I'm not interested in a fair fight."

"I keep on hearing Zoubek's words," Kazin said. "The ship was death. He said it like a prophecy."

"You don't think we can beat *Canar Calethari*?"

Kazin shrugged. "I don't know. We've never met a ship like her until now. *Magpie*'s always been the best privateer around, but a large part of that's been due to the skill and training of her crew. From all reports, *Canar Calethari* is also well crewed and well led. If the crews are matched, and the stories we're hearing about the enemy ship's weapons fitout are true, *Magpie* won't stand a chance."

"Not in a stand-up fight, I agree. But I have a plan."

Kazin laughed. "You're a bloodhound, Aruzel, and you've got a scent. Tell me your plan. I can see you're going to, anyway, whether I like it or not."

Chapter 16

As *Kudu* passed low over the human settlement on Radik, Teonar had the satisfaction of watching its population scatter in several directions at once. As was now his usual practice, Nomelet ignored the settlement's satellite and the deserted transport that had brought the colonists to Radik, and sent the battle cars straight down to attack the settlement without warning. Now the gamble was paying off. No fixed defences, the laser batteries not even powered up, and the best loot still not hidden away. This would be their most successful raid yet.

Teonar was beginning to enjoy the life of a privateer, and understood what humans like Kidron saw in it. The excitement, the booty, the honour.

She ordered the pilot to put the battle car down 300 metres from the centre of the settlement. Even before *Kudu* landed, she slid open the hatch and leapt out. Sixty soldiers followed her. She drew her blaster from its holster and waved forward with her other hand. Her troops fanned out, guns ready and eyes looking for the first sign of resistance. First went the Actane, fast and nimble, half running, half leaping as they advanced. Behind them the Mendart, slower and less agile than the

Actane but very strong and single-minded in the attack. What the Actane could not handle the Mendart would take care of. Last came a squad of highly trained Calethar: aggressive and efficient. They were better soldiers than the Actane or Mendart mercenaries, but were used in combat only if the situation became desperate; Nomelet had to pay compensation for every Calethar killed. Teonar was the only Calethar in the front line, as befitted her rank.

By now troops from *Anma* would be securing the laser batteries in case some of the humans shot at the grounded transports while their occupants got on with the business of looting.

Some humans had run in their direction when they started their advance but, on seeing their numbers, changed direction or just stood still, arms raised in their gesture of surrender. Teonar ordered two mercenaries to round them up. The invaders encountered no resistance until they were 200 metres from the settlement's centre and beginning to enter streets and alleyways. There was that strange, percussive sound that human side-arms made, and an Actane mercenary near Teonar dropped noiselessly to the ground. Another mercenary stooped to check the casualty while four others charged the house the gunfire had come from. They broke the door down and disappeared inside. There was another shot from the human weapon and then a weird and unnatural silence. The mercenaries reappeared a few moments later, one wounded in the leg, dragging the corpse of their attacker between them. The mercenaries had taken their trophies, and what was left of the body was dumped at the front door of the house for all the other humans to see. Teonar checked on the Actane mercenary who had first been shot, but no one could do anything for him. His throat was cut and his body left on the street to be picked up later. The advance continued.

Teonar's communicator buzzed three times, the signal from Raenar that the laser batteries had been secured. Good. The battle plan was proceeding perfectly. She worked well with Nomelet, almost as if they were matched. The thought excited her: he would make an excellent mate. The sound of another shot startled her, and she cursed herself for letting her thoughts drift. This time the shot had come from a large building Teonar thought was probably a meeting hall.

The mercenaries found cover behind corners or abandoned vehicles and waited for orders. If the settlement was going to offer any proper resistance, this was logically the building they would use to anchor their defence. Teonar calculated how many humans might have had time to arm themselves and get here before the arrival of her force. She ordered a team of ten mercenaries to check out for snipers in the surrounding structures. The other mercenaries fired into the large building in an attempt to draw return fire so they could calculate how many armed humans they had bottled up.

Teonar buzzed Raenar on the communicator.

"We've reached the centre of the colony. The enemy is sheltering in the main building. We are determining their strength now. What is your position?"

"All the humans here are dead," Raenar said gleefully.

"Then send two of your platoons into the colony from your end. Once we have the main building isolated and surrounded we can attack."

She turned off the communicator before Raenar could answer. She was still counting the return fire from the humans when a mercenary told her Raenar's two platoons were in position. She stood up and raised her blaster to give two shots, the signal for the assault to begin, when there was a flurry of human fire from one of the surrounding buildings. She heard the whip-like sounds of the mercenaries' blasters firing in return, followed by more human fire.

Teonar thought back to how easy their progress into the settlement had been, even allowing for the surprise they had achieved. Suddenly the mercenaries' fire abruptly ended.

My people lost the firefight, she thought. *That's a tenth of my force.*

The cold realisation that she may be in an ambush made her shiver.

"Withdraw!" she cried. "Get back to your battle cars!"

She tried to signal Raenar to tell him what was happening but could not get through; the signal was being jammed.

Suddenly the fire from at least forty human weapons opened up from several of the surrounding dwellings. Bullets spat at Teonar's feet, whizzed past her ear. Several mercenaries fell.

"Keep your order!" she shouted, but chaos had set in. The Calethar force began to break up and lose its cohesion. She physically restrained those soldiers she could reach. "Use your weapons! We need covering fire!" But the human attack continued and more of her force fell. The mercenaries ran back through the streets.

Teonar swore and joined her Calethar regulars, then led a fighting retreat down a narrow alleyway. They stopped every few seconds to return enemy fire. They emerged onto a much larger street and their pace picked up. All the way back to the edge of the settlement she heard the sounds of the human assault and the screams of her troops left behind. "I will destroy this place!" she swore aloud. "I will bomb it out of existence, and then personally decapitate any survivors!"

They reached the open fields around the settlement. She ordered her troops to hold there and cover those still retreating. She tried again to contact Raenar, this time burning through the jamming.

"There are at least thirty well-armed humans attacking my position," he told her calmly. "I don't know how much longer I can hold the batteries. I suggest we embark and leave as quickly as possible."

"What do you think I'm doing? Leave the batteries and get going. Most of the attack seems concentrated against us."

"I will continue to hold this position with my detachment until you make it back to the ship," Raenar said.

Teonar swore. Raenar was far too important to leave behind.

"Destroy the batteries *now* and escape as best you can," she ordered him.

Next she contacted Nomelet.

"It was an ambush, Ship-Captain. There are too many human fighters for them all to come from the colony. I am getting our forces back to the battle cars."

"Why did the plan go awry? This makes no sense. Unless . . ."

Teonar realised where Nomelet's logic was leading him. Her limbs went cold.

"Kidron!" she hissed over the communicator. "Ship-Captain, do you think *Magpie* is here?"

"It must be!" he replied. "Withdraw your forces as soon as possible. We will deal with the settlement later."

Teonar signed off. Her small force grew in numbers as mercenaries who had evaded death or capture in the settlement joined her depleted squad.

"War-Captain, they're charging!"

She looked across the field. A line of humans were running straight for them, shouting war cries.

"Back to *Kudu*!" she cried.

All discipline deserted her troops, even the Calethar. Ashamed, Teonar watched them run like frightened herbivores.

She followed them at a trot, stopping frequently to turn and fire. By the time she reached the battle car only thirty-five of her command were left alive, many of them wounded.

She ordered her troops on board. With one last look at the advancing enemy she boarded and told the pilot to lift off.

Kazin cursed when a Calethar detachment chose to search a house hiding a fireteam from *Magpie*. He stood back against the wall of his own hideaway to watch the proceedings. It was not long before he heard gunfire. There was a short exchange and then an uneasy silence. Kazin watched the Calethar leader, a huge female, to see what she did next.

He heard her bark the order for a retreat. Cursing, he poked his pistol outside a window, aimed at the leader and fired. He missed. He shouted a command and a withering gunfire opened up on the mercenaries. Most of the enemy panicked and fled, but he saw a small group gather around the Calethar female.

He signalled Spiez on his communicator.

"They've figured out it's an ambush," he said. "Start your assault on the laser batteries now!"

He looked down again into the square. The Calethar had gone. He rushed downstairs and found Santa organising a squad to give chase.

He contacted Kidron on *Magpie*.

"I'm sorry, Captain," Kazin began. "The surprise party went off earlier than expected. The enemy are retreating back to their transports."

"Which means their captain may know we're *Magpie* and not a colony ship. See what you can do to finish them off – if possible get their transports. I'm launching the attack against *Canar* now."

Kazin joined Santa's squad, already moving down the alley used by the Calethar for their retreat. Enemy fire was wild but persistent. Kazin let Santa give the commands – close-order fighting was her specialty, not his. He followed, taking cover when he could, shooting back when he saw a target.

He heard a whoop to his left. An Actane wielding only a long knife leapt at him from a side street. He fired twice, hitting the alien in the body. The mercenary fell, groaned, tried to stand. Kazin ignored him and jogged to catch up with the squad. He was passing alien dead and wounded, many of them Calethar.

A blaster bolt bit into a nearby wall. Fragments of stone nicked his ear and cheek, drawing blood.

The humans reached a wider street. There was more cover here and they redoubled their assault on the retreating enemy, but a flurry of blaster fire blunted the attack and claimed two of the squad.

Santa turned to Kazin. "I need more troopers! I want that Calethar bitch leading them!"

She ran off to organise another assault, but the aliens retreated again and the squad set off in pursuit.

Kazin signalled for reinforcements, but was told Spiez had gathered all spare units for his attack on the laser batteries.

He went off after the others, found them crouching at the edge of the settlement. Santa pulled him down just as a blue bolt crackled overhead. In the distance he could see the aliens' transport, and hear its engines already warming up.

"They've gone down about a hundred metres away," Santa told him. "Waiting for stragglers." She shook her head in grudging admiration. "Damn, she's a fine combat leader."

"Wonderful," Kazin agreed. "Let's kill her."

"That means charging across open ground," Santa said.

He met her gaze. "I know."

Santa shrugged. "What the hell." She drew a deep breath. "*Magpie*!" she cried. The word rang out across the field. "Up and at 'em!"

As a single body her squad got to their feet and charged. Kazin's heart leapt for joy. Washed with battle frenzy he ran as fast as he could, shouting "*Magpie*!" and shooting wildly with his pistol.

The enemy fled. The humans redoubled their efforts, but could see they would not reach them in time to stop them escaping. They screamed in frustration as the aliens scrambled on to their battle car.

Their leader was last on board. The battle car lifted into the sky and accelerated towards them.

The humans halted their charge, exhausted. They looked up, saw the enemy leader framed in an open hatch.

Kazin raised his pistol and fired until he ran out of ammunition. He heard Santa shouting something at him. He looked at her.

"Get down! For God's sake, get down!"

The words made no sense to him. All he knew was that his quarry was escaping. He was furious. He did not see the Calethar female aim her blaster, did not see her fire.

He was thrown to the ground with terrific force. He tried to get up, but he could not move. Neither could he hear anything. He looked up to the sky and though it was getting darker he could see no stars.

The battle car swooped over the colony and climbed like a great bird. Santa raced to Kazin's side. His injury was terrible, and the smell of burnt flesh made her gag. His lips moved but he made no sound. All Santa could do was watch him die.

Kidron ordered *Magpie* to battle speed and put the ship on full alert. For a moment his thoughts lingered with Kazin and the crew he was leaving behind on Radik, but they were safer down there than he and the remaining crew aboard the privateer. The plan had gone so well at first. The Calethar captain had sent his raiders planetside without properly reconnoitring the surface or the transport innocuously orbiting the planet, relying on his ship's reputation to keep away any suicidal attack. But chance, the single factor no captain can command or predict, had intervened, and now *Canar* was probably on full alert and ready for battle, a situation Kidron had hoped to avoid. He knew his best chance in defeating the Calethar ship had been in surprise. Now that was gone, he had to rely on a swift attack and his crew's experience and ability.

Navigation Officer Lieutenant Marin picked up *Canar* within seconds of the alert. He confirmed she was moving and Kidron's worst fears were realised.

"All sections, we're going in to attack," Kidron told the crew. Then to Marin alone: "We'll aim for a low pass, between the enemy and the planet. After we swing by I want a full-G boost to a higher orbit. Position us for an attack against their stern."

Lieutenant Obe told him two Calethar transports had left the planet. Kidron asked Danui to calculate the possibility of hitting them without compromising their attack on *Canar*.

"We have time for one salvo, sir, but it's a long shot," Danui replied.

Kidron gave the order to fire. If they were lucky they might destroy the transport carrying the Calethar's war-captain, restricting *Canar*'s future raiding activities.

He heard the salvo leave the ship.

"Sir . . ."

Kidron looked at Obe. He was as white as a sheet.

"What is it, Lieutenant?"

"I'm sorry, sir, but . . . Commander Kazin is dead."

Kidron stared at Obe. He did not believe him.

"He was killed attacking one of the transports."

Kidron felt numb. *Oh, God. Why him?*

"Who's . . . who's in charge down there?"

"As far as we can make out it's Lieutenant Robinson. Spiez is wounded."

"Confirm that with Robinson," he said.

"Captain?" Danui was standing by her station. "Toma is not a line commander. She has never led troopers."

"You're right," Kidron said, abashed. *Forget Michael! You still have a battle to fight!* "Obe, who's senior ground combat officer?"

Obe checked his computer. "No officers, sir. Next in rank is Santa."

"Alright. Let Santa know she's in charge. Tell her if things go badly up here she's to surrender to the Calethar. Any further resistance will only result in the complete destruction of the settlement."

"Aye aye, sir."

Kidron forced his attention back to *Canar Calethari.* The two ships were now fully in range of each other's sensors. Kidron wanted to land the first blow.

"Launch two salvos against the primary target, then give me that high-G climb."

He heard the torpedoes leave *Magpie.* He sent a prayer after them, and another for Michael Kazin.

Nomelet listened with great displeasure to his helm-captain, an old and experienced secertor named Makarin.

"Ship-Captain," Makarin began, "any attempt to pick up the ascending battle cars will place *Canar* in even greater danger.

"Teonar and Raenar will have to take their chances. *Magpie* is coming in much faster than expected. They realise their stratagem has failed. To manoeuvre to retrieve our battle cars will give the enemy an advantage they probably don't need. Sir."

Nomelet nodded grimly. The helm-captain was right. The first and most important mission was to destroy *Magpie*. The humans had come so close to carrying out their ambush, it made Nomelet quiver. He had been overconfident and foolish. If Raenar had been aboard he would have had good reason for usurping his command. Thankfully, Raenar was on a battle car and in no position to threaten anyone.

Makarin issued a string of orders. As he did so Nomelet received two communications. The first told him *Magpie* had fired a salvo of torpedoes towards the two vulnerable battle cars; the second informed him that a further two salvos were headed for *Canar*.

"Can we evade them?" he asked Makarin. The helm-captain checked his sensors.

"No, at least not without throwing away our own chance of attacking this pass.

"Our defences will be good enough to destroy most of the incoming torpedoes. My calculations indicate those that do get through won't inflict any serious damage. On the other hand, our attack could severely damage or cripple the enemy."

"Continue on course. Is there something we can do for Teo . . . for the battle cars?"

"No, sir."

"Very well."

"War-Captain, the battle has begun and we are caught in the middle of it." *Kudu*'s co-pilot, a drone called Stax, pointed to the screen. Teonar saw an incoming flight of torpedoes.

"A complete salvo," she said. "Six torpedoes."

"Can we avoid them?"

"We can try."

Stax was suddenly slung hard against one of the bulkheads. A bright flash winked across his field of vision.

Teonar cursed and pushed *Kudu* through another tight roll. A second torpedo narrowly missed them.

"It's done," Teonar said matter-of-factly. "We're through . . ."

Her voice trailed off into a whisper.

"What is it?" Stax asked.

"*Anma* didn't make it."

There was cheering on the bridge of *Magpie*. One enemy shuttle had been destroyed.

Kidron himself was less enthusiastic. He knew more than a few lucky shots were needed to destroy *Canar* or force her to surrender.

"First salvo has reached the enemy ship," Danui reported. "All six torpedoes destroyed. No damage. Incoming salvo reported."

Kidron studied his own battle screen. Green registration lines showed the progress of *Magpie*'s second salvo against *Canar*, and the new red registration lines indicated their counterattack. At least eight torpedoes. *What a monster. This is no privateer. It's a dreadnought in privateer's clothing.*

"Start the high orbit boost two minutes before calculated impact of incoming salvo."

"Aye aye, sir. Second salvo has reached the enemy ship . . . two misses, one destroyed . . . three hits!" Danui had trouble keeping her voice under control. Kidron's hands clenched into fists.

"Estimated damage is minimal," Danui continued, disappointed. "Reduced engine function. Perhaps one of their port defence banks has been taken out."

"Ten seconds to high orbit boost," Marin reported.

Kidron tensed himself for *Magpie*'s high-G manoeuvre. He wished the second salvo had done more damage, but at least they had blooded the enemy, which was probably more than any ship had yet done to *Canar*. The breath was taken out of his body as the privateer's main drive fired. The red registration lines altered course to match their target's new trajectory, but Kidron could already see they were safe from that attack.

Suddenly his screen exploded in his face. Shards of plexiglass bit into his cheeks and forehead. His body recoiled with shock. Smoke, thick and acrid, filled his nostrils. Somewhere in the back of his mind he heard Danui.

"Critical hit! A bloody particle beam! Extensive damage to port wing, computer axes . . . *our* beam weapon has been destroyed . . ."

Kidron felt himself passing out, and he struggled against the black wave rolling over him. He thumbed the communicator on his couch's armrest. Excruciating pain shot up his hand. He looked down and saw that his right arm, from the elbow to the tips of his fingers, was a bloody mess.

"Engine room, sir."

"Damage?" Kidron asked, gasping for breath.

"None, sir."

"Full boost. I want us in a high elliptical orbit, or we're finished."

"Aye aye, sir."

But Kidron did not hear the confirmation.

Makarin grunted with satisfaction. His sensors showed that *Magpie* had changed course to avoid any more combat. He ordered a second salvo released, knowing its chances of hitting its target were small. The other ship had flung herself into an orbit that was either highly unstable and unpredictable, or long and elliptical where no torpedoes would have the speed or range to reach her. He considered using the beam generators, but the chance of getting a good fix on *Magpie* was too remote to make it worthwhile. *Magpie* was at least badly damaged, and possibly useless as a warship. *Canar* could take her time and there was still the surviving battle car to pick up.

He gave his conclusions to Nomelet. The ship-captain nodded and praised Makarin for his skill. *Magpie* defeated! A great dream fulfilled! The Uzdar would celebrate this victory for a long time to come! He felt relief rather than exhilaration: a great responsibility had been lifted from his shoulders.

And Raenar was dead. Compensation to Floran would be expensive, but Nomelet's position as ship-captain was now secure; because of his foolish charge into the Radik system, it had been shaky indeed.

His communicator buzzed and Teonar's voice came over the system. "Praise to Nomelet, ship-captain. Praise to Makarin, helm-captain. Praise to *Canar Calethari*, proud and mighty warship, sword of clans and curse to her enemies."

Nomelet's chest swelled. "And praise to Teonar, war-captain. Praise to all who serve our cause. We are glad you survived the battle and welcome you back with joy."

Robinson and Lynch were checking the camouflage nets over the cutters when Santa and a dozen troopers ran up. Santa took Robinson aside and spoke to her. Lynch saw Robinson sway on her feet. Santa put out a hand to steady her but the pilot stepped back, warning her away. Santa spoke again. Robinson shook her head violently, walked away from the sergeant.

Santa breathed heavily.

Lynch saw her face was drawn, her eyes red. She walked over to him.

"Where's your side-arm?" she asked.

"In *Lark* –"

"Then get it and put it on, Ensign."

Something in her voice stopped him asking any questions. He boarded *Lark*, retrieved his weapon belt from the cockpit and returned. Santa and her squad were waiting impatiently for him. There was no sign of Robinson.

"Come with us," Santa ordered and started off at a fast trot. Lynch caught up with her.

"Santa, I'm *ordered* to stay with *Lark* –"

"We're in trouble, Aaron. Our attacks on the laser batteries have been repulsed and we've suffered casualties. We need all the guns we can get."

"Then what about Toma –"

"Someone has to stay with the cutters." She threw him a sidelong glance. "Aaron, she's the best pilot we've got. We can't afford to lose her."

They reached the settlement in a few minutes. They passed grim-faced colonists throwing alien corpses onto a blazing pyre. The stench was almost unbearable.

"What did you say to Toma?" Lynch asked the sergeant.

"Why do you ask so many *fucking* questions?"

"She's my friend," he said simply.

They heard firing ahead. Santa increased the pace.

"Santa?"

"Kazin's dead," she said.

Lynch stumbled. Santa dragged him along until he regained his footing. Neither of them said anything more.

When they reached the human positions around the laser batteries they were met by a young corporal named Grace. He was wounded in the arm. Blood stained most of his tunic. Lynch was surprised he was still standing.

"What's been happening?" Santa demanded.

"We've lost two more. Wounded, but out of action. Spiez is in a bad way. I estimate fifteen enemy are holding the batteries. They're all Calethar. The mercenaries fled to the battle car when our attack started."

"You've got two fire teams here. Where's the third?" she asked.

Grace indicated their position with a nod. "Behind the settlement's port controls. They're giving us fire support when we move up and preventing the enemy from escaping south towards the hills."

"Can you bring them up without the Calethar seeing them?"

"Sure," Grace replied, puzzled. "But what about covering the way south . . ."

Santa shook her head. "They don't want to escape. This is a do-or-die effort for them. We have to secure those batteries before they decide to turn them on the settlement. I'm going for a look-see. Get the third fire team up here and let me know when they arrive."

Grace left to carry out her orders.

Santa peeped over the shallow dirt redoubt the humans had built up in front of their position. The batteries, and in front of them the Calethar redoubts, were about fifty metres away. At the moment they might as well be fifty kilometres. Even with three fire teams an assault would be cut to shreds. She had to figure out a way to increase their chances.

Santa called Grace back and asked him where the remote controls for the laser batteries were. He shrugged. "I didn't even know they had remotes on a backwater like this."

Santa's shoulders drooped. She had not thought of that. *What now, Sergeant? You've got forty troopers waiting for you to do something to turn everything around.*

"Uh, Santa?"

She glanced up. Lynch was shifting from one foot to another. He looked slightly ridiculous with his weapon belt around his flight suit. *I should have left him back with Robinson,* she thought.

"The corporal here mentioned the settlement had port controls. Isn't that where the laser remotes would be?"

Santa blinked. A second later she was grinning from ear to ear. "You're a genius," she said.

She ordered her squad to deploy with Grace's people, then set off, keeping low to the ground. She did not object when Lynch chased after her.

The port building was constructed like a pillbox to survive a close landing or a take-off that went wrong. They entered the building, waited a moment for their eyes to adjust to the dark, then searched the room's panels for anything that looked like remote controls for the batteries. Lynch's gaze fell on a black box shoved under one of the panels, and he pulled it out.

"Is this what you're looking for?" he asked.

Santa grabbed the box from his hands and opened it. "Eureka!" she cried.

She contacted Grace. "We've found the remote controls. I'm going to try and overcharge the battery's power source. If it works they'll go with one hell of a bang. Tell your people to keep their heads down. When you hear the explosions, make your move."

There was a long, thick cable extending from the back of the box. She attached it to one of the room's several power sources, took one quick glance out of the room's single, armour-glassed window and depressed a switch marked '1'. A ready light flickered on. She flipped open the charge indicator and thumbed it to full, she repeated the procedure for the other three batteries then returned to the window.

In the sudden pause, Lynch became aware he was not afraid. Everything was happening too fast for his mind to catch up. He remembered then the news about Kazin, and realised he felt nothing about that either right then.

"Toma took it badly," he said to Santa.

She stared at him. Her dark eyes were filled with pain.

"They were lovers," she said.

A warning beep came from the box.

"Go to hell," she said.

Raenar was feeling very pleased with himself. It looked as though his gamble was going to come off. Like a true Uzdar, he had seen the long chance and embraced it, trusting in the favour of the clan gods and his own courage. He would be the first to admit it was a close-run thing, but staying behind to hold the batteries had provided him with the key to unlocking Nomelet's power. The ship-captain had already shown he was unworthy of his office by blindly leading them into this ambush. Now, by a display of bravery and tactical wit, Raenar, son of Floran, was showing all who served on *Canar* that he was fit to assume the mantle of ship-captain. By holding the laser batteries he had allowed the battle cars to escape without danger, and now he was holding down a human force that outnumbered him by as many as three-to-one.

His small detachment was down to fifteen, but they were all Calethar. Behind their makeshift redoubts their position was too well defended for the humans to take by assault, and even if they were to try and succeed they would find only corpses to greet them. Raenar would kill himself to avoid capture. And then, Raenar told himself with grim satisfaction, he would still win. Nomelet would return in shame to Dramorath, and his position as leading contender for clan leadership would be assumed by his father, the sire of a hero and the builder of the ship that had already proved itself far superior to any other vessel.

He slowly became conscious of a high-pitched humming coming from behind him and he turned. He noticed nothing unusual at first, then saw the base of one of the lasers was starting to glow with heat. The humming was now clearly audible and insistent.

Raenar stood up, careless of his own safety, and walked towards the batteries. As he realised what was happening he broke into a run. He had to reach the power source and destroy it before it was too late.

"No," he said, and then to the world: "*No! Curse the gods, no – !*"

A searing light burned into his brain and the ground ruptured beneath his feet. He felt himself picked up and flung around like a leaf in a storm. He hit the ground hard and lay there stunned.

There was an incredibly bright flash followed by an ear-thumping explosion. A second later there were three more.

Santa and Lynch rushed outside and ran towards the batteries. Ahead of them the others were already charging.

Lynch made the first redoubt, stumbled and slid down, landing on top of a dead Calethar, one of its eyes a bloody pulp. Lynch jumped up with a frightened yell, dropping his pistol. Someone pushed him hard in the back, shouting: "Get down, you idiot!" Grace dropped in beside him, ignoring the dead alien beneath them.

Lynch groped with his hands for his pistol, finding it to one side.

There was a scream behind him. He turned on his back, saw a human standing there, blood pouring from his mouth. The man stumbled back, fell.

Grace fired twice then scrambled up, dragging Lynch with him.

Lynch looked around for Santa, saw her standing over a wounded Calethar trying to crawl away on his hands and knees. She calmly placed her pistol to the back of his neck and fired. The Calethar collapsed to the ground. She turned, met Lynch's gaze.

"Oh, God," he whispered hoarsely.

Santa saw a shape on the ground not far from the destroyed batteries. It was not moving. She walked towards it.

Lynch ran to join her and reached the body first. He carefully rolled it over. There was a sudden flash of movement and he instinctively jumped back, but not quickly enough. He felt a sharp pain in his left shoulder, and saw the short, bloodied knife wielded by the Calethar draw back for another lunge. There was a second when nothing seemed to happen, when everything was frozen in time and space, and then the Calethar's knife was spinning into space.

Santa was standing over the alien, her foot on its chest. She leaned over, placed the barrel of her pistol inside its mouth and started squeezing the trigger.

Lynch saw her freeze. She stayed like that for several long seconds, then stood up and reholstered her pistol without firing a shot, her face suddenly pale.

When Kidron regained consciousness he felt no pain and the bridge was free from smoke, although the devastation was clear enough. Most of the screens had been blown, and he noticed blood stained many of the instrument panels and couches.

"How many did we lose?" he asked the paramedic leaning over him with a syringe in her hands. She ignored the question and turned away from him.

"Doctor . . . it's the captain. He's regained consciousness."

Doctor Bingham – short, squat and gory – floated into his field of vision. "You've been out for over two hours. You're not wounded seriously, but you won't be using that arm for a while."

"How many did we lose?"

Bingham did not answer, but then he saw the warning look in Kidron's eyes. "Thirty-two so far. There's another nine or so who probably won't make it. Another sixty or more who are badly wounded. Most of the crew have an injury of one kind or another. Most of those who weren't wounded when we were hit by the enemy's beam weapon were bounced around pretty severely when we boosted into this orbit."

"What's our situation now? Who's in command?"

"We're safe for the moment," replied Bingham. "Danui's in command."

Kidron sat up with the paramedic's assistance. "Danui – here, please."

"I've other patients to attend to," Bingham said. "If you'll excuse me." He didn't wait to be excused, but left anyway, looking tired to the point of exhaustion.

Kidron ordered Obe to get in touch with Santa back on Radik, then Danui appeared.

"I expect the doctor's already given you a run-down of our casualties. Other than that there's not a great deal to tell. The engine room's about the only section of *Magpie* not damaged. There's been no attempt by the enemy to pursue us, though it's surely only a matter of time. There seems to be little we can do about it one way or the other, but jump and run. We have no other options that I can see."

"And leave our troops behind," said Kidron.

"Our destruction will not save them, Captain," Danui observed softly.

"Very well. Thank you for baby-sitting. I agree with your conclusion. We'll jump as soon as *Magpie* is secured. I assume you've already taken some action along that course."

"Yes, Captain –"

She was interrupted by an excited call from Obe. "Captain! It's Santa! We've re-established communications with Radik, and she has a prisoner!"

"A prisoner?"

"A bloody Calethar noble, Captain! A real, live dyed-in-the-socks trading lord!"

The crew on *Canar*'s bridge shuddered as Nomelet's roar echoed around their heads. All of them understood what the sound meant – someone was about to have their stomach ripped open by the ship-captain for some unforgivable transgression. Even Makarin, the most steady and experienced Calethar on board, could not repress a shiver. When the echo finally died, he turned to face his commander. He was surprised to find no bloody remains at his feet, only a terrified messenger from the communications room.

"Raenar!" Nomelet screamed. "That imbecile son of an idiot shipbuilder! Raenar!"

Makarin waited for some of the rage to dissipate, and gently enquired what the deceased Raenar could have done. Nomelet turned his gaze to Makarin, much to the relief of the messenger and the discomfort of the helm-captain.

"Raenar is *not* dead," answered Nomelet, "though I'm sure he wishes he was. Has *Kudu* docked yet?"

Makarin was confused. Had they not all seen *Anma* destroyed by *Magpie*? How could Raenar possibly be alive?

"Well?" prompted Nomelet, his tone threatening.

Makarin shook himself from his confused thoughts and checked his instrument panel. "The bay is pressurising now, Ship-Captain."

"Get Teonar up here as quickly as possible," Nomelet ordered, and dismissed everyone with a swipe of his claws. The messenger ducked and darted back to his communications room, relieved to be alive.

If not for the devastation surrounding him, Kidron might have enjoyed the irony. While his ship was crippled and perhaps a third of her crew wounded or dead, he had never been in a more powerful bargaining position. He held in his hands, or more accurately, in Santa's hands, the life of a Calethar noble. With that he might not only be able to save his ship but perhaps even salvage a victory. *But carefully,* he warned himself. *Step as if you are walking on rice paper.*

Danui waited nervously by Kidron, occasionally glancing expectantly towards him. Normally so unflappable and efficient, the sight of the fretting weapons officer emphasised for Kidron the danger of their situation.

"Nothing yet, sir," Obe reported.

"It will be a while," Kidron said, and wondered how his own voice sounded to the others on the bridge. "I doubt they have any contingency plans for a captured Calethar noble. It isn't something that happens every day." Kidron fought the sudden urge to laugh, but the returning pain in his arm rapidly quelled any exultation he may have felt. *Laughter just wouldn't do,* he reminded himself.

"Message from Santa, Captain," Danui announced. "She has determined the clan. Uzdar."

Uzdar! Kidron allowed himself a smile this time, in recognition of his own shortsightedness. Of course. What other clan would go to so much trouble to kill him except the same one which had bankrolled Jimmy Tolstoi? The settlements *Magpie* had hit during her long and varied service had, until Tunius, belonged to other clans, but the Uzdar were considered the unofficial leader among the Calethar outworlds. He should have known they would be behind this operation. He also realised then who *Canar*'s ship-captain must be.

"Put another message through to *Canar*," he told Danui. "'To Ship-Captain Nomelet, Pillar of the Uzdar, nephew of Great Enilka, Trading Captain of the Cale-thar. Greetings from Captain Aruzel Kidron of *Magpie*. Victory was yours. Through no fault of your own it has been taken away from you. The battle was won, but not the contest. Will you not talk to me?'" Kidron looked up. "Let's see if that doesn't speed things up."

Teonar hurried to the bridge as soon as she received Nomelet's message. The courier had subtly warned her about the ship-captain's mood, so she was not surprised to see him angrily pacing the bridge. Nomelet turned to her and said between clamped jaws: "That idiot Raenar is still alive. Why didn't you tell me he'd stayed on the planet?"

"Ship-Captain, I didn't know. My orders were for a complete withdrawal."

Nomelet stared at her for a moment and then nodded sharply. "Yes, of course. I'm sorry, War-Captain. I didn't mean to imply the blame was yours. It appears, then, that he attempted to take matters into his own hands for his own personal glory . . . and subsequently failed. Unfortunately, he has not only failed himself, he has failed us all."

"I don't understand," Teonar said, keeping her voice as consoling as possible.

"He was captured by the humans," Nomelet explained. "And now they are using him to get themselves out of their predicament. Our victory is being stolen from us by Raenar's blundering."

Teonar let Nomelet's words sink in. She could not hide her disappointment. All that they had planned and hoped for had come to nothing.

"Excuse me, Ship-Captain, War-Captain," Makarin interrupted. "But if Executive Raenar has allowed himself to be taken prisoner, can we not continue the battle irrespective of his safety? He must realise the consequences."

Indeed, Nomelet had pondered the same option, but had discarded it almost immediately. "No, Makarin. I cannot be responsible for his death, through action or inaction on my part. He is the son of Floran, recognised as a possible heir to Enilka. That places Raenar in the line of succession as well. To desert him would be seen by the clan as a betrayal."

"Ship-Captain," Teonar began carefully, "perhaps all is not lost."

"What do you mean?"

"Consider these points. First, under your leadership *Canar Calethari* has obtained great wealth from the humans. Second, she has proven her worth beyond any reasonable doubt. No one, within your own clan or outside of it, can criticise the logic behind her construction. Third," and here she dropped her voice so that only Nomelet could hear her, "Raenar has damaged his father's cause, perhaps beyond repair. Instead of his father gathering the rewards he deserves for the excellent design and construction of this ship, he will instead see his family's honour diminished by his son's actions. Fourth, Raenar will be in your debt, and no longer a threat to your own captaincy and claims to clan leadership."

"But the conditions of his ransom!" Nomelet shouted. "The humans are demanding that *Canar* return to Calethar space immediately, causing no more harm to humans or their settlements –"

"With respect, sir, that is the minimum we could expect them to ask. The captain of the *Magpie* is a clever and determined leader. He knows he has much bargaining power with Raenar in his hands. At least they are not asking you to swear never to return to human space, or to surrender all of our booty."

"They know I wouldn't do such a thing. Even the clan would recognise Raenar's life is not worth such a price."

"Exactly. Kidron is asking for a fair trade. He knows his business, down to the last bolt of cloth, the last coin, the last life. In this case his own life and the lives of his crew."

"And of his ship," added Makarin, who thought of any ship as a living thing. Teonar grunted in agreement.

"Ship-Captain," said a courier, hanging back until he was called to deliver his message.

"What is it?"

"Another signal from the human captain."

Nomelet tensed. What now? Had they asked for more? Would he have to shoulder the responsibility for Raenar's death after all? He clacked his jaws and the courier relayed Kidron's last message.

"You see, Ship-Captain," Teonar said, pushing her point home. "Kidron has deduced who you are, and his words are both noble and fair. What he says is true. The victory was yours, and was taken away through no fault of your own."

Nomelet snorted. "Still, the victory tasted sweet, and it is hard to surrender it for the life of a worthless noble, even if he is my cousin."

"A cousin who will be forever in your debt," Teonar reminded him. *And out of my way,* she thought to herself. Nomelet and she had been at fault for leading *Canar* and her crew into an ambush. Raenar's decision to stay behind on the planet had been a shrewd one politically, if selfish from any other point of view. But now, through either ill fortune or some blunder, Raenar had removed himself as a threat to either her or her captain. Teonar was already calculating the consequences. Future paths all seemed less hazardous now.

"As you say," Nomelet agreed wearily. "Courier, signal to *Magpie*. 'We accept your terms.' No honorific. There is no need to swell Kidron's head any further."

Kidron watched *Canar Calethari* accelerate to her jump point and disappear, in awe of her power and grace. He felt exhausted, and wanted to do nothing but sleep for a week. But there was too much work to do. *Magpie* had to be repaired for the jump back to Hecabe. Once there, the ship would need not only an extensive refit but also major upgrading to match Nomelet's vessel. As well, he needed replacements for all the crew he had lost. *But how will I ever replace Kazin?* he asked himself.

He stared at the now empty screen. "One day, Nomelet," he said softly, "one day we'll meet again, and you'll wish you'd never let me out of your grasp. I promise this on the body of Kazin, and all the others who died. I promise this on my life."

Chapter 17

Hecabe filled the main viewing screen on *Magpie*'s bridge. Lynch looked at it with wonder. When he had left the planet all those months before he had felt no regrets at all. He had thought of Hecabe as merely a dull speck in a dull part of space, and yet now it seemed to him beautiful indeed. He realised he thought of it not just as the place he came from, but as *home*. He said the word slowly to himself, letting the sound of it roll around in his mind.

His emotions had been pulling quite a few surprises on him. First the change in his relationship with his uncle caused, ironically, by his leaving Hecabe. Then the fire in the cargo bay, which destroyed forever the adolescent belief in his own invulnerability. He felt bone-chilling fear for the first time during the encounter with *Uzir*, and a kind of blind anger during combat that evaporated as soon as the battle was over. There were the unexpected and emotionally disarming feelings he suddenly felt for Robinson when she told him about her parents.

And most of all there was jealousy.

Even thinking about it now, weeks after the event, made him ashamed. To be jealous of Kazin, of a dead man. Was his reaction so strong because of the difference in age between the lovers? Or because he had never suspected Robinson had a life apart from being a pilot, apart from being *his* teacher, *his* friend?

Lynch found no answers to these questions. He knew that when Kazin's remains had been shot into Radik's sun, the small coffin tracked by *Magpie*'s sensors for its entire journey to obliteration, he had felt nothing. While the rest of the crew were in deepest mourning for the mates they had lost, he was simply angry; irrationally angry at Robinson for betraying his undeclared feelings, at Santa for telling him the truth, at Kazin for being Robinson's lover and for *dying*. How could he confront a dead rival? How could he hate a memory? He felt ambushed.

And now, here he was returning to Hecabe – to home – the prodigal misfit, his emotions all a jumble.

He did not notice Kidron standing behind him until he spoke. "It's an amazing sight, isn't it, Aaron? It always fills me with a kind of peace. In a strange way spacers are more sentimental about their homes than idlers ever are."

Lynch smiled briefly and left. Kidron watched him go then took his seat. He gazed at Hecabe floating on the screen. *I lied to the boy,* he thought. *I find no peace here any more.*

As it had for Lynch, the loss of Kazin had proven a pivot for Kidron's emotions. He understood with unwelcome clarity that peace – the inner peace all humans strove for – was the illusion either of exhaustion or narrow-mindedness. The only true peace was that found by Kazin, the peace of oblivion.

Again, as he did every day, he wished desperately his friend was by his side once more.

Lynch was given leave to recuperate from his flesh wound. He went down with Robinson in *Swallow*. They spoke little.

At the spaceport he contacted his uncle, who was overjoyed to hear from him. He would not hear of his nephew staying anywhere but with him, and so it was arranged.

On their first night together, Lynch gave his uncle an account of *Magpie*'s voyage. N'Djama listened with patience, his eyes growing wider with the telling.

The conversation slowly turned to friends, acquaintances and trade.

"How is Mahmed?" Lynch asked.

N'Djama sighed. "As always. He slowly climbs up the ladder of success in the fiercely competitive field of stevedoring. One day he will reach the top, look down and realise he isn't really so far from the bottom."

"And I trust no consignments from Newton have gone astray since my departure?"

"Indeed, since your departure we have lost no consignments from Newton, or any other planet for that matter. Do you think there is a connection?"

Lynch shook his head. "It is nothing more than coincidence."

The two laughed suddenly. N'Djama reached out and slapped his nephew's shoulder. At that moment a lot of Lynch's emotional pain evaporated. He was with someone who had always loved him no matter his faults, and a flood of affection for the big, gruff merchant almost brought tears to his eyes.

"Are you going back out with Captain Kidron when *Magpie* has finished her refit?" N'Djama asked.

"Yes. The Captain seems willing to take me on again."

"There was never any doubt about that. He was quite full of praise for you when I talked to him earlier. He wouldn't leave without his new pilot unless the new pilot didn't wish to leave with him."

"I want to go," Lynch said softly.

"Then can this old merchant give the young warrior a word of advice? Get to know your enemy."

"I know about the Calethar."

"I mean get to know them, not just *about* them. Get inside their heads. Learn their language. Learn their customs. Learn how they interact with each other, how the clan system works, about clan leaders . . . Aaron, learn everything there is to know!" He was leaning against the table, surprising Lynch with his sudden intensity. "Learn to think like a Calethar!"

"How? There are no teachers, and there isn't enough time –"

N'Djama held up his hand to stop his nephew's objections. "There is plenty of time. It will be weeks before *Magpie* is ready to leave again, and even after she's left you'll have opportunities on the voyage to continue your study. As to whom . . ." N'Djama smiled, ". . . why, one of the best scholars on the Calethar is serving with you on *Magpie*."

Lynch looked blankly at his uncle.

"She is an exologist, and her specialty is the Calethar.

"Her name is Ranjeeka Patha. *Doctor* Ranjeeka Patha. Whenever *Magpie* returns home she teaches at the

Salem college. If you wish, I can arrange for you to meet her there."

Lynch looked dubious.

"Well, what is your decision?"

"You haven't given me any time to think about it."

"What is there to think about? After all, if you don't do this, what are you going to do to pass away your time? Work in my factory?"

Lynch knew Robinson planned to give him more flying hours on *Lark*, but that would hardly fill in all the spare time in the coming weeks, and he could not fly while he was recovering from his wound. As well, he still felt uncomfortable around Robinson and wanted some time apart from her.

"When do I meet this mysterious expert?"

His uncle smiled. "Is tomorrow too soon?"

At mid-morning the next day Lynch was in the lobby of Hecabe's only college. Following his uncle's directions he found Dr Patha's room without difficulty and knocked gently on the door. He heard a muffled "come in", and entered.

It was a small, neat office. There was a work station, some memory cube storage space, and a second desk with a chair on either side, laden with spools, cubes and even a few antiquated books. Dr Patha was sitting behind the desk, filling up a good-sized chair.

"*Santa!*"

"Hello, Aaron. Your uncle told me you would be here this morning."

"Santa?"

"You're repeating yourself."

"You're the Calethar expert?"

"No, I'm Dr Patha's chair-warmer. Close your mouth, you idiot, you're making a spectacle of yourself."

"You know my uncle?"

She looked at him with wide brown eyes. "You'd be surprised at the number of people your uncle knows." She waved him into a seat. "So, you want to learn about the Calethar?"

"I can't believe it's *you*."

Santa looked offended. "I have been an academic almost as long as I've been a trooper. Space voyages are often long and tedious, and study is a good way to fill up the time.

"You would be surprised how many troopers like me, and engine crew and pursers and maintenance staff, have degrees."

She studied him for a few seconds, then threw him a batch of spools.

"What are these?"

"Homework. I want you to read them all. I guess you could call them Calethar primers. When you've done that, say by this time two days from now, I want you to come back here so we can begin some proper study."

"Are you going to teach me the language?" he asked.

"Walk, don't run, son. Let's see how you handle the basics first. We've only got a few weeks before we lift off again – I assume you're signing on for the next voyage – and then things are likely to get a little hectic. We'll continue the work on *Magpie*, but it will be piecemeal. I want you to have a proper grounding by then. Remember, the Calethar are as complex a subject as we humans are, perhaps more so, since their relationship with other races goes back farther than our own, and that's all a part of it."

Lynch collected the spools and put them in various pockets. He rested back in his seat, waiting for further instructions.

"Are you still here?" she asked. "I teach here, remember? I've got work to do."

Lynch's formal education to date had taught him to read, to write and to hate school, so he was surprised to find his interest captured by subjects like comparative anthropology and alien history, the two main streams of exology, the study of alien life and its physical cradle. As his knowledge of the Calethar progressed, his desire to learn their language grew. He wanted to leaven all the data Santa was throwing at him with some primary sources. He knew reading or hearing material in the original had to be more revealing about how the Calethar actually thought.

Whenever he had any questions he found Santa more than helpful, and for the first time in his life Lynch discovered what it meant to actually enjoy learning, to revel in the sheer pleasure of knowing things for their own sake.

His favourite subject was history, especially the intricate and messy period after the Calethar became a spacefaring species, and the convoluted interactions that then took place between their civilisation and others, leading up to what in human terms was the climax: their first contact with humans. As he read, the information formed patterns in his mind; sometimes this happened consciously, often with a great amount of effort on his part, and sometimes subconsciously, when things just seemed to slip into place and sort themselves out.

The Calethar had originally been a predatory and nomadic species, evolving from an ancestor that looked like a mix between an otter and a preying mantis. It was essentially mammalian, or as mammalian as anything on the Heartworld ever got. The Calethar were a particularly territorial and efficient species and any other candidates for sentience were soon relegated to the dustbin of failed evolutionary experiments. The Calethar never developed agriculture and so never had the societal base to move on to industry. That they reached space at all was due entirely to their adoption as mercenaries by several spacefaring species. As individual Calethar returned home after their tours of duty, they brought with them disparate slices of knowledge and pieces of technology that slowly developed into a technological society peculiarly their own. Because they had never passed through the equivalent of cultural growing pains, their application and use of that knowledge was, though at times erratic, quite direct. In very little time they had learned to dominate their near neighbours in space, and lessons learned here helped them to dominate most species they came in contact with in the following centuries.

The secret was, as Santa once told him, that they had gone into space with their more primitive instincts infecting them like persistent viruses, principally their fierce territorialism and combativeness. However, because their combativeness was instinctive, it was also highly controlled. They never completely conquered any species and were not interested in taking direct control over territory already settled. Instead they neutralised potential threats while concentrating on spreading their own species through the exploration, settlement and eventual transformation of previously undiscovered worlds. So good were they at this that within a few millennia they had settled more worlds that most of the other species combined, and this gave them the base for their incredible trading empire. They easily captured any markets taking their interest, and this taught them that the tyrants of supply and demand maintained the status quo more effectively than force of arms could ever hope to. And then humanity appeared on the scene – a new spacefaring race with an evolution more conventional than the Calethar, but with a few strange twists that surprised them. The Calethar found their dominant position under threat for the first time.

Humanity had made it into space the hard way, fighting nature and themselves every centimetre. The species had burst on the universe like a broken sore, spreading quickly and indiscriminately. Their unique penchant for violence was not revealed until the Mendart, an old and outrageously proud species, had tried to squash a human settlement intruding into what they considered their private hunting grounds. At the time, the humans had been prepared to pay compensation for a mistake they did not know they had committed, but the Mendart refused to listen to calmer voices, the Calethar among them.

In the war that followed, which was as abhorrently destructive as it was short, the Mendart found themselves suing for peace and trying to gather together the broken shards of their once thriving empire. Even now, decades later, they had only recently recovered enough to renew a rudimentary trade with other species. The

Calethar found in the Mendart a good source of mercenaries – a species that millennia before had hired the Calethar for exactly the same purpose.

The Calethar took more notice of the newcomers. Before the war with the Mendart they had a peculiar respect bordering on affection for the strange newcomers. In many ways their temperament and attitudes were similar, and the Calethar even considered becoming their patron. That changed after the war. The Calethar's primitive and still strong territorial instinct hardened and sharpened their attitude to humans. A feeling of amused amiability was replaced by one of guarded, even hostile, caution. The humans, still new to the game, reacted like any child would. They rebelled.

The Calethar language was the hardest thing for Lynch to learn. He found it easy enough to memorise an extensive vocabulary of Calethar words, but being able to put them in the right order was difficult. The problem was aggravated by Calethar society being so highly structured and class-ridden (even within a clan – indeed, even within a family) that not getting the words in the right order could result in the speaker delivering a mortal offence. Interlingua, a mixture of languages developed by merchants of all spacefaring species over the decades, was restrictive and without the nuances of a single tongue belonging to a single culture; great for trading goods, but lousy for understanding Calethar intentions or attitudes.

Santa was a good teacher, and Lynch was in awe of her seemingly boundless knowledge of the Calethar and their language. Every day she would impart some piece of information invaluable to understanding the aliens not covered in any text or document.

One of the most interesting aspects of Calethar culture was that sex played no part in determining status. Strength and stature varied from individual to individual, but not because of sex. A female had as much chance as any male to develop into a big and hefty Calethar. They even *thought* the same way. Their attitudes to war, killing, parenthood, social responsibilities, trade, whatever, could not be differentiated by gender.

Lynch learned that even though Calethar behaviour was virtually unchanged by the huge technological advances they had made, it still held up. It was as if the vast and empty plains they used to inhabit had been replaced by the vast and empty distances of space. In a strange way, the Calethar were uniquely evolved for life off-planet.

"We can learn so much from them, Aaron," Santa told him. "I can see us humans making mistakes we shouldn't be making because we're not learning from them. They're a proud and honest species, without the arrogance and rudeness that usually accompany such virtues. And they see something similar in us.

"They really are fascinated by humans. Much more than they are by any other species. If only more humans were as interested in them."

In time, Lynch grew to like the Calethar.

When he talked about it with his uncle, N'Djama said: "Your affection for them is a natural by-product of your admiration for them. I like many of my trading rivals, for example, but that doesn't stop me trying to find ways to outwit them or catch them wrong-footed."

"Rivalry in trade and rivalry in war are two different things, Uncle," Lynch said.

"True – the stakes are higher. But liking the Calethar doesn't mean you want them to control our destiny."

Chapter 18

Marie Uvarov looked more worn, but she still carried her responsibilities remarkably well. Kidron thought he understood how great those responsibilities were, but only because he had had such close professional contact with her over a long period of time. In some years, the only fresh intelligence she got on the Calethar was from Kidron's voyages into their space.

"I need help," said Kidron.

"I don't think the Hecabe government can give it to you. You need the Federation." Kidron didn't answer. "But I suspect you already knew that."

"Tell me, Marie, is the help not forthcoming because Hecabe hasn't the technology or because Hecabe is afraid?"

"Oh, I'd say the latter. But Hecabe has always been afraid. That isn't new, Aruzel; it's just that *Canar Calethari* is."

"Surely, then, they understand how important it is to destroy the ship."

Kidron tried unsuccessfully to keep the anger out of his voice. Why did this always seem to happen when he was with her? he wondered. She was always so calm, so pleased with whatever scraps of information he was able to bring back to her. He felt like a school kid who desperately wants to impress his teacher, and feels ashamed and worthless when he fails.

"Of course some of them understand how important it is," said Uvarov. "But many don't. And even some of those who do don't give it the same priority as you. After all, you're very involved in all of this . . ."

Kidron looked at Uvarov as if to say, "Oh, not you, too". Uvarov let the sentence die. They both knew what the appearance of *Canar Calethari* meant for human colonies not only on the frontier but among the border worlds. The Calethar now possessed a greater capacity than ever before to threaten humanity. And if they built a fleet of the new ships before the Federation could develop a counter then humans could lose the frontier sector forever.

"Do you have any particular Federation contacts in mind?" Kidron asked.

"I'm looking around. My office here is nothing more than a shop-front. You'll probably have to take a trip deeper into human space, or visit a Navy port, to get the assistance you need. But I must say, Aruzel, I don't think you'll get it. I believe you should leave *Canar Calethari* alone."

"That's hardly the point. *Canar* has to be destroyed as quickly as possible. The Calethar will think twice about seriously attacking human space if their best ship is destroyed in an encounter with *Magpie*. Imagine the effect on the High Council, on all the great clans from the Heartworld.

"But I need better weapons and equipment. *Canar*'s carrying beam weapons with capabilities I've never heard of. And her drive makes *Magpie*'s engine look like a windmill. Also, navigation equipment. Somehow *Canar* can track across hyperspace. I need that, too. I need whatever the Federation weapons research laboratories can give me."

"You want miracles."

"If it's miracles that are needed to take out *Canar Calethari*, then one way or another it's miracles I'll get. If I can't get them from the Federation, I'll get them from somewhere else. But I will get them."

"Somewhere else?"

"Wherever the Calethar got them from, Marie," Kidron answered. "We both know they don't possess the research base to have come up with all the innovations *Canar* was equipped with. I'll lay odds the nav gear came from a Terran world, maybe even some of the weapon systems."

"Perhaps," Uvarov admitted gravely. Kidron was certain then she knew more than she was letting on.

"I need that gear, or better. Can you get it for me, or do I go solo?"

Uvarov snorted. "Solo? You've never been solo. We've been interested in your activities for some time. We could never officially sanction your work, but we've learned a great deal from it. We will do for you what we can. But even the Federation has its limits." She looked at him sadly. "Aruzel, I want to help you. If you are determined to pursue *Canar Calethari* I will do anything I can to get you what you need, but *I* can't perform miracles."

"Oh, Marie, you're too modest by half. Miracles fall from you more easily than tears."

"That's meant to be a compliment?"
Kidron laughed for the first time in weeks.

Chapter 19

During *Canar Calethari*'s voyage home, Raenar was treated by the crew with every courtesy befitting his rank, as though nothing untoward had occurred. This was on explicit instructions from Nomelet, who wanted to ensure there was no possibility of Floran accusing him of insulting his family. Nomelet was determined to hold and use his new-found advantage, whatever the crew's feelings.

Raenar himself felt his shame deeply. His attitude changed completely. He never questioned any orders and acted with extreme deference to both Nomelet and Teonar. When not on duty, he confined himself to his cabin, dwelling on his dishonour and steeling himself for the meeting with his father. He determined to make up for his gross error. Somehow, someday, he would repair the damage to his family's reputation.

Dramorath greeted *Canar*'s arrival with great excitement and praise for the ship and its crew. Enilka gave a special reception for Nomelet and Teonar.

The profits from the expedition were huge, more than compensating the clan for its initial outlay on the ship. Their reputation rose tremendously on the Heartworld and on the High Council. The Uzdar seemed certain to sell the vessel's patent to the Calethar Fleet as well as to other clans, promising a huge increase in the clan's revenue. The Calethar would soon be equipped with an armada of the invincible ships, and then let the humans beware. The Calethar would resume their rightful place as the dominant species in all of known space.

The most important effect on the long-term welfare of the Uzdar was the impression the *Canar*'s success made on the scattered clans of the outworlds. The Uzdar had always been looked upon as the most important clan of the outworlds, but now as well they were looked upon as the *leading* clan. The distinction was vital. Importance was attached to wealth and trading success, leadership to prowess and honour. From now on, whatever the Uzdar proposed would be taken up and supported by most of the outworlds, a sizeable chunk of the Calethar population and the race's economic and military power. Furthermore, the secertor tribes, and these numbered in the hundreds, would manoeuvre to ally themselves with the Uzdar, who would become the patron of several new full clans; the respect and authority accruing from that would place them among the most powerful of the Calethar anywhere. All of this Nomelet had foreseen, and his disappointment at not destroying *Magpie* was alleviated by the realisation of so many of his other dreams. Anyway, Kidron could not forever avoid *Canar*, or one of her sister ships that would now almost certainly be built.

Enilka had already talked about ploughing some of the profits from *Canar*'s maiden voyage into the construction of a second vessel.

"Imagine the destruction we would wreak and profits we would win with two such ships!" the clan head declared, his eyes widening.

Nomelet did not voice his own doubts on the issue. He knew the vessel was only a means to an end, but many of the Uzdar, as well as other Calethar, were beginning to see the new class of ship as an end in itself. They dreamt of plundering not only the riches of the human worlds but whispered of raiding the settlements and ships of other species as well. Nomelet found all this talk distasteful. It was not for the Calethar to take up piracy as an occupation. It was appropriate to make the occasional foray if only to teach the humans an object lesson, but a species could not survive on plunder alone. Trade was the key to power and wealth, not privateering, and the more the Calethar indulged in piracy the smaller the returns as less and less booty was found. An even worse prospect would be the full militarisation of humanity as a defence against constant attacks. Nomelet had every faith in the ability of his own species to dominate another in the normal run of things, but he was also keenly aware of the human potential for warfare and the natural fecundity with which they so easily made up for any disaster or defeat. The Calethar had a history of war and violence no worse and no more exemplary than most other species, but the humans operated on a different order altogether – their history was the bloodiest of any known species, and as far as Nomelet was concerned the incredibly short period of time it had taken the humans to utterly defeat the Mendart was a lesson too few Calethar took to heart.

If it was through war that the Calethar were to initially regain their supremacy, it had to be a short and devastating one. The Calethar must force the humans into a position where peace would be seen as the only logical alternative to an otherwise prolonged and absurdly expensive war of attrition. Once a peace favourable to the Calethar had been settled, his species' natural predilection for trade and dominance would win through. Nomelet knew there was no other way.

And for all that to happen, the other clans, especially those of the Heartworld, had to be convinced. It would entail the clans working together as they had never done before so an armada of sufficient size could be constructed. The less warning the humans had about the coming conflict the easier and more certain a victory it would be.

Until then, Nomelet still had one dream to fulfil. The destruction of *Magpie*, and her cursed captain, the human Kidron.

Teonar was enjoying the pleasures of Dramorath, a world which offered so much more than her own planet, a relative backwater. Her share of the profits from *Canar*'s first voyage had already been credited to her clan and she felt no compulsion to return home yet. As well, she sensed that her fate, and that of her people, was tied up with the ambitions and plans of Nomelet, and she wanted to stay around to see what he did next. She was surprised, however, when Nomelet made the first move by calling on her in the luxurious dwelling Enilka had given her for the duration of her stay.

Teonar thought Nomelet looked strange in the formal robes of clan elder, and she said so.

"You are used to seeing me in battle and ship gear, Teonar. And yet that role has occupied only a small fraction of my life."

"I know. But I think it suits you better. You are predisposed to action, not intrigue."

Nomelet smiled. "It is about our future courses of action that I have come to see you."

Teonar looked at Nomelet, trying to guess his intentions. She offered him the guest lounge, reclining on her own. She liked this home a great deal. A bubbling stream ran through it, surrounded by a small, low forest of native shrubs and herbs. The place was always full of the smell of living things, of nature. She was looking forward to her first hunt on Dramorath. Enilka had promised to arrange something special for her, and a clan head always kept his word.

Nomelet accepted the couch gracefully, and let his long claws dangle in the stream's cool waters. "How refreshing," he sighed, closing his eyes momentarily, an indication of how much he trusted her. "I have come to ask you for two favours. To begin with, I am planning a second voyage with *Canar* against the human worlds, and I want you to serve again as my war-captain. This voyage will be different in nature from the first, however. It is to be more of a reconnaissance than a raiding mission. Short-term profit will not be its objective, though I see many long-term benefits accruing to it as well as great honour."

Teonar nodded, containing her excitement. Honour was almost as important as profits in raising a clan above the status of secertor. She would do anything to assure her own clan's success in this.

"Could you be more specific?" she asked, and then added a little too hurriedly: "I am, of course, interested in any proposal involving *Canar Calethari*. I regard her as . . . well . . . my ship in a way, if my saying so does not offend you."

"Indeed, I'm glad to hear you say so. All I can tell you about the projected voyage at this time is that we'll be leaving quite soon. If my plans are successful, perhaps as early as Year's End."

Teonar clacked her jaws. She was still willing to go, despite the short notice. "What is your second favour?"

Nomelet scratched his snout carefully with a claw, a sign of hesitation. *Rare for him,* Teonar thought to herself, surprised. *It is so out of character . . .*

"Before I leave Dramorath again, I want to ensure my family's . . . succession," he began breathlessly, and then blurted the rest out in a quick jumble of words. "I want offspring and I would be honoured if you would provide the egg and in return I will make special efforts to see that your clan is raised from secretor status and if you wish it see that you yourself are accepted as part of the Uzdar. As my mate. If you want. Teonar."

She could not help laughing, but it was not to humiliate him.

Nomelet ventured a nervous smile. "Do you agree?"

Teonar became more serious. "I agree to all except the timing."

"You will not offer your egg before we leave?" He seemed disappointed.

"Of course I will. My own line would thus be guaranteed as well. But not to the rest, at least not until we have returned. I do not want my own judgment –"

and here she looked hard at Nomelet "– or the judgment of my ship-captain – affected by ties of mateship. An egg is an impersonal thing, no more a part of my essence than a piece of my skin. But to link us together formally involves far more. Do you understand?"

Nomelet clacked his jaws, and looked at her with pride. His mind soared with the knowledge that she had accepted his offer. He had never felt so nervous before in his life, nor so unsure of success. Emotions were vices normally belonging to others which he manipulated to suit his plans, but now he was a victim of them himself.

"You do me honour," he said humbly.

"The honour is mine," Teonar returned, and bowed her head.

Nomelet had expected resistance from Inglas to his proposals, but not for her to be so vitriolic about it. Her anger was barely under control, and he noticed with satisfaction that Enilka seemed almost as taken aback as he.

"There is no need for a second mission, Enilka," she stated. "The new ship has proven its worth. Why should the clan risk a second venture into human space? Nomelet himself has said that the profits will not be as great. I see no advantage in this plan, and my advice is to reject it."

Nomelet squatted patiently in front of the pit, his head inclined as if in meditation. He pitied his cousin for her shortsightedness. For the clan's own good she must not be allowed to become its head.

Enilka gazed upon the three Calethar before him. Nomelet, Inglas and Floran. The three principal elders, the main contenders for the succession. He wished he could make them work together, but understood their ambition to succeed was a vital element in their getting as far as they had above their other cousins. There were forty families in the clan, forty possible contenders for his position, but only three had shown the necessary qualities.

"Well, Nomelet? Inglas's arguments are valid. What answer do you have?"

"Only this, Enilka. That if our clan is to be guided only by what profit it can gain in the short term, then we will not take our rightful place among the Calethar."

"We already have our rightful place among the Calethar!" interrupted Inglas, risking a reprimand. "We are a member of the High Council, the first outworld clan to achieve such an honour!"

"It is not enough," Nomelet said simply.

Inglas stared at him in amazement. "Not enough? What more is there?"

"Explain yourself," Enilka ordered Nomelet.

"I don't see why we shouldn't strive for leadership of the High Council itself."

Enilka actually rocked back on his heels. "Are you mad, Nomelet? We are an *outworld* clan! We have already achieved much more than any such has a right to expect."

"With respect, Enilka, I disagree. We are in the perfect position to achieve much more. The outworld clans are the ones which grow. Those from the Heartworld are stagnant, and rely on our trade with other species to make their profits for them. They turn us, to coin a human term, into nothing more than 'middlemen'. They are extraneous. Furthermore, the brunt of the coming war with the humans will be born by us outworlders. We will provide most of the crews, and the bulwark against any human counter-attacks. The Heartworld sits safe and fat and rich because of our efforts. It is time things changed. When the humans have been defeated, and Calethar dominance reasserted, it will be largely because of our efforts and those like us."

Floran found himself nodding in agreement, but stopped when he saw Inglas glaring at him. This was not a good time to make her an enemy. If Nomelet got what he wanted, then Floran's primary benefactor and protector would be off-planet for a second time, and Inglas would need little excuse to try and destroy him.

"There is something in what you say," Enilka agreed, "but how does this bear on your planned second voyage?"

"A reconnaissance of the human border worlds will reap for us invaluable intelligence. No matter how large an armada the High Council can organise to attack them, without intelligence it cannot strike effectively. The clan with that intelligence will lead the armada and determine its strategy."

Enilka grunted in agreement. Nomelet was right. Such information as Nomelet proposed to gather would prove invaluable in any assault on the human sector. He was in awe of Nomelet's imagination and ambition. He began to see why Floran held him in such respect, and why Inglas was so determined to stop him.

"The risk is still too great," Inglas said, sensing the way Enilka was thinking. "If the humans should somehow capture *Canar Calethari*, the loss in our prestige would be enormous. Not to mention the fact that the humans would then have access to the new ship and all her improvements. Can you imagine the armada succeeding if it was opposed by a human fleet equipped with similar vessels? The Calethar would never regain its rightful place among the spacefaring species. And the Uzdar would be condemned from one end of our civilisation to the other."

"The armada will take place no matter how well armed the humans are," Nomelet said. "The High Council has determined on a course of war, and I don't believe anything will dissuade it. Only the proper intelligence can hope to guarantee its success."

Enilka held up one clawed hand. The debate ended. Nomelet, Inglas and Floran waited in silence while their clan head came to a decision. Nomelet could hear his cousin's hard breathing. She was in distress. Nomelet knew then he had won, even before Enilka spoke.

Nomelet needed great patience. Despite his constant urgings, and the encouragement and support of Enilka, it was taking much longer than anticipated to get *Canar Calethari* ready for duty. At first it had been minor things, mainly administrative, but Nomelet's concern grew as time wore on. Investigations on his part revealed that most of the delays stemmed from the office of the master shipwright. This puzzled Nomelet, for he assumed the shame his son had brought the family would inspire Floran to greater efforts, not lesser.

Petty administrative and clan-related tasks kept Nomelet from confronting his cousin for several days. He had to arrange replacements for the crew he had lost, some to battle and some who left *Canar* because of other commitments (no Calethar would voluntarily leave a ship with such honour now attracted to it); he had to re-negotiate contracts for his ship's mercenary detachment (again, a task made easier because of *Canar*'s reputation); and he had to arrange for supplies and the maintenance of the ship's new and expensive weapon systems.

Eventually, however, he caught a shuttle to the giant orbiting shipyards, and confronted Floran in his own territory. He allowed time for the minimum amount of courtesy, and then went straight to the point.

"Why are you holding up *Canar*'s refit?"

Floran looked away from his cousin and stared out the window. Nomelet's gaze followed, and he could see furious activity clustered around a dock at the extreme end of the shipyards.

"What's going on there?" he asked. He could not remember any orders for the construction of a large ship coming to the clan in recent times. And then he recognised the vessel.

"That, cousin, is the reason for the delay," Floran told him.

"That's *Canar Calethari*!" Nomelet exclaimed with alarm. The ship was barely more than a frame. It would be weeks – months – before she was ready to travel.

Floran laughed in genuine amusement. "No, Nomelet. It's not your beloved ship. But nonetheless, it's the reason for your delay."

Nomelet looked at Floran warily. "What are you talking about? Where is *my* ship?"

"On trials. She has been completely refitted. Indeed, you could leave, if you so wished, within hours of her return, assuming your crew could be assembled that quickly."

"It could," Nomelet said, relief washing over him. "Why all these constant reports that all is not ready? And what is that ship?"

"Haven't you guessed?" Floran shook his head sadly. "Her name is *Kahunna*."

"'Hunter'? And what will she hunt?"

"Whatever you order her to. She will be leaving with you for human space."

Nomelet said nothing, but his look told Floran that he still had a lot of explaining to do.

"*Kahunna* is *Canar*'s sister ship. You will be commanding a small squadron when next you leave Dramorath. You will become the terror of the humans. They will tell stories about you to their young to keep them disciplined."

Nomelet was puzzled. "My next mission is a reconnaissance, not a raiding venture. The more ships I command the harder the job will be. I'm going in quickly and getting out even faster. And I'm going to leave *soon*, Floran. Do you understand?"

Floran nodded. "You will be delayed by only a matter of ten days. The wait, I promise you, will be worth it."

"Ten days? It would take ten times that for *Kahunna* to be finished, even allowing for her being the second of her class."

"Perhaps I should have described *Kahunna* as *Canar*'s little sister. She will be no match for *Canar*. Mostly empty hull. Fast, some firepower, but short on screens and crew. Minimal auxiliary equipment and backup systems."

"I don't understand," Nomelet said, impatient now. Floran was speaking in riddles.

"Think about it, cousin. While you're away on your reconnaissance mission, *Kahunna* will be raiding human settlements. Everyone will assume it is *Canar* again, leaving you to do your job in whatever manner you wish."

"Why?" Nomelet asked.

"I have just explained why –"

"Why are you doing this for me?"

Floran sighed deeply. "Because I want my son to redeem himself. He has shamed me, my family, the clan. I want him to make up for it. I am asking you to let him do this by making you a gift of *Kahunna*. I have built her with my share of the returns from your first mission. Let Raenar captain *Kahunna* under your command."

"And what does Raenar think of your plan?"

"When I mentioned it to him he showed the first joy since his return home. It is as if he is born anew. If you refuse him, I fear for his life."

"I do not wish to see him dead. But you know as well as I do why he put so much at risk. He wanted the captaincy of *Canar Calethari* for himself, and the clan leadership for you. How can I trust him again?"

Floran's arms shook slightly. Nomelet understood the pressure the shipwright was under, but he could not afford to grant Floran's wish from pity. Too much was at stake.

"He is different, Nomelet. Shame has made him so. You know as well as I how proud he was. Well, his pride has been replaced by guilt and self-hate. He will be no risk to your position. But to guarantee it I now make you this promise . . . on our clan's seed."

Nomelet gasped. What Floran was offering was the most sacred of promises, a vow so binding that to break it would destroy for decades any influence he and his family could have within the clan.

"What promise?"

"That I will support your claim for clan leadership, forgetting my own until you so wish it."

Nomelet could hardly believe Floran's words. For it all to be so easy!

"I cannot guarantee your son's safety, Floran," he warned.

"I know. Neither he nor I expect – nor wish – you to heed his safety. Only the most dangerous tasks will allow him to redeem his honour."

Nomelet nodded slowly. His hearts were racing. Inglas would not be able to stand against both he and Floran. When the time came, clan leadership would be his.

"Tell me something, Floran."

"Yes?"

"What do you mean you will forget your own claims to the leadership *until* I so wish?"

Floran snorted. "Don't play games with me, Nomelet. I know your ambition goes beyond the clan. Indeed, your ambition is so great that I can see no end to it. It has been a long time since any of the Calethar have wanted to reach as far as you, or dreamed so deeply. If you succeed, you will want someone you can trust to succeed you as clan leader. Me."

"And if my plans don't succeed?"

"You will still need someone in the clan to back you up, be your sword or shield. Either way I will have more power and influence than I do now."

Nomelet saw the wisdom in Floran's choice, and realised how useful an ally the master shipwright would make. As an enemy, things would have been much harder. An ally at last, he thought to himself, and one who seems to understand why he believed the clan could not be the beginning and end of Calethar policy. The artificial parameters and constraints the clan system imposed on the species were strangling their future, and he was going to change that. And then he thought: *if Floran has read this in my actions and words, who else? Inglas? No; she was clever, but not that perceptive. Enilka? Perhaps, but if so he was keeping it to himself. Ah, Teonar. Of course. She would have seen it quite early on. In which case she may have expected my proposal.*

"Your offer is acceptable," he told Floran.

The shipwright visibly relaxed. "Then all is well, cousin."

Nomelet wasted no time in procuring Teonar's eggs, a painless operation that took a clan doctor five minutes to perform. As the container holding the eggs was taken away in preparation for their insemination, Teonar considered her decision once more. She still felt it was the correct one, and a worthy sign to Nomelet of her commitment to him. But in one way it worried her. It was as if she was admitting that something could happen to either or both of them on *Canar*'s next voyage, and that was a bad thought for a war-captain to have. She quickly dispelled the notion with a confident grin, showing her teeth to no one in particular but feeling the better for it. She needed a hunt. She was getting stale and had not tasted blood for far too long. Enilka had arranged for one in two weeks' time, just before *Canar* was to leave, and she was impatient for it.

The doctor returned and eyed her warily. "Are you alright?"

"Restless," she said, without explaining further.

"I am often jealous of you among our people who are as comfortable in space as the rest of us are on the surface, but not at times like this. I have seen so many eaten up by their eagerness to be away again. To never know peace, or calm, or contentment."

"I have known all three, Doctor, but only on a ship."

The doctor shrugged. "A ship can never be a home," he said quietly, showing just how little he knew or would even be capable of understanding. Teonar was not angry at his presumption; she felt sorry for him.

"Don't you ever wish you had a home?" he persisted. "I mean a permanent home. Something not subject to the whims of solar flares or space flux."

"No," she answered.

The doctor extended his claws briefly and retracted them again, the Calethar equivalent of a shrug. "I am sure that deep inside every Calethar's soul there is a yearning to make a home."

The doctor's babbling was starting to irritate Teonar. "What are you driving at?"

The doctor busied himself with some instruments, pretending only to be casually interested in the conversation, but Teonar could see the tension in his shoulders, the muscles clamping like a vice along his back.

"I mention it from whimsy, mainly. But if one was interested in settling down permanently, there are ways it could be made easier. Certain land with generous tithes belonging to them could be made available to one whose reputation was so high within the clan – even for a secertor."

"Oh? And who would arrange such a tempting deal?"

The doctor smiled. "Perhaps I have already said too much. But I know of parties within the Uzdar who would gladly assist such an arrangement in any way within reason. A pension could also be arranged, and favours for one's own clan. Important favours."

Teonar had heard enough. She knew who was really making the offer. She reached out quickly and grasped the male by his arm. Her claws were extended, but she did not hold so tightly that they pierced his skin. She drew him close to her, and whispered: "Tell Inglas for me, Doctor, that this secertor vagabond needs no favours. I am a war-captain, and will make my own fortune."

The doctor shook with fright, and Teonar let him go with disgust.

"I was only carrying a message –"

"Enough," she spat. "You have already talked too much. And see that my eggs are well looked after. I want no witch interfering with my property. If, on my return, they are not all producing offspring I will have your eyes for decorations on my weapon belt. Do you understand?"

The doctor nodded vigorously. "I meant no offence," he said meekly.

"None taken," she replied lightly. "But for your health's sake, do not forget my warning."

Teonar left the surgery before her disgust made her do something she would regret. The Uzdar were a tolerant clan, but probably not too forgiving of those who killed their doctors. They were so expensive to train.

Chapter 20

Captain Aruzel Kidron wished he was on the bridge of *Magpie*. Instead, he was in Marie Uvarov's dark office again, feeling more claustrophobic than he ever did in his own small cabin, and confronting a woman who, like Uvarov, was nothing like the image she projected. She reminded Kidron of everyone's grandmother: short, a little squat, grey hair like steel wool cut short, weathered skin . . . she even possessed the twinkling eyes. Her name was Soo Lee, and she was the most senior line officer in the Federation Navy. Uvarov mentioned her full title, but Kidron lost track after the word Admiral. Admiral Soo. Every human knew that name, but Kidron had problems relating it to this inoffensive looking woman sitting on the edge of her chair talking to him as though he was a favourite relative.

"Captain Kidron," Soo was saying in her sweet voice, "Commodore Uvarov has told me about your encounter with *Canar Calethari*. We suspected the vessel was a new kind of ship, but your report even took us by surprise."

Kidron nodded, not sure what to say. This old, homely woman was the commander who had led a

Federation fleet to victory over the Mendart battle squadrons all those decades ago. How many other surprises would come his way before the meeting was over?

"And Commodore Uvarov also informs me that you intend to meet and battle with this ship a second time. I feel it is my duty to advise you not to pursue this course of action."

"I understand that. However, my mind is made up. *Canar* has to be destroyed."

"The Commodore and I have had several frank discussions over this matter. I understand the situation perhaps better than you know. Indeed, I have been following your career with some interest." Admiral Soo smiled. "In fact, Aruzel," she said, leaning towards him, "you might even say I regard you as a kind of wayward son." She watched Kidron's startled expression with interest. "Oh, yes. It might also surprise you to learn that the Navy also regards you as something of an *ex officio* naval officer.

"Commodore Uvarov tells me that you need . . . now let me see here . . ." She fumbled with a piece of paper and squinted as she read it out. Kidron wondered if the squint was an act. *She can probably see like an eagle.* ". . . free-directional beam weapons, additional anti-missile pods, and a hyperspace tracking system. Anything else, Aruzel? No first-class cabins for your crew? Or perhaps a company of marines? An escort of a dreadnought or two, maybe?"

"If you have them," Kidron replied, stern-faced. The way Soo had read the list you would have thought he had asked to be President of the Federation.

Soo laughed lightly. It was *exactly* the sound his grandmother used to make. A shiver went up Kidron's spine. In a weird sense he found her image almost macabre. The bits just did not fit together.

She stopped laughing, rested back in her seat and sighed, rubbed her eyes with the thumb and first finger of one hand. When she opened them again they were like two hard pieces of coal. Kidron held his breath. The transformation was incredible. Now there was no doubt he was staring at the conqueror of the Mendart Empire. She had conceived and carried out a strategy that crippled a civilisation already ancient when humanity's ancestors first dropped out of the trees.

"You're a fool, Captain."

Kidron sat rock-still. He was being reprimanded and it did not enter his mind to defend himself or answer back.

Soo twisted around in her seat to face Uvarov. She threw the piece of paper onto the desk and snapped her fingers. Uvarov pulled a sheet from one of her drawers and handed it to the admiral.

"However," she said, more to Uvarov than Kidron, "we need a fool. So this is an authorisation for you to obtain most of what you need, plus some extras you haven't thought of, from the Navy Supply Station on Diarmaid. I know it's a long haul from here, but you can't get the stuff anywhere else in human space. Diarmaid is the chief weapons research station for the Navy."

A small fire of joy kindled in Kidron.

"Naturally, there are conditions," Soo added.

"Go on," he said, suddenly suspicious.

"First – and I know this will be difficult – only you, your crew and those Naval personnel involved in installing the equipment are to know of this. I cannot stress how important this is for Federation security."

"Of course," Kidron replied.

"Under most circumstances we would not even admit that these weapons existed. But the Navy agrees with your summary of the situation. To forestall a war between humanity and the Calethar, this new ship has to be destroyed. Under present conditions the Navy isn't able to do the job itself, at least not officially, and in the Navy any other way is virtually impossible.

"The second condition is that *Magpie*'s next mission be specifically to hunt down and destroy *Canar Calethari*, which I have been given to understand is your intention anyway. But a rider to this condition is that on completion of that mission, should you survive, you return immediately to Diarmaid so that the weapons can be dismantled and returned to naval stores."

"Accepted." Kidron was relieved that so far the conditions were so lenient.

"Third. *Magpie* is commissioned as a naval vessel from the time you are equipped with the new weapons to the time they are returned to stores."

Kidron could not help himself. "A *naval* vessel!" he exclaimed. "A naval *vessel*!"

"You heard. It will be commissioned as the Federation naval ship *Vendetta*, destroyer escort class, experimental. Don't worry, Captain, we won't expect you to change the name on *Magpie*'s hull. I told you the Navy likes to do things by the book. You and everyone else in the know will still refer to your command as

Magpie. But commissioning the ship is not simply a bureaucratic nicety. Effectively, you will be going to war, Captain. A small, hopefully tidy war that will not spread beyond the clash between your ship and *Canar Calethari*. But like it or not, it is now Federation business."

Kidron nodded, feeling numb.

"There is a small rider to this condition as well, I'm afraid, Aruzel," Uvarov said. She looked at Soo, and the admiral nodded to her to continue. "When *Magpie* joins the Navy list, so do you and your crew."

"I beg your pardon?"

"You will become Captain Aruzel Kidron, Commanding Officer of *Vendetta*, operating under the warrant and regulations of the Federation."

"Are you serious?"

"I have never been more serious in my life, Aruzel."

"Commodore Uvarov is telling you the truth, Captain. Technically it means you come under the direct command of the Navy. In fact, you will carry on as you normally would, except that any order you receive from either myself or Commodore Uvarov must be obeyed. Failure to do so will result in a court-martial, and believe me, you don't want to know what that could mean to you or your command."

Kidron believed her. An officer in the Federation Navy! Poor old Kazin must be turning in his grave. Thinking of Kazin hardened his resolve. He nodded his agreement, though he could not find the will to voice it.

Neither Soo nor Uvarov said anything then, and Kidron looked at them impatiently. "There is another condition?" he asked.

Uvarov looked away. Soo stared him straight in the eyes. She opened her mouth to speak, hesitated, and then seemed to make up her mind to get it over and done with.

"You must make every attempt to kill the Calethar noble called Nomelet."

"Of course I will," Kidron said, wondering what the sudden drama was about. "In any space battle involving . . ." And then he realised what she really meant. "You actually mean . . . even if he surrenders . . ."

"That's right, Captain. We want Nomelet to die even if he surrenders *Canar Calethari*."

"That's impossible," Kidron blurted. "If Nomelet surrenders his ship I can't just blow her away –"

"Under no circumstances would we expect you to destroy any vessel that surrenders to you. We are talking about Nomelet. Just Nomelet. He *must* die."

"You don't know what you're asking . . ."

The admiral sighed deeply. "You're wrong. I know exactly what I'm asking, and I know how much it goes against the grain.

"But understand this. I have been watching Nomelet's career for even longer, and much more closely, than I have been watching yours. He, and not *Canar Calethari*, poses the greatest danger to humanity. He is that rare thing among his people, a Calethar with ambitions and dreams that go far beyond clan politics. He intends to see the Calethar as strong – stronger – than they were before humans entered the scene. And he believes, quite rightly I might add, that it can't be achieved unless humanity is reduced to a fraction of its present size and power."

Kidron swallowed. "But to *murder* someone in cold blood . . ."

"I won't play games with you, Captain. It is murder. But his death would almost certainly avert a war between his species and ours. We have been working on the High Council over the last twenty years, ever since we discovered it was considering an invasion of human space. We believe we can persuade it to agree to a permanent treaty with the Federation as long as Nomelet does not become too powerful an influence in the High Council. A year ago we received intelligence that the clan Uzdar had been accepted as a member, giving Nomelet a voice at the highest level of the Calethar central government."

Soo paused for a moment and studied her hands. Kidron guessed that what she was asking from him she herself found abhorrent.

"Nomelet is even older than I am, hard as it may be to believe. I know I probably look like I'm a hundred if I'm a day, but in fact I'm still under the ton. I am an old woman, Aruzel. Nomelet is 103 Terran years in age, but is considered by his long-lived people to have just reached the time for mating. He has another century or two of active life ahead of him, all dedicated to making his dreams come true. And he will, Aruzel, he will . . . if he lives."

Chapter 21

To Lynch's eyes the Navy Supply Station orbiting Diarmaid was a disorganised junkyard. There seemed to be no pattern to the agglomeration of girders, domes and modified ship hulls slotted together wherever a loose airlock could be fitted. Though the station contained some of the greatest minds in human space (and some great minds *not* from human space), none of them had the ability or will to organise the station into some semblance of aesthetic order.

As *Magpie* slowed her rotation for the final approach to her dock, Lynch stared out of one of the common room screens, agog at the amount of metal in orbit around the blue and yellow world suspended at the bottom of the screen.

"It's like someone's idea of hell," said a voice behind him. He turned to see Santa watching their approach from over his shoulder.

"You've never been here before?"

Santa shook her head. "We're a privileged few, Aaron," she said lightly. "Except for a handful of politicians keen to see where all the research funds go, no one but Federation Navy personnel ever see this place. Up until now, that is. *Magpie*'s the first civilian ship ever allowed this close to Diarmaid."

"I thought the Navy would have assisted at least some privateers in the past."

"I've never heard of any. I guess they figure *Canar Calethari* is a big enough threat for them to break some of their own rules."

Lynch grunted and returned his attention to the station. *Magpie* was floating by an amazing construction of peculiar angles made up from bits and pieces of what appeared to be a dozen ships.

"Look," Santa said, pointing to a flat sail projecting from an environment dome. The sail had a white star painted on it, surrounded by a blue circle. "Pre-One Earth gear. Nothing goes to waste, it seems. That might not even have come from a starship. Probably the remains of a twenty-first century intrasystem freighter or scout boat."

Lynch peered at the sail with more interest. It *looked* very old, though he couldn't explain exactly *how*. Maybe the way the sheet of metal had been cut, or the faint suggestion of welding along some of its seams. Or the white star in a blue circle. Pre-One Earth? He shook his head. That was so long ago it wasn't worth worrying about. As *Magpie* drifted closer he could see the sail had suffered from the impact of thousands of micro-meteoroids. The symbol looked as though it had been recently retouched. Someone at the station enjoyed their history, he thought.

Magpie continued on her way, sometimes observed by interested technicians working outside the protective domes and second-hand hulls. Occasionally one of them waved, but most just seemed curious at the sight of a civilian vessel. They were not surprised. If the ship had gotten this far without being stopped, detoured or simply destroyed, it must be expected. Soon enough, they went back to their work. They would find out what the ship was doing here, even if the news was unofficial . . . every sailor could get hold of accurate scuttlebutt without difficulty.

Lynch, by craning his neck, got a good view of *Magpie*'s destination. They were only a few kilometres away from the only structure he had yet seen that even faintly looked as though someone with a flair for design had been involved in its construction. It was a huge, tree-shaped affair, resembling a fir or cedar. The branches were passageways, and the needles silvery environment tubes containing laboratories and other facilities. The construction spun slowly on an axis that ran from its apex through the middle, a giant metal trunk.

"What's that thing we're heading for?" he asked Santa.

She pushed Lynch out of the way in order to get a good look. "We're supposed to be docking at the main administration centre. They call it the Pyramid." Then, a little dryly, she added: "I guess that's it."

Lynch peered ahead. *Magpie* was now floating by a series of meshed tubes and girders that seemed to have no organised thought behind them at all, but they covered a large area. Just behind this mishmash of metal he could make out the silhouette of a huge spaceship.

"Is that a dreadnought?" he asked a little breathlessly. He had never seen one up close before. All he knew was that they were big. *Really* big.

"Yes. It's large enough to be one of the new 300,000-tonne *Trafalgar* class. They're monsters, the size of small asteroids. I've heard they have enough firepower to obliterate a whole planet."

Lynch shivered. "Could it take on *Canar Calethari*, do you think?"

"Well, it's about five times the size. I guess it'd have the firepower and armour. But it wouldn't have the agility. I think in a stand-up fight *Canar* would lose out, but that isn't what the Calethar built her for. *Canar*'s meant to be more like a big cat. It stalks and strikes very quickly and violently, and then gets the hell out. If that behemoth was in orbit somewhere, and *Canar* suddenly popped into normal space right on top of it, fired all its missiles and got off a few beam shots, then I reckon the Calethar would have a huge scalp to share among their weapon belts."

Lynch whistled. "And we're going after her," he said, more to himself than to Santa. He was not afraid, merely overawed at the task Kidron had set himself and his crew.

Santa gave a short, unpleasant laugh. "Sure enough. We'll be like a cat, too. Only our game is another predator, not some fat freighter or defenceless settlement. We'll catch her, and we'll win."

"You're sure of that, aren't you?"

"Of course." She looked down at him with some surprise. "Aren't you?"

Lynch shook his head. "Hell, no. I'm not sure of anything."

Robinson watched with a mixture of curiosity and impatience as the station's technicians fitted a new weapon system into *Swallow*. It was a lozenge-shaped turret that sat in the cargo section, about two metres long, half a metre tall and three metres wide. Projecting from its front were two barrels that looked like thin metal tubes reinforced with glass figure eights.

The senior technician stood back to view her handi-work, then turned to grin at the pilot. "It's beautiful, isn't it?" she said, obviously pleased.

"I'm sure it is," Robinson agreed, and added, a little quizzically: "But what is it?"

"Laser turret, but not your everyday kind. Mac's up front in the cockpit fitting the aiming device. It will track up to ten independent targets and automatically select priority threats and fire at them. We've been working on this beauty for nearly a decade now. This is the first operational unit."

"Is it entirely automatic?" Robinson asked.

"No. You'll have an override. Sits low, doesn't it? Hardly takes up any cargo space. When we've finished here you won't actually be able to see the turret. It will be encased in an exit pod. When you go into action you lower the turret below the belly of the cutter. Until then, your enemy won't have a clue you're armed. They'll assume you've only got the standard mining grade laser most cutters are equipped with. A nasty surprise for someone, eh?" The technician looked at Robinson suggestively.

"Indeed," Robinson agreed, saying no more. If the technician did not already know whom it was going to be used against, she was not going to blab. "What about a power source?"

"Runs off your main engine, just like the old laser. No power loss to your batteries at all, unless you're drifting.

As long as your drive lasts you have an active weapons system. Same goes for the turret drive. Revolves on two axes, so you can fire in virtually any direction below the shuttle's equator. Ideally, you'd carry two turrets, one dorsal and one ventral, but we only have two of them at the moment and your captain wanted one on each cutter."

Robinson nodded. Kidron had wanted the cutters' weapons systems upgraded after they had proven so useful in the action against *Uzir*. She left the technician to it, curious to see what other new gadgets *Magpie* was acquiring. She made her way to the common room, stationing herself in front of a screen. Four large main-tenance craft were attached to the privateer by lifelines and cables, and floating around these craft and the ship were several white-suited technicians doing things to *Magpie* that Robinson could not identify from her observation point. What she could make out though were some wicked-looking pieces of equipment being hauled from one of the carriers and manoeuvered beneath the ship's cross-spar.

"Beam weapons," said a voice beside her.

"Hello, Danui," she said without turning. "How many? And what's happened to our old one?"

"Four, all multi-directional and rapid firing. I had no idea the things were even being developed let alone in existence. I guess the old one's been consigned to the rubbish dump, or more likely it's already part of some new experiment. Nothing gets wasted here."

"Not surprising," said Robinson, still gazing outside. "If you have a few thousand scientists and you give them all the room they want, eventually everything will be put to use. It must be like working in a giant toy factory for them."

"I suppose so. I wonder if they ever give any thought to how their inventions are used?"

Robinson shrugged. "I doubt it. The technicians and scientists I've talked to are like a gaggle of excited children. They just want to know if their inventions work. They probably never consider what it actually means if they do work. By the way, do you know what all those modules that have been dumped in the main hold are for?"

"Something to do with navigation. The captain's being tight-lipped about it. Ever since his meeting with that admiral on Hecabe . . . I don't know . . . something somehow seems different about him. More grim, if you know what I mean."

"You're forgetting *Canar Calethari*," Robinson said. "Thinking about that ship is enough to make anyone grim."

"Velocity: 10,000," Robinson said.

Lynch glanced out *Swallow*'s starboard porthole. The kilometre beacons along Diarmaid's testing range were flashing by at nearly three a second. It was the only external indication of their speed.

"Laser on," Robinson ordered.

Lynch flicked a switch. A graded crosshair appeared on his visor display and followed the movement of his right eye.

"Laser on," he said.

"Alright, let's see how it works."

Lynch gave control of the new weapon system to its own computer. Immediately yellow alphanumeric target co-ordinates appeared on the cockpit screen, flickered for a moment. One of the co-ordinates was chosen as a priority, its colour changing to red.

As co-pilot, Lynch now had nothing to do except watch proceedings. A second later Robinson was no longer working as pilot. The computer had taken over every function of the cutter. *Swallow* rolled, pitched, yawed and fired her own engines as she lined up for her attack run.

"Don't we do anything?" Lynch asked.

"Stop complaining," Robinson said. "Enjoy the ride."

The computer beeped. The chosen target alphanumeric flashed. They heard the laser hum briefly. The alphanumeric disappeared off the screen.

"That's it!" exclaimed Lynch.

Even Robinson looked disappointed. "I thought we would see what we were firing at . . ."

Swallow rolled, her engines fired. Another target had been chosen.

"This is going to be one boring flight," Lynch said.

"You could always try talking to me," Robinson suggested.

"I do talk to you, Toma –"

"About flying, yes. There was a time we also talked like friends."

"That was before –" Lynch stopped himself, shutting his mouth.

Robinson's eyes widened with sudden understanding. "Before you found out about Kazin and me."

Lynch could not look at her.

"I didn't know you felt that way about me," she said, her tone faintly amused.

"I wasn't sure I did," he said quietly. "I'm still not sure."

"I don't know whether to be flattered or angry."

"Angry?"

"Why didn't you come and talk to me about it?"

"I thought you wanted to be left alone."

"I *did*, at first. I still grieve for Kazin. He was my best friend. But I didn't cut myself off from everybody else. You're the one acting like a widow."

"What do you mean?"

Robinson sighed. "I mean you're behaving as if all the pain in the universe was your responsibility. You're employed as a pilot, not a martyr."

"You *are* angry," he said defensively.

The computer beeped again and another target was destroyed.

"No, Aaron, I'm not angry. Disappointed, maybe. My relationship with Kazin wasn't a secret. We were friends; we were lovers. I wish he was still alive. But I had a life apart from him and I still have. He too had his own circle, and his first love was always *Magpie*."

"And what's your first love?" Lynch asked.

Robinson blinked. "I don't have one, Aaron. All I have is a first hate."

"The Calethar."

For a while neither talked. *Swallow* continued selecting targets and destroying them, then navigating and flying herself through the testing range to her next victim.

Lynch tried sorting through the conflicting mass of emotions and thoughts that filled his mind.

"Do you want to be my lover?" Robinson asked abruptly.

"I don't know any more," he replied honestly.

"When you do know, tell me, and *then* we can talk about it properly," she said, smiling.

Lynch nodded.

The computer beeped.

"So, what do we talk about right now?" Robinson asked plaintively.

Kidron was alone on the bridge. Most of *Magpie*'s systems were down so the Navy's specialists could work on them. Only the main screen was operating, filled by the crystal image of the Pyramid, a floating vision that seemed out of place at a military research facility.

All over his ship hundreds of scientists and technicians were changing *Magpie* into something new. She came to Diarmaid a privateer, a converted trader, but would leave metamorphosed into one of the most powerful warships in known space.

But as powerful as Canar Calethari? Kidron wondered, knowing he could only find out in combat.

The changes to *Magpie* were more than physical, however. Since she was built she had been an extension of Kidron himself: her voyages made to pursue his ambitions; her computers and systems analogs of his own senses; her weapons his teeth and claws. *Magpie* had been his life-mate, his abiding love.

And now she was becoming something else, a tool not only for his revenge but for Federation policy as well. It was no longer his mind alone that guided her course, but the foreign minds of admirals and strategists.

He shifted the view on the screen. The Pyramid disappeared, replaced by the deep gulf of space and the scattered stars. Out there, somewhere, was Nomelet. Kidron neither hated nor feared the Calethar, and yet he had agreed to hunt him down and kill him.

No, Kidron reminded himself, *murder him. To cast him into the vacuum.*

Kidron's hands balled into fists. He wanted to be away from here. He wanted the confrontation with *Canar Calethari* to be done with. He wanted to be free from his prison of circumstance, a prison he created by attacking Tunius all those months ago.

Kidron at last realised what Kazin had tried to warn him about. He was no longer his own master. His destiny now was truly out of his own hands.

He felt as if he had lost everything.

Chapter 22

Canar Calethari and *Kahunna* left their orbits around Dramorath within minutes of each other and accelerated towards the edge of their home system. Those in ships and the dockyard watched in awe as the two vessels, metal sisters, soared into space. They were like two long needles of death, their very shape a portent of destruction and war. They were gods, and their crews god-like. Those watching the departure felt as if they were witnessing the beginning of something momentous. Times were changing. The Calethar were fighting back and the good years would return.

Fight well, they whispered as the ships disappeared into the black sea. *Fight well*.

Raenar listened to the reports coming in from his crew. *Kahunna* had not had time for a shakedown voyage, and her crew were scuttling along and in between her bulkheads, checking instruments and readouts, listening for any telltale sounds of something going wrong. All spacers knew how a ship *should* sound, and the slightest buzz or crackle or clang that should not have been there would immediately alert the crew. So far nothing had gone amiss.

Raenar contacted Nomelet in *Canar Calethari*.

"*Kahunna* flies like an arrow," he reported.

Nomelet was relieved, but not surprised – Floran had worked hard and long on *Kahunna*'s construction.

On the bridge with Nomelet were Makarin, helm-captain once again, and Teonar. Although Teonar had not been enthusiastic about the change in plans, after Nomelet had explained to her the advantages of going out with two ships she turned around. When Raenar had offered his personal oath of loyalty to Nomelet she dispassionately viewed the advantages and felt more confident about the outcome of their mission. She no longer had any doubts about Raenar himself, only about *Kahunna*.

Nomelet noticed her expression. "What is wrong?"

"It is *Kahunna*," she explained. "I am distrustful of an empty ship. A stripling dressed as a warrior is still nothing more than a stripling."

"I believe the deception will work," he said, and pointed to the screen where they saw pictures beamed back to them from Dramorath of the two ships piercing through space.

God, he thought, *the humans would quake in their boots if they could see this sight.*

Teonar later joined Nomelet in his cabin.

"When do you think *Kahunna* will be ready to raid?" he asked.

"She's as ready now as she'll ever be," Teonar replied. "Raenar has trained his few troops hard and well. His crew, spacer for spacer, is as good as our own. The sooner they're in combat the better, so their training doesn't go stale on them and their eagerness isn't frustrated waiting for something to happen. Have you seen Raenar's crew manifest?"

Nomelet nodded. "Many are Calethar who have shamed themselves or their family in some way. Raenar has chosen wisely. These spacers will follow him wherever he goes for a chance to regain their honour."

"And I think the sooner they're used, the more potent a weapon they'll be. Also, the greater the opportunity we'll have of completing our mission undisturbed. It will take a while to map and chart the defences and movement webs of the human border worlds. The more distractions *Kahunna* offers, the better our chances."

Nomelet called up a chart on his cabin's small work station. "Study this. It shows the planet Hecabe. It's a border world and Kidron's home base. Hecabe isn't as well defended as some and richer than most. I want *Kahunna* to raid there first. In fast, out fast. When reports begin to spread that *Kahunna* has penetrated their territory, the humans will panic."

Teonar grinned. She liked the plan. "I hope Kidron appreciates the irony."

Raenar knew he was being honoured; at the same time he was painfully aware that only a Calethar who had been shamed would feel such gratification at being admitted before the ship-captain's dais on board *Canar Calethari*. For all that, Nomelet's face was stern, and Teonar's impassive. Raenar understood the gravity of the situation, and the importance of what Nomelet was saying.

"Your helm-captain already has the co-ordinates and specifications for the Hecabe system. I want you to inflict as much damage as you can in as short a time as possible. Under no circumstances are the humans to suspect, or be given any reason to suspect, that they are not facing the real *Canar Calethari*. I would rather see you send *Kahunna* into the sun than give away that secret."

"No less than I," Raenar responded, and Nomelet saw he was speaking the truth. "When do you want us to go?"

"As soon as possible. I expect you to leave as soon as you return to *Kahunna*."

"It will be done," Raenar said, confident and eager. Nomelet smiled, then, and Raenar felt the cloud of shame that hung around his mind like a black miasma begin to clear. He almost laughed with joy, the joy of release, and the joy of anticipated battle; battle, what was more, against the hated humans on Kidron's home world. Oh, they would pay for his disgrace.

Nomelet stood up and clasped Raenar's claws within his own. "Good luck, cousin. Our prayers will be with you."

Then to Raenar's surprise, Teonar too came forward and repeated the ritual. Raenar suddenly felt he could die for these two.

"Our next rendezvous, should everything go according to plan, will be here in twenty ship days, where we will review our success and you'll be given your next mission. If we do not appear, wait five days. If we still haven't appeared in that time, you are to assume we've been destroyed. Under no circumstances are you to seek revenge for us." Raenar opened his mouth to object, but Nomelet held up his hand. "Instead, you are to return to Dramorath. Your father, noble Floran, will then fully outfit *Kahunna*, and then, and only then, with you in command, will she return to exact retribution for *Canar Calethari* . . . and this time, under her own name. Do you understand?"

Raenar nodded, silent and in some awe. Nomelet was giving him a gift more precious than life. He turned, and without looking back left the audience chamber.

When he had gone Nomelet glanced at Teonar. "Do you think I've done the right thing?"

"What else could you do?" she asked in turn. "If we are destroyed, and if Raenar returns with a fully out-fitted *Kahunna*, he too will meet his end. He deserves that chance. You owe it, I think, if not to him, then at least to his father."

Nomelet nodded. "You see the right of it."

"And there is another reason," Teonar continued.

"And what might that be?"

"That if *Canar* is destroyed on her reconnaissance mission, any real hope of a successful Calethar invasion of human space is impossible. The war parties will not accept the fact unless it's made painfully obvious to them. That can only be achieved by sending *Kahunna* to certain destruction as well."

Teonar studied Nomelet's face closely. For a moment his eyes clouded over, and she thought she could actually see great pain there. She resisted the urge to reach out and comfort him. He would not appreciate it at this time and in this place. In some ways their closer relationship made certain things much harder for the two of them.

"Yes," he said slowly. "Again, you have the right of it." He sighed deeply, left the dais and rested his sceptre in its place against the wall.

"The Calethar can only regain their previous position of dominance at the expense of the humans. But the blow struck against them must be at exactly the right time and with exactly the right amount of force. Anything else will only end in disaster, and our species' eventual subjection beneath the human . . . what is their word? . . . heel." There was a note of disgust in his voice, as though he was discussing a part of anatomy belonging to a herd animal.

"Are you so certain, Nomelet?" His fierce conviction sometimes frightened her.

"How can any of us be sure about anything? These humans are so unpredictable, as unpredictable as the cosmos we inhabit. Sometimes, contemplating the combination of the two makes me tremble. I wonder if other species saw us that way before we became the powerbrokers?"

"Perhaps," Teonar said. "If so, and if we are fated to fall under the sway of humanity, they will be nothing more than the new powerbrokers and one day will in turn give way to some other species."

Nomelet shook his head. "I don't think so. The humans are truly different to any who have come before. If they win the coming struggle, there will be no need for powerbrokers any more. All will thrive or perish at their peculiar and erratic whim. For all our sakes, that mustn't be allowed to happen."

They returned to the bridge when told Raenar had reached *Kahunna*.

There were no more signals between the two ships. *Kahunna* changed course as they watched, accelerating to her jump point.

The bridge crew silently watched her go. In a short while she was out of sight, and a few minutes later normal space was fractured by a brilliant burst of energy. *Canar* tracked her sister ship's progress through hyperspace for as long as she could.

"It has begun," Nomelet sighed.

Chapter 23

As *Magpie* slid away from the Naval Supply Station orbiting Diarmaid, Kidron called his officers to a meeting. He confirmed Danui's promotion to Commander and the position of Executive Officer. Danui was in her forties, small, lean and as feral-looking as a weasel. She spoke few words, but listened attentively, and interrupted only when there was something that needed saying. She had served with Kidron almost as long as Kazin. Santa was appointed to Lieutenant, replacing Spiez – still on Hecabe recuperating from his wounds – as head of *Magpie*'s ground combat units. Finally, he announced Lynch's promotion to Sub-Lieutenant.

Lynch had never felt so proud as he did when the other officers congratulated him.

Kidron cleared his throat and looked at each of them in turn before producing a message sheet.

"This came in just over twelve hours ago." He began to read. "'Signal to Captain Aruzel Kidron, Naval Supply Station, Diarmaid; from Commodore Marie Uvarov, Hecabe Defence Forces.

"'Hecabe raided three hours ago by Calethar warship, believed to be *Canar Calethari*. Damage extensive to

Salem and adjoining space- and shuttleports, together with their facilities. Casualties not yet determined, but believed to be high. Enemy vessel left system three hours ago. End message.'"

There were soft exhalations from those assembled. The message struck at the hearts of all of them, for they either came from Hecabe originally or had since made their homes there.

"We are now heading for the frontier sector. I see no point in returning to Hecabe. We can do nothing more there now that *Canar* has already gone."

"Why the frontier?" Obe asked.

"*Canar* will not try to hit one of the border worlds again. The warning is out, and the element of surprise is gone. Even that ship would not be able to stand up to the defences of a reasonably populous world if it was ready and waiting for her."

"Hecabe was just unlucky then," Obe said.

"Luck had nothing to do with it. Nomelet knows Hecabe is *Magpie*'s home base. He may even have been hoping to catch us there, under refit."

"Letting us know that nowhere is safe," Danui muttered, smiling thinly.

"Wait till he sees what we're bringing him as a present," Robinson said.

"One question, Captain," Danui said. "Has Commodore Uvarov sent any subsequent messages? Do we have any idea about *Canar*'s present capabilities? Has she improved her weapon systems? Not that they need any improving."

Kidron shook his head. "No, though I expect she will send more information when she can. I'm sure one of

Canar's objectives would have been communication facilities, and *Hecabe*'s probably down to only one or two transmitters. If that's the case, Uvarov will just have to wait until her turn comes round again before sending another signal." He paused and then said: "Any other questions?"

There were none. Kidron called up a holograph of the frontier sector, and all gathered around it.

For the next six days Kidron spent all his time either on the bridge or in his day cabin behind it. In that time reports came in of *Canar Calethari* raiding two human planets in the frontier; reports also came in of four human traders not arriving at their destination.

Then on the sixth day Kidron received information that a third colony had been hit.

"Danui, look at this."

A three-dimensional map of the frontier was displayed on his personal screen. Red circles showed the colonies *Canar* had raided.

"Now, if I add the routes of the missing traders –" he entered a string of co-ordinates "– what do you see?"

Danui stared at the screen, trying to discern a pattern. "Nothing," she finally admitted.

Kidron smiled, pushed a button. The image on the screen rotated on its axis.

"A fan!" she cried. "*Canar* is weaving back and forward across the frontier, each new plot closer to Calethar territory."

"Precisely. If Nomelet continues in this way, then his next target is one of these two human colonies."

He pushed a second button and two green circles appeared, close together.

"But which one?" Danui asked.

Kidron pointed to one of the circles. "Maluka."

"How can you be so sure?"

"It's the richest," Kidron said.

Chapter 24

Raenar was in his cabin with *Kahunna*'s war-captain. Derin was an experienced and very tough warrior, and his report on the recent raid on Maluka was brief and concise.

"Congratulations, Derin. The humans will never forget this day."

Before Derin could reply the duty klaxon sounded. Raenar immediately contacted the bridge.

Odore, his helm-captain, answered. "A ship has been detected coming in from hyperspace."

"Arrival time?" Raenar asked sharply, dismissing Derin with a wave of his claw. The war-captain bowed once and left.

"No more than three minutes, Ship-Captain," Odore answered. "It's coming in very fast."

"Warship?"

"The register doesn't indicate as such, but . . ."

"Out with it. We have no time for courtesies."

"Traders don't register as warships, but traders don't come in this fast."

"*Magpie*?"

"It's possible, sir."

"Work us up to battle speed," Raenar ordered. "Get us between this cursed planet and the ship's incoming trajectory."

"Yes, sir."

"I'm on my way to the bridge."

"Yes, sir." Odore signed off.

Raenar dressed in his battle gear, cursing fate. He did not understand how Kidron could possibly have known he would be here. *Kahunna* and *Magpie* had been destined to meet eventually, but Raenar wished it had been under more favourable conditions. He could not run. Under no circumstances must Kidron learn this ship was not *Canar Calethari* – and that ship would never run from *Magpie*. Nomelet's instructions had been explicit. Honour must be done: for his sake, his family's sake, his clan's sake, and most important of all, he reminded himself grimly, for the sake of the Calethar. Battle he could understand, and in the heat of combat even forget his own lingering shame. Battle was the great leveller, the great purifier.

Magpie flashed into normal space ten planetary diameters from Maluka. The ship's sensors immediately told Kidron the settlement's defence satellites had been destroyed and that *Canar Calethari* had not only been the instrument of their destruction but was even now in orbit around the planet. Kidron ordered battle speed, and waited for detailed reports to come from Lieutenants Marin and Chapman, Danui's replacement as weapons officer.

Canar had been caught unprepared. Undoubtedly her equipment had picked up *Magpie* tearing through hyperspace just before she re-entered the temporal universe, but she had not had time to work up to full speed or to manoeuvre between *Magpie* and the planet, where *Canar*'s signal would be disfigured by the background radiation all planets reflected. Kidron saw all this by studying his battle screens. He asked Obe if they were getting any signal from the settlement.

"No, sir."

"*Canar Calethari* is picking up speed very quickly," Marin said. "Intercept course, aligned with the planet. It won't give her much protection, though. She's an easy target."

"Did you get all that, Chapman?" Kidron asked.

"Yes, sir."

"We proceed with the attack plan we discussed earlier. Torpedo salvo with covering beam fire."

"Sir." There was a pause as Chapman did some quick figuring, and consulted his computer. "Two minutes is optimum release time for the first salvo."

"Authority," Kidron grunted, and returned to his screens. Nomelet was forgoing subtlety. *Canar* was charging *Magpie* like a wild animal, all brute strength and aggressive confidence.

By the time Raenar got to the bridge Odore's suspicions had proven correct. *Magpie* was rushing in at battle speed, taking advantage of her enemy's surprise. There would be no running away this time, no tricks, no foolish Raenars to foul things up. When he laughed at this last thought, some of the Calethar on the bridge laughed with him, thinking the ecstatic rush of battle blood was behind it.

"She's coming in very quickly, Ship-Captain," Odore said. "Too quickly for us to get a good lock on her with the beam weapon."

"Fire anyway," Raenar answered. "It might persuade Kidron to slow down or alter course. Anything to give us more time to reach battle speed."

Raenar felt tense. This was his first ship-to-ship battle as a captain. He was confident he could win, but still there lingered that knowledge that his future career and status hinged on what happened next.

"Firing," Odore said.

Kidron blinked as his screens temporarily whited out.

"Minor damage to bow sensors," Chapman reported.

"That's some beam weapon they've got," Danui muttered.

"One degree alteration to course," Marin announced. There was a slight jarring as the modified *Magpie*, still loose in the joints after her major refit, changed course.

"First salvo away," Chapman said.

Kidron saw the green registration lines light up on his battle screen as *Magpie*'s greeting raced towards the Calethar vessel.

"Beam attack!" Kidron ordered, and the weapons officer fired the most powerful of the privateer's new weapons. Four bright lines shot out from *Magpie*'s wings, and converged to a point where the battle computers predicted *Canar* would be.

Raenar watched *Magpie*'s evasive manoeuvre on the battle screen, startled by the privateer's quick response. Then he saw that *Magpie* herself had opened fire.

"Torpedoes," Odore announced evenly. Kidron was repeating his earlier, fateful tactics.

All the better, Raenar thought to himself. "Prepare defensive missile screen and a course manoeuvre," he ordered.

"Beam weapon almost re-energised," reported a Calethar to Odore's right.

"White out!" Odore shouted, with such a startled voice that Raenar's gaze snapped back to the battle screen. He had time to notice the screen register *Magpie* firing a four-beam weapon when *Kahunna* suddenly shook from bow to stern. Lights flickered. One of the navigation screens exploded in a shower of splintered plastic and molten metal. Raenar heard someone cry out in pain. A couple of Calethar rushed to the victim's assistance. Everyone on the bridge felt the ship decelerate.

"They've hit the dorsal engine," Odore reported.

"How bad?" Raenar demanded.

Odore spoke to someone through his communicator, and turned to Raenar, his face grim.

"We're losing power steadily. Pressure's down. Fuel leakage. Local fires."

"Alright," Raenar said. "One good blow. We have to get *Magpie* before she can fire again."

"What else is *Magpie* armed with?" Odore wondered aloud, but Raenar silenced him with a look. He did not want the crew frightened.

The Calethar next to Odore said, "Ship-Captain, our own beam weapon is fully charged."

"And we have a full salvo of missiles armed and loaded," Odore added.

"Continue our course straight for the privateer," said Raenar. "The faster we close, the harder it is for them to aim."

Odore altered course to match *Magpie*'s new trajectory.

If we can do nothing else, Raenar thought, *we will ram the cursed ship.* The thought renewed his determination. His mouth was set in a tight grin, his eyes sparkled with battle lust. He wished he could meet this Captain Kidron face to face and tear his throat out with his own teeth. His hearts beat faster. *But I will kill you any way I can, Kidron. And I will kill the female who took me prisoner that shameful day.*

His reverie was disturbed by Odore's frightened voice. "Incoming salvo! It's going to hit!"

Kidron rapped out orders as quickly as he could press channels on the communicator by his chair. When *Magpie*'s first shot damaged *Canar* he ordered a second salvo fired. Marin reported the Calethar ship altering course to intercept *Magpie*, putting the privateer's first salvo off the scent. Kidron ordered its destruction, and eyes brightly flashed in space then faded into the blackness.

"Keep on course," he told Marin.

"*Canar* is losing power," Marin reported. "Damage was greater than we thought." And then a moment later: "Sir, our second salvo is almost on top of them and *Canar* is not manoeuvring."

"What!" Kidron studied his own screen carefully, and saw that it was true. He picked out *Canar*'s defence missiles hovering around the ship like a nebulous cloud, but not enough of them to stop all the torpedoes.

The salvo hit.

Raenar knew he was going to die.

The bridge erupted in a gout of flame, intolerably hot. He felt his lungs burn. Air was being sucked out into space from a gaping hole that had eaten away half the main screen. He looked down and saw that his hands were shredded like old straw. He wished the pain in his chest would stop. The young female who had been working with Odore was alight, ablaze like some ghastly candle. Of Odore there was no sign – Raenar assumed he was sucked out into space. The air was getting thinner. A warning klaxon wailed uselessly in the background, its sound getting fainter as the atmosphere escaped from the bridge.

Oh gods, Raenar thought, *let it end.*

Kidron had optical scopes trained on the ship. He saw the alien vessel had been reduced to a hulk, gaping holes and drifting tendrils of cables and girders obscenely decorating the scarred hull. Bodies slowly drifted away from the wreck like bits of discarded garbage.

He ordered *Magpie* to move in when the enemy ship allowed itself the last word. There was an explosion, then a flash so bright Kidron thought he could feel the heat even from where he was, thousands of kilometres away. When the filters on the scopes dropped down to an acceptable level, nothing was left of *Canar*.

The crew cheered.

Kidron felt uneasy. He went over the battle tapes twice with Danui.

"Do we have a spectral analysis of the explosion?" he asked her.

"Yes, sir. They show an unusually low carbon count for a vessel that size, but otherwise nothing out of the ordinary."

"Why such a low count?"

"It's possible the ship was undercrewed, or that *Canar* really did operate with less hands than would another ship that size."

"Even if the crew itself was smaller than logic dictated, what about all its troops? Information from Maluka indicates the ship carried at least sixty soldiers, mainly mercenaries. If we deduct that from the number the analyses suggest were killed in the explosion, *Canar* operated on less than a skeleton crew."

Danui shrugged. "It was a new kind of ship, Captain. We don't know how it operated."

"Alright. The crew deserves some rest. Signal Maluka asking permission for the crew to be cycled down for a break. Usual arrangements, we'll pay for all damages, et-cetera. But I want a full watch kept on ship at all times." *I'll allow myself that concession, at least.* "I don't see Maluka refusing, since we're the heroes of the hour. Three days, no longer. Then we head back to Diarmaid and return the equipment to the Navy."

"They'll be pleased it worked," Danui said. "What are our chances of keeping it, or even just one or two items?"

"I don't know. They certainly owe us something. I'll contact Uvarov and see what she says."

"Captain," Danui said quietly, "something's still bothering you."

"Something's not right with the way it all happened. *Canar* being here, for example."

"But we expected her to be here."

"At the back of my mind is the thought that it shouldn't have been this easy. It's as if *Canar* was here only because the Calethar knew we hoped to find her here. It's all too easy. I feel as though we've been set up.

"And the battle itself. I can't put my finger on anything concrete, but how did we destroy *Canar* so easily? Our new weapons aren't the explanation. The beam weapon certainly helped, but Nomelet had proven himself to be . . . I don't know . . . more canny, I guess.

"We could have won that battle with the old *Magpie*, and that definitely worries me." Kidron's eyes widened. "That's it, by God!"

"Sir?"

"Nomelet wasn't on the ship!"

"You mean he's back on Dramorath? Some other Calethar had command of *Canar*?"

"Exactly. It all begins to make some kind of sense. I wasn't prepared to consider Nomelet wasn't on the ship. But if some other Calethar was commanding, then the dilemma resolves itself."

"That still leaves us the problem of Nomelet," Danui said.

Chapter 25

Canar Calethari waited two days for *Kahunna* to appear at the rendezvous point. Both ships had been late on previous occasions, but not by such a margin.

Nomelet was in his cabin when Teonar knocked and entered.

"We have intercepted a signal between the two border worlds," she said.

"Why wasn't I informed by com?"

"The signal says *Magpie*, captained by Aruzel Kidron, encountered and destroyed *Canar Calethari* in a battle near the planet Maluka."

"How many others know of this?"

"Just the signals officer. Should we keep it a secret?"

"No. I will not deceive my crew."

"Their anger will be greatly roused," Teonar said. "They will want revenge."

"Good," Nomelet said. He poured drinks from a decorated decanter into two mourning cups, and gave her one.

"To Raenar and his crew," he toasted. "They did a great service and bestowed great honour on all of us. May their souls reside in all the glory they deserve, and may it reflect on their families and clans."

They swallowed their drinks in one gulp.

"It was as you planned," Teonar commented, not accusingly.

Nomelet hesitated for a second, and then nodded slowly. "Raenar suspected, I think, his part in all of this. He knew he wasn't meant to return home. I think even his crew understood that."

"And Floran?" she asked. "Do you think he knew how it would end?"

"I am sure he wanted it this way. Perhaps he suggested it to Raenar for this very reason. I owed them, for the clan's sake, this opportunity for Raenar to find his honour. It was an obligation, and this was the best way for it to be fulfilled. But knowing that doesn't alleviate the pain I feel in my heart. Raenar wronged me – us – terribly, but his willingness to discharge his obligation made him valuable to the Uzdar. The clan will miss him, and is the poorer for his passing."

"Floran will be comforted by those words," Teonar said neutrally. Though she understood what Nomelet was saying, she still remembered the old Raenar. It was almost as if he had two sides, two personalities. Two fates. "If it had not ended this way," she continued, "I think the future fortunes of your clan, and mine, would not have been so promising."

"That is hard of you," said Nomelet quietly.

"I am your war-captain, Nomelet. I must say these things, whether they be hard or not. It is my duty to advise and affirm."

Nomelet scraped his foot-combs along the floor. "I know this. And as my war-captain, you also must know what comes next."

Teonar let her head move slowly from side to side. It was a relaxing movement, but also one indicating thought. Nomelet waited, watching her with interest.

"Most of our reconnaissance work has been done," she said. "What is left is unimportant. We have a new duty now. Or rather, an old duty that had been put aside for more pressing business. The hunt for *Magpie* should be resumed."

"The hunt? No. I know where the vessel is. At least, where she is right now. Off Maluka. Kidron believes he has destroyed *Canar* and –" his lips curled in a half-smile "– her captain. We must move quickly if we are to succeed. Our prey awaits us, but it won't wait much longer."

"I will order our reconnaissance data to be compiled and transmitted immediately. We will be ready to leave for Maluka before another day has passed."

"Inform the crew, Teonar, of our new task. It should raise their spirits tremendously."

"It will raise all our spirits," she said. "Unfinished business is so distracting, and now the debt is even greater."

Everyone on the bridge was tense. The feeling infected all on board, and made their bodies fairly scream with the need to release energy, preferably in battle. Makarin, a veteran of numerous conflicts, understood the feeling and welcomed it. No ship could hope for success in battle without it, for it gave the edge that could mean the difference between winning and losing. In all the actions he had been involved in, this tension, stretched almost to snapping point, had always impregnated the crew and the ship itself.

He cast an approving eye over his people. All were at their stations, watching their screens with a determination that was eager rather than grim. They, too, understood a part of what they were embarking on, perhaps not as well as Makarin or Nomelet or Teonar, but well enough to feel they were a part of something vitally important to all their futures, and certainly more important than the narrower concerns of their own individual destinies. The path they were set on would affect all the Calethar. *And all humans,* Makarin added.

"Has the signal been sent to Dramorath yet?" Nomelet asked.

"Yes, sir. The ship is ready to depart. We have discharged all our other obligations."

The words were formal, more formal than Makarin would normally have used, but the occasion warranted it.

"Then set course for the human world of Maluka. Get us as close as possible to the planet without dropping us in its atmosphere, and above the hemisphere opposite the settlement. They wouldn't yet have replaced all their warning devices. I'm sure *Kahunna* would have been thorough in that regard. I want us to gather as much signal intelligence as possible before we come over the settlement. If *Magpie* isn't there, I don't want the humans alerted to our presence. If she is, I want our arrival to be a complete surprise. That cursed pirate ship is not to escape us this time, Makarin."

"I understand, Ship-Captain. I will bring us so close to Lagash you will be able to reach out and touch it."

"That would be suitable," Nomelet agreed.

Makarin set to work.

"Captain?"

Kidron turned to Obe. "What is it?"

"A human trader has notified the Federation it intercepted a signal to Dramorath as she entered normal space to complete some minor repairs."

"So?"

"The signal was in code and will take weeks to break, but the source of the signal could not be traced to any planet or known vessel."

Kidron's heart beat faster. "Give me a trace line for the signal and put it on my screen."

The Dramorath system appeared as a blue spot, with a red line extending from it and disappearing into infinity . . . or, rather, off the screen's edge, indicating that the source of the signal had not been located. A thought nagged at his brain briefly but slipped away. He opened a line to Robinson down on Lagash, and got Lynch instead.

"Aaron, tell Toma to get the crew together. Fun's over. It's time we got going."

"Aye aye, sir," Lynch answered and signed off.

Again that elusive thought drifted back, and this time Kidron latched on to it. He keyed in possible jump routes for *Canar Calethari* from Hecabe to Maluka. The new lines on the screen meant nothing to him. He then keyed in possible jump routes using the red signal line as an axis. The result made his head jerk up.

Obe looked up from her work. "Sir?"

Kidron ignored her and got onto the cutter again. This time he got Robinson.

"Captain, Aaron tells me you want all the crew up. It might take a while to –"

"Get as many as you can, Toma. Now!"

"Yes, sir," she replied, suddenly alert.

He punched off and sent for Danui. "Freyr – on the bridge, immediately."

Kidron switched on the yellow alert. Alarms sounded all over the ship.

The small spaceport on Maluka was in a state of chaos. Robinson moved like a woman possessed. She ordered Lynch to get both cutters ready for an emergency take-off, then rushed off to round up as many crew as she could find.

Lynch convinced the authorities to give them immediate clearance even though it meant delaying the landings of shuttles belonging to two freighters which had entered orbit around the planet the day before.

As soon as things were cleared with the authorities, Lynch checked the cutters were fully fuelled and powered up. Though there would be complaints later about all the unnecessary noise, he wanted to make sure they could leave as soon as Robinson returned. There was a third quick call from Kidron, giving him co-ordinates for the rendezvous with *Magpie*. When he fed the co-ordinates into the computer, he noticed the rendezvous point was away from the ship's parking orbit. *Magpie* was already boosting under emergency power.

Robinson returned in twenty minutes with over eighty crew. They boarded the cutters, taxied onto the tarmac and took off vertically, wasting a lot of fuel but reaching space in record time.

As soon as Danui was on the bridge, Kidron showed her his screen.

She studied it for a moment, then swore under her breath. "A second ship," she said.

"I'll bet all the profits from our next voyage that's the case. Now everything makes sense. What we destroyed wasn't *Canar Calethari*, which is why the readings were so odd. Now I'll bet all the profits from our last voyage that the real *Canar* is on her way to Maluka right now. If we don't get in a better position than this we've had it."

"And if we don't get more crew we've had it. Where are *Swallow* and *Lark*?"

"On their way up." Kidron indicated the rendezvous point on his screen. "We'll be meeting them here, but I don't want to have to slow down for them." He turned to Obe. "Get the cutter bay ready for a special delivery. As soon as the crew's off, I want Robinson and Lynch to take them out again, fully armed and with combat squads on board kitted up for a vacuum assault."

"Got it," Obe said.

"Any signs yet of an incoming vessel?" Kidron asked Marin.

"Not yet sir, and we're stretching the new scanner to its limit. That should give us at least a twenty-minute warning."

"Fine. Let me know as soon as you pick up something . . . no matter what you think it is!"

"Aye aye, sir."

Kidron returned to his screen.

"Where do you think Nomelet will appear?" Danui asked.

"There are so many places, so many approaches. From sunwards, to blind our scanners? Or into the sun to pick up extra velocity from gravity boost? Or a sneak attack from the planet's opposite hemisphere?"

"Maybe that's it," Danui said. "Nomelet doesn't know about *Magpie*'s refit. He might think that approach would effectively keep us blind, with no idea of where *Canar Calethari* would appear, or how close."

Kidron nodded. "And he'll plan on us being a sitting target – just squat in orbit. That's two points to us."

"We have a trace, Captain," Marin declared. "Large ship, coming in very fast. Our computers indicate it's *Canar Calethari*."

"Arrival point?"

"Just getting the data now, sir." He faced Kidron. "Other side of Maluka."

Kidron slapped the arm of his couch. "Nomelet, that may have been your greatest mistake. And it only takes one. Ask Jimmy Tolstoi."

Five minutes later he punched through to Robinson in *Swallow*. "*Canar*'s going to appear behind Lagash. You have to leave now. I can't afford to have your wash detected by the Calethar when they come around. They'll blow you to kingdom come if they stumble across you first."

"Aye aye, sir. Good luck."

"And you." *My God, Toma, you and Aaron are going to need all the luck you can get.*

He switched channels to the engine room. "As soon as the two cutters are clear I want full power."

Chapter 26

Canar Calethari slipped into normal space so close to Maluka it seemed to Nomelet he could have reached out and scooped atmosphere. He congratulated Makarin on his navigation, and ordered a wide passive scan of the planet and surrounding space.

"The only traffic we're picking up is some confused reports from a couple of freighters in parking orbit over the settlement," reported a specialist. "No alert that we can detect."

"I wonder what they're confused about?" Makarin wondered aloud.

"Could be anything," Nomelet said. "The raid by *Kahunna*, the battle between her and *Magpie*."

"Or our arrival," Makarin added.

"Not likely, Helm-Captain. I think their reports would then reflect panic rather than confusion."

Makarin nodded and returned to his controls. "Forty minutes for us to complete the half-orbit at this altitude, picking up battle speed as we go."

"Will we reach optimal velocity by then?"

"Sixty per cent, but increasing rapidly. It should be more than enough to catch a sleeping *Magpie*."

Nomelet told Makarin to proceed, and ordered all sections to maintain battle stations. "It may be a long haul. Any sign of something out of the ordinary, let the bridge know immediately. Ship-Captain out."

Nomelet turned his attention to the beautiful world below. "This would make a good planet for a Calethar outpost," he said.

"Most planets with human colonies would," said someone else on the bridge.

"More signal traffic from those freighters. Still a little garbled, but I think they're upset about take-off privileges."

"Let them argue. Soon the problem will be solved for them."

A red vector line appeared on *Magpie*'s battle screen.

"Heads up, everyone!" Danui cried.

"That's it," Kidron said. "Our guest's arrived."

Reports came in from all over the ship. Danui expertly regulated the traffic.

"Can verify it's *Canar Calethari*," Marin said after a minute.

"Weapon systems on line," Chapman said. "Torpedoes armed and loaded."

"Ship ready for combat, sir," Danui reported formally.

"Word from *Swallow* and *Lark*?" Kidron asked.

"In position."

"Captain! *Canar*'s just broached the horizon," Marin said. "She's heading for our old parking orbit, and accelerating. She'll have our true position in a few seconds."

Kidron faced Chapman. "Salvos one and two, fire immediately. Marin, course alteration. Take us around and behind her. We have the edge on speed. Let's see what those bastards can do with a privateer on their tail."

Magpie thumped slightly as the two salvos were fired. The patterns were as wide as possible, and Kidron knew *Canar* would not have much trouble avoiding them; in fact, he was counting on it.

The artificial inertia generators countered some of the stress of *Magpie*'s violent course change, but Kidron still had to hold on to the armrests of his couch. His stomach swung viciously and then tried climbing up his throat and into his mouth. He swallowed hard and concentrated on watching his battle screen.

"Broad beam message to *Swallow* and *Lark*. Prepare for intercept."

"Aye aye, Captain," Obe answered.

"I hope you have the good taste to die on your vessel Ship-Captain Nomelet," Kidron said.

"I beg your pardon, sir?" Obe asked, puzzled.

"Never mind. Just send that signal." *Keep your mind on the job, Aruzel. Fate will take care of itself.*

"*Magpie* isn't there," Makarin said flatly. "We have just two freighters. Undoubtedly the source of the garbled communications we've been following."

Nomelet leaned forward in his chair and peered closer at the main screen. He had been so sure Kidron would still be in orbit. Where had he gone wrong?

"Perhaps one of the freighters . . ." someone on the bridge tentatively suggested.

"He wouldn't try that again," said Nomelet. "Anyway, it would assume he was ready for us."

"And neither of the two vessels have the mass to be *Magpie*," Makarin added. He turned to Nomelet. "I'm sorry, Ship-Captain. I agree with you the pirate should be here, but . . ."

He let the evidence speak for itself. Nomelet was still leaning forward, as if by peering closer to the screen he would be able to pick up something the sensors could not. His disappointment would be keen, thought Makarin. *What am I saying? All of us feel the same way.* Something in the top right-hand corner of the screen drew his attention.

"*By the gods!*" he cursed, and slammed his fist down on one of the attitude jet controls. *Canar* pitched wildly. Several bodies lost their balance. Even Nomelet was almost flung out of his chair.

"Torpedoes!" Makarin cried, and slammed down on the control of a second jet. The crew who had regained their feet were hurled around a second time. At the back of his mind Makarin registered the sound of someone breaking a bone, and he desperately hoped it was not serious. *Oh, gods,* he thought, *if I don't pull this off it will be more than broken bones we'll have to worry about.*

Nomelet knew what Makarin was trying to do, and did not interfere. *Leave the manoeuvring to the expert. You figure out what happened, Ship-Captain, that's your job.*

Figures and lines formed spectacular tracery on his personal combat screen, and his experienced eye immediately located the source of the attack. *Magpie. So, Captain Kidron was here. Well and good.*

Now it ends.

"Helm-Captain, will any of those torpedoes hit?"

"No, Ship-Captain, not now," Makarin said grimly. "And our computers have locked on to the devil. We can fire when ready."

Nomelet nodded and studied his screen again. *That was clumsy of you, Kidron, giving yourself away like that. Why so wide a fan? What did you think you were doing?*

His answer came with a shuddering blow that made *Canar Calethari* groan like a wounded animal. Electrical fires sputtered from several places on the bridge.

"That was a beam weapon!" Makarin shouted, and sent *Canar* on another wild manoeuvre. This time the confusion was more severe. One Calethar did not get up again. Others were variously trying to put out spot fires or attend to their stations, but the cloying smoke filling the bridge made even the simplest task difficult.

"Damage report!" Nomelet demanded.

A female Calethar squinted through the haze at her console. "Midsection leaks. Some damage to latitudinal engines. Mid-range sensors damaged but still operating. Rear port sensors destroyed, backup system running."

"Makarin – get us out of here!"

"You mean jump, sir?"

"No, damn you, I don't mean jump! Get us back up to battle speed! *Magpie* will be swinging behind us for a killing shot. Use our defensive missiles to blow a path through any torpedoes that get in our way."

"That will deplete them too quickly," Makarin said.

"Do it!" Nomelet ordered, and returned his attention to his battle screen. The computer was now showing three possible positions for *Magpie*, either because the damage to the mid-range sensors was worse than reported or because the computer was having trouble isolating the privateer from among all the debris that had suddenly appeared on its screens. Nomelet cursed, but chose the signal accelerating in a wide curve to their aft as the one most likely to be her.

Is that you, Kidron? What else have you planned for us, I wonder?

Marin reported *Canar Calethari* was accelerating to battle speed, giving little to manoeuvre. Kidron had already deduced as much from his own screen. He ordered *Magpie* to give chase.

"Damn the torpedoes, eh, Nomelet?" he said aloud. "Alright, then, let's play your game." He turned to Chapman. "*Canar's* trying to ram her way through the torpedo net. Launch a third salvo."

He felt the torpedoes, large, dark angels of death, leaving *Magpie*. On his screen *Canar* stood out like a bright beacon, chased by several torpedo lines that looked like spider threads shot out to catch a fly.

"Return salvo," reported the war room. "We're heading directly into them."

"Defensive missiles. Prepare another beam shot."

"Weapon recharged."

"Fire when ready," Kidron said.

There was no reply to this last order, just a satisfied grunt. Kidron could see *Magpie* was catching up with the Calethar ship. He signalled the cutters to close the net.

Makarin was performing miracles, weaving *Canar* between torpedoes and space debris. At the same time he kept the ship on a level enough course for her to pick up longitudinal velocity. Nomelet found it almost hypnotic watching his helm-captain at work.

By now the computer had determined exactly which of the three signals was in fact *Magpie*; Nomelet had guessed correctly.

"*Magpie*'s fired another salvo," Makarin reported calmly.

"Another?" Nomelet felt confused. Kidron knew a pursuing salvo was easy to pick off. "That means there'll be another beam shot! Ten degrees starboard!"

Nomelet ordered a return salvo to slow down *Magpie*'s progress. At this point he did not hold out much hope for its chances, but any advantage he could gain at this point in time would be welcome. A thought flashed across his mind.

"How many mines have we?"

"Mines, Ship-Captain?"

"You heard me."

"Seven, sir. All meant for orbiting roles. They have a limited homing range."

"Do you think you can let one of their torpedoes hit us without causing too much damage?"

"Hit us, sir?"

"Must you repeat everything I say?"

"Sorry, Ship-Captain. I could let one hit us. We've already received damage on the rear port sensors. If I let a torpedo hit there the extra damage to *Canar* would be slight."

"Do so. And when it hits I want all the mines released. Let them float among the debris."

Makarin's wizened face opened in a comprehending smile. "By all the gods! It might work!"

"*Carefully*, Makarin, ever so carefully."

As the enemy salvo came closer Makarin guided the ship to catch one of the torpedoes without making his intention obvious. His face was contorted by the effort, and he held his breath. His movements were deft and precise, and Nomelet again found himself marvelling at Makarin's skill. He thanked his gods and good fortune for his choice of crew.

"*Magpie* has evaded our salvo," Makarin reported, and then: "Hold on, here it comes!"

Nomelet had time to grip his seat before the ship was rocked by the explosion.

"Mines away!" said Makarin.

"Fire a beam shot to keep their attention on us," Nomelet ordered.

Makarin took a moment to aim and fire.

"We almost got her then," a young Calethar reported, stomping his feet excitedly. Nomelet felt like laughing despite the danger.

"This is a battle, Migas, not a game," Makarin warned the youngster. "Keep your attention firmly attached to the here and now."

Kidron was not concerned about the approaching salvo. *Magpie* easily edged around its fan and continued the chase without losing velocity. But *Canar* was still accelerating, and every second Chapman waited before firing the beam weapon increased the likelihood of a miss.

The enemy ship performed a complex series of manoeuvres.

"Captain," Chapman said, "I think one of our torpedoes is going to hit."

Kidron studied his screen more closely. The enemy helm-captain must be experiencing difficulties in disengaging from the whole salvo, and had chosen the lesser of several evils by risking a strike by a single warhead. Even as he watched it struck home, and debris scattered into space.

"Well done, Chapman."

"Thank you, Captain," Chapman replied, mystified. He obviously had not expected any hits.

Just then the whole bridge lit up as if their own private sun had risen. Kidron felt a great heat on his skin. *Shit,* he thought, *that was close. A beam shot. At least it will take them a while to recharge, especially if they are using all their energy to accelerate.*

Marin, his voice relaxed, said: "Debris ahead, largely from *Canar Cal –*"

Kidron did not hear any explosion. A wall of rapidly moving gases picked him up from his couch and threw him onto the deck. He had an impression of everything being tinted red and yellow, like a glorious sunset, and then things went grey, as though he had lost colour altogether. Somewhere in the back of his mind he heard a desperate voice screaming. Something about another one coming. He tried to hold on to that voice, that warning, to use it as an anchor to drag himself back to the real world. There was another eruption, and he was picked up and thrown again. There was intense pain, and then nothing, just a swallowing numbness.

When Robinson and Lynch received Kidron's coded message they fired their cutters' engines, slipping out of their hiding place against the surface of the moon and into free space. Their powerful rockets accelerated them towards *Canar*. The two cutters maintained radio silence, their laser turrets hidden in their bellies. They needed to get as close as possible before being detected, and closer still before revealing their deadly new stings.

Santa left her squad in the passenger section to sit in the cockpit with Lynch. He tried to explain some of the information the screen was displaying.

"Red for baddies, white for goodies," she repeated, feeling herself buoyed by the abstract information represented by one red dot and three white.

"A strike!" Lynch exclaimed when one of *Magpie*'s torpedoes slammed into *Canar*. "Torpedo this time. Port and rear, not far from where the beam hit."

Santa was studying the screen when a vibrant red line slaked across its surface from *Canar* to *Magpie*, and then continued off the screen. "What the hell was that?"

"Enemy beam," Lynch answered. "And a close one. *Magpie*'s going through debris left behind . . ."

His voice trailed off as a series of hatched red figures started flashing next to *Magpie*'s icon.

"What happened?" Santa asked, suddenly alert.

"I'm not sure." The red figures changed abruptly, were joined by new ones. "I think *Magpie*'s been hit, and badly."

"By what? I didn't see anything come from *Canar*."

"The debris! The Calethar must have ejected something with the debris after their ship was hit."

His attention was drawn to *Swallow*. She was drawing ahead. Lynch boosted *Lark*'s velocity to match. He saw on the screen that *Canar* was decelerating and turning to finish off the stricken privateer. *Magpie*'s velocity had decreased only slightly, but there was no hand behind the helm. She was a sitting target, unable to manoeuvre.

Lynch waited until the last moment before lowering the laser battery. It would give his shuttle a higher profile for the enemy sensors to detect, but hopefully the Calethar were so involved with *Magpie* they had no thoughts for her chicks.

As soon as the first mine exploded against *Magpie* Nomelet ordered Makarin to swing *Canar Calethari* around. Even as the helm-captain was carrying out the command the screens showed that a second mine had homed in on the enemy ship and gone off, causing even more extensive damage.

Nomelet did not feel exultant, nor did anyone else on the bridge. There was a curious silence, as though they had witnessed the death of a great animal, and they felt a peculiar mixture of privilege and awe at being present as it drew its final breath.

"Position us for a killing blow, Makarin. It's time the enemy was put out of its misery."

Makarin fired *Canar*'s forward verniers to slow the ship down, then manoeuvred her to fire into *Magpie*'s flank. There was no defensive fire, no more salvos from the stricken vessel. She continued on her course, battered and exhausted. Makarin took his time lining up the beam shot which would tear into the hub of the vessel and strip away *Magpie*'s wings.

Nomelet ordered a salvo to follow it up.

The helm-captain placed his hand over the beam firing switch, and turned to Nomelet for the final word.

He heard Migas say something. At first the words did not register, and Migas repeated himself.

"There's something coming in very fast. Two vessels, I think."

Makarin swung back to the screen. He heard Nomelet curse behind him.

"*Magpie*'s cutters!" the ship-captain shouted.

Without thinking, Makarin fired the main engines, and inadvertently performed the one action that was most dangerous to his ship.

Robinson held off communicating with *Lark* for as long as possible. The two cutters were converging on *Canar Calethari* as fast as they could while still leaving some margin for manoeuvring. They were a thousand klicks from the enemy ship when Robinson flicked on the radio and ordered Lynch to concentrate on the ship's midsection. *Swallow* would aim at the prow.

Even as they fired, *Canar* lurched forward. Instead of damaging just two sections of the ship, the cutters' powerful new weapons travelled along almost *Canar*'s whole length. The lasers left tracks like dark, smouldering scars. The two cutters swooped over the ship, their lasers still firing.

"Turn the blasted alarms off!" shouted Nomelet, his voice almost drowned out by the ringing.

Makarin tried to obey, but the controls were damaged.

"Report!" Nomelet ordered.

Makarin read from his control board. "All stabilisers destroyed. Main engines overheating. Gas leaks along the whole ship. No weapons except defensive missiles –"

"Use them! Get those cutters!"

Makarin targeted the cutters as best he could. "All missiles launched!"

Lynch used the yaw controls to turn *Lark*'s prow 180 degrees so it faced *Canar* again, then fired his engines. The cutter decelerated so quickly the breath was knocked out of him and Santa. Without the inertia generator they would have been smeared against the bulkhead. It took over a minute for *Lark* to accelerate back towards the enemy.

"She's fired something!" Santa yelled, pointing to the screen.

Lynch saw several small red dots heading straight for him. He slammed the port verniers control to change course but it was too late. One missile hit on the port wing. *Lark* shuddered and rolled wildly on her axis. Lynch heard screams over the intercom coming from the troopers in the passenger section.

"God!" cried Santa, fumbling at her harness buckle. "I've got to get back –"

"Stay where you are!" Lynch shouted. "There's nothing you can do for them until we finish with *Canar*!"

He fired the starboard verniers and the rolling stopped.

"Aaron! Are you okay?" It was Robinson on *Swallow*.

"We're okay, Toma! Continue your attack! We're on our way!"

"How badly damaged are we?" Santa asked.

Lynch called up the damage screen. "The targeting computer's down."

"So we can't use the lasers?"

"No, we can't use the turret. We can only fire straight ahead. If we aim *Lark* at *Canar* the lasers should hit her."

Lynch adjusted *Lark*'s trajectory. They watched as *Swallow* made her second pass, from bow to stern. Debris blew off into space. Gas fires flared.

Then it was *Lark*'s turn. Lynch fired the lasers.

His attack struck *Canar*'s stern. The lasers hit for only two seconds, but it was enough. Explosions fluttered in the ship's hull like lightning behind heavy cloud, racking *Canar* from one end to the other. Pieces of her flew off into space with frightening force. Lynch twisted *Lark* aside to avoid striking a pod mounting.

"Quick, Aaron, return to *Magpie*! *Canar*'s had it!" Robinson shouted over the radio, and two shuttles accelerated towards their mother ship.

"Ship-Captain, there is nothing we can do. We have no power. Most of our crew sections are open to space. We have no weapons. We are adrift."

Nomelet stared at Makarin without really focusing on him.

"Where are the cutters?" he asked, his voice distant.

"Heading back to *Magpie*. They've done their work here." Makarin's voice was bitter. He looked down at poor Migas. The youth's head was smashed to a pulp.

Fires crackled around them, surviving bridge crew hurriedly putting them out. Fibre ganglions hung dislocated from the roof. The alarms still rang and warning lights flashed like strobes. The main battle screen was scorched and torn. Fine particles of smoke filled the air.

"We must surrender," Nomelet said forlornly.

Makarin nodded. "We will need a transmitter. I will see if I can repair one."

Lynch and Santa could see *Magpie* was as badly damaged as *Canar*. Unless the cutters attached themselves to the ship and used their own engines to slow her and put her into orbit around Maluka, she would continue on her way for eternity.

Lynch felt he was in a nightmare, piloting a small craft around tonnes of debris and the hulking corpses of two great warships.

Beside him, Santa was silent, her mouth open. Her eyes reflected the explosions still rippling through *Canar Calethari*. "Oh God," she whispered, her voice hoarse.

Chapter 27

While Santa went back to check on her squad, Lynch attached *Lark* to *Magpie*. Robinson connected *Swallow* to the other side of the hull. Using their engines and verniers they slowed *Magpie* enough to place her in a reasonably stable orbit around Maluka. Lynch attached a boarding tube from *Lark* to one of the ship's hatches and pressurised it.

Santa returned to the cockpit.

"How are your people?" Lynch asked.

"A few broken bones and bruises. Nothing serious."

"You and I will go to *Magpie*," Lynch said. "Robinson will stay with *Swallow* in case we need the cutter's engines again."

Together, they carefully made their way down the tube, opened the hatch and entered.

Lynch thought he had stepped into hell. Acrid smoke hung in the air, making it difficult to breathe. Red emergency lights winked on and off. A body tumbled against him and he gently pushed it away. Globules of blood floated along the corridor.

He looked around. The smoke and poor light made it hard to pick out details or get a clear idea of the extent of damage. He saw a second body jammed between a girder and the bulkhead. Its head was missing.

Santa called out and a voice shouted back: "Stay there!" Lynch saw someone gliding towards them through the gloom like some apparition. A moment later he recognised Balkowski. The man was streaked with grime and gore. His eyes were two dark pits in a drawn, pale face.

"Santa? Lynch? Where . . . where did you come from? I thought you were on *Lark*."

Santa indicated the hatch. "We've just come through. *Lark* and *Swallow* have placed *Magpie* in orbit around Maluka –"

Balkowski suddenly grabbed Santa by the shoulders so tightly she grimaced. "*Canar Calethari* – where is she?"

"It's alright," Santa said, releasing his grip. "She's no threat to *Magpie* any more."

Balkowski floated in front of them, shivering.

"How many casualties have you?" Lynch asked. "How badly damaged is *Magpie*?"

Balkowski turned to face him. "Casualties are heavy everywhere . . ." He started to cry. "Oh, God, I'm sorry."

Santa held him until he regained some control.

"Is there any word from the captain?" she asked.

Balkowski shook his head. "All lines have been severed with the bridge. No one knows what the situation is like up there. We can't get to any vacuum suits to find out –"

His voice broke again. Lynch turned away. He saw another body, a young woman's. She was tumbling slowly towards them along the corridor. Blood seeped from a gash in her throat, leaving behind her a trail of small round rubies. As she passed he stopped her and used a loose cable to tie her to the bulkhead. He recognised her but did not know her name.

"We have suits in the shuttle," Lynch said. "And the squad on board is fully kitted up. They can access areas out of touch with us here, and recover . . . bodies . . . and any equipment we need. Santa, you and I should get to the bridge."

"We'll contact Maluka before we start off," she told Balkowski. "There are two freighters orbiting the planet; they'll give us some assistance. We'll have to work on life support first off, then the engines and navigation. How many of you are there here?"

"Thirteen. We've set up a surgery in the crew's mess. Bingham's there doing what he can."

"Okay. Get this section cleared up. Take the bodies somewhere, try and ventilate the smoke, turn off the bloody emergency lights. We'll send any survivors we find back to you."

Balkowski nodded, encouraged by having something to do.

Lynch and Santa returned to *Lark* and quickly suited up. Santa assigned troops to explore sections of *Magpie* that Balkowski had heard no word from.

Lynch got in touch with the freighters and explained the situation to them. One freighter agreed to come to *Magpie* with all haste to assist however she could, the second would guard the remains of *Canar Calethari*.

Lynch then got in touch with Robinson and explained the situation. They agreed she would stay on station until the trader arrived. Santa then assigned sections of the ship for her contingent of troops to visit and explore.

Finally, Lynch and Santa left the shuttle through the airlock and jetted their way forward along the main hull to the bridge. On the way they saw that many sections in the hull and wings were gutted and exposed to vacuum. They saw dead crew caught up in the twisted wreckage. Unless Kidron and Danui were still alive, Lynch realised, Santa, as the next line officer, was in charge. And then Robinson and himself, he thought gloomily.

From outside, the bridge looked intact. Lynch asked Santa how they were going to get in, and she indicated a small emergency airlock aft of the bridge plates. Santa cranked open the airlock with a hull tool she had brought along for the job. Once they were in she forced shut the external door, shifted the tool to a second port and began to pump air in from the bridge. A gauge on the airlock wall showed pressure was rising.

"That's a good sign," she told Lynch. "It means there's plenty of air on the other side." The pumping was hard work, and Lynch took over from Santa halfway through. When the gauge indicated the airlock was fully pressurised, he cranked open the internal hatch. It opened with a slight popping sound and a flurry of particles.

At first neither Lynch nor Santa went through. They could see metal beams, wires and fibres hanging and crisscrossing like vines in a rainforest. Most of the lights were out, and the bridge was eerily illuminated by those that remained, many of which flickered like fireflies. One control board was hissing, gas rising like a miniature geyser.

"Do you see any bodies?" Lynch asked nervously.

Santa pointed to a shapeless huddle only ten metres from where they were. It was, Lynch could see now, vaguely human in form, and covered in strands of wire. A wreath of smoke wafted past, settled over the body like a halo and then slowly dispersed.

Lynch moved forward carefully, using fallen beams as handgrips, avoiding the trailing ends of dangling wires, some of which still fizzled and sparked. He breathed in deeply as he came up to the body, reached down and slowly turned it over. He gagged, but was able to hold his stomach down. It was Danui, her face untouched, almost peaceful, and belying the terrible abdominal wound that had killed her. Intestines glistened like wet plastic in the ghostly light.

"At least it was quick," Lynch said, trying to be as clinical as possible. He had liked Danui a lot. "Arteries are shredded. She wouldn't have known anything."

"Can you see any others?"

He twisted around, finding the suit's helmet too restrictive. He unsealed it and slowly drew it back until it flopped against his right shoulder. The air was pungent with the smell of burnt plastic and flesh, and the back of his throat immediately felt raw, but he could breathe and now see most of the bridge. There were four other bodies, all still. Lynch felt as if he had broken into an ancient tomb. He was determined to find out who all the bodies belonged to, and then get out. He could not take much more of this.

Suddenly weary, he looked around towards the captain's couch. Thankfully there was no corpse sitting in it, staring blankly back at him. He could not have taken that. For a moment he had the wild idea that the captain may not have been on the bridge when *Magpie* was damaged, but in his heart he knew it would not be. His eyes wandered slowly back towards Danui, and then he saw the fifth body, half hidden under one of the control stations near the main screen. He knew it was Kidron because of the captain's sleeve with its four circlets.

Lynch booted his way over to the body, and gently pulled it from underneath the station. The face was unmarked, but coagulated blood spread fan-like from the nose and mouth. The back of the skull was loose and spongy. He did not investigate any further. "He's dead," he said simply. And then: "Let's get out of here."

"We have to put names to the rest," Santa said, sounding more determined than she felt, and made her way to the others. "Marin . . . Chapman . . ." Lynch heard her choke. She went to the last body. "Obe! He's still alive!"

"What?"

"I saw his chest rise! Help me! Quickly!" Santa had already taken off her helmet and gloves by the time Lynch had made his way across to them, and was cradling Obe in her arms.

Lynch pulled his helmet back on and clicked the radio on with his chin. "Toma, get a med team up to the bridge right away." He clicked off again and removed the helmet, ignoring the pilot's question. He knew what it was, and he did not want to answer it. Not yet, anyway.

A two-person med team arrived within five minutes, carrying enough equipment with them to require four adults under normal gravity. Aaron helped them through the airlock procedure and pointed them towards Obe. They stared at Kidron's remains as they floated past but said nothing. They doffed their vacuum suits and went to work, one moving Obe into a position where they could inspect him thoroughly, the second setting up the equipment.

"He's in a bad way," said the one handling Obe, "but he'll live. Any . . . others?" There was a hopeful note in his voice.

"No," Santa answered.

The medic sighed. "I've counted seventy dead so far. This makes seventy-four."

"See what you can do for Obe," said Santa, and looked at Lynch.

"I agree," he said in response to her unspoken question. "There's nothing more we can do here. Let's get back to *Lark*."

They replaced their gear and left the two medics to their work. It took an infuriatingly long time to leave by the airlock. Now that they were leaving, Lynch wanted to get out as quickly as possible.

When they got back to the cutter, the communicator light was flashing. Lynch switched the transceiver on.

"Aaron, why haven't you been answering?" came Robinson's voice, demanding and already emotional.

"Toma, I'm sorry . . ."

"No."

"Toma, the captain is dead."

"*No!*"

"I saw him, Toma. I'm sorry. There's nothing anyone can do. He couldn't have known what happened." Lynch knew no such thing, he had not inspected Kidron's body that closely.

"Who else knows?"

"You and me, Santa and the med team. Perhaps the med team has passed the word on by now, I don't know. Do you want it hushed up?"

"No. The crew deserves to know as soon as possible. But don't let the merchants know. They might try for salvage rights."

"We can't stop them getting *Canar*, Toma. One freighter's already on its way there."

"I wasn't thinking of *Canar*, Aaron. They might try and claim *Magpie*."

"They can't do that, it belongs to the capt . . ."

"That's right, Aaron, and he's dead."

Santa interrupted. "One of our merchant friends has just arrived."

Lynch looked up to see the freighter manoeuvring to within grappling distance of *Magpie*. Magnetic lines were already snaking out from the ship towards the privateer. Then a new voice came over the cutter radio, interrupting Lynch's observation.

"*Magpie*. This is Ship-Captain Nomelet commanding the Uzdar warship *Canar Calethari*, calling for assistance. The battle is over. We cede to *Magpie*. We need assistance. We require medical aid and equipment to –"

The message was interrupted by a scream of fury and hate. Lynch was so surprised he did not recognise the source at first. And then he knew.

"Toma! Get off the channel –"

"They destroyed *Magpie*! They *killed* Kidron!"

"Captain Kidron is dead?" came Nomelet's shocked voice.

"Toma," Santa said, ignoring the Calethar, "get off the channel! Now!"

In reply, *Swallow* fired her engines. The cutter arced over *Magpie* and headed towards *Canar Calethari*.

"Damn!"

Lynch spoke urgently into the transceiver. "Ship-Captain Nomelet, this is Sub-Lieutenant Aaron Lynch of *Magpie*. Lieutenant Toma Robinson is approaching your vessel in one of our cutters. Under no circumstances allow her to board your vessel. Do you understand?"

"I must confess, Sub-Lieutenant Aaron Lynch, that I do *not* understand," Nomelet said.

"Please, Ship-Captain, just do as I request," Lynch said curtly. He switched on the main engines. Even before Santa had managed to buckle herself in *Lark* was off, knocking the breath out of both of them. The boarding tube connecting the cutter to *Magpie* tore loose and automatically sealed itself to stop precious air escaping.

"What are you doing?" Santa yelled.

"We've got to stop Toma," he replied, his voice low and urgent. "If we don't, she'll murder every being on *Canar*, whether they want to surrender or not."

By the time *Lark* matched courses with *Swallow*, Robinson had already lowered the laser battery. Lynch tried desperately to raise the pilot on the intercom, but she ignored him. Then Santa tried, without success. On his screen Lynch saw the second freighter positioning itself near *Canar Calethari*. In desperation he contacted its captain.

"Merchant Ignozu Ardel here, pilot. What can I do for you, and what is your companion on the other cutter up to?"

Lynch quickly explained the situation. "Captain, you have to evacuate *Canar Calethari*."

"Evacuate the Calethar? Are you crazy? What would stop them from taking over the ship?"

"They would do no such thing. They have surrendered. You know how important honour is to them."

"But why should I? What if this mad pilot wants to finish them off? Why should I hinder her? The Calethar are no friends to us humans."

"Imagine the effect on your trade with Calethar worlds if word got out you let one of their nobles be slaughtered by a mad human after officially surrendering," Lynch replied.

"That's blackmail."

"Call it what you like. But the Calethar have surrendered formally. I can play you the recording if you like."

Captain Ardel sighed heavily. "That will not be necessary. I will evacuate the Calethar as you request. This will cost me fuel, however."

"You already have salvage rights over the Calethar vessel. I don't think you'd make as much from a year's trading as you will from that."

Ardel laughed. "You are very shrewd for a pilot. If you require work after all this is over, look me up."

"Thank you, Captain, but I already have a ship."

"The offer was not made from a sense of altruism."

Ardel signed off, and once again Lynch hailed Robinson. "Toma, the Calethar are being taken off *Canar* and put under the protection of Captain Ardel of the free trader *Blenheim*. Pull in the laser. Ardel has salvage claims on *Canar*, and would look dimly on any attempt to destroy her, or members of her crew."

The intercom crackled static for a while, and then Robinson said: "Alright, Aaron. Meet me at *Blenheim*. At least we can see this Nomelet. I want him to *know* me. I want him to know he has a *new* enemy."

"Please, Toma, let's see him together. Don't leave the *Swallow* until we get there. Agreed?"

"Agreed," she said, and signed off.

Ardel allowed both cutters to dock in *Blenheim*'s loading bay. When the two craft were secured the bay was sealed and pressurised. Lynch and Santa were met by a young ensign who introduced herself as Mayer, and together the small group proceeded to the bay airlock where they waited for Robinson to join them. When she arrived she looked haggard and apologetic, her cheeks stained with tears. She said nothing to them.

Mayer escorted them through the airlock and led the way up to a smaller bay where *Canar*'s surviving crew were being held. There were about twenty Calethar, and an equal number of mercenaries. Working among them were three human medics doing what they could for the wounded. To one side of the bay nestled a group of six beings, three human and three aliens. Mayer led them towards this group, and introduced the visitors to Captain Ardel, a short, paunchy man with a goatee.

"Pilots Robinson and Lynch, I assume, and . . ."

"Lieutenant Ranjeeka Patha," Santa said, introducing herself and firmly shaking the trader's plump hand. Ardel winced. He turned to the three Calethar.

"Ship-Captain Nomelet, War-Captain Teonar, and Helm-Captain Makarin."

The three Calethar bowed, the stiffness in their movement stemming from anatomy and not pride. Lynch and Santa bowed back. Robinson did not budge an inch. If the Calethar noticed the slight they gave no indication of it.

"And these," Ardel continued, waving at the two other humans present, "are my Executive Officer and the ship's purser." The humans all shook hands.

There was an embarrassed silence for a moment, then Nomelet said in Interlingua: "I'm sorry Captain Kidron did not survive. In battle it is always the objective to destroy your enemy, but now that the battle is over I would have liked to meet him."

Teonar and Makarin both made motions indicating agreement with their leader's sentiment.

"If he were alive," Santa said carefully, keeping one eye on Robinson, "I'm sure he would have been as interested in meeting you, Ship-Captain. When he spoke of you it was always with respect."

"We should adjourn to more comfortable quarters while we discuss our respective futures," Ardel said.

The Calethar bowed again, and Santa agreed for those from *Magpie*. Still Robinson said nothing. Her face was as blank as a wall. As the assembled beings followed Ardel out of the bay and into a long corridor, she said: "No one move, please. I would hate to kill the wrong one."

Lynch turned around despite the command, and saw her standing a little back from the group, her pistol in her hand.

"Toma, put the gun away. This is madness."

"Perhaps, Aaron. But don't push me. I don't want to have to hurt you."

Her eyes reflected no madness, just grief. He saw it had overwhelmed her whole being.

"It's over, Toma," he said as calmly as possible. He faintly heard the others shuffling behind him, trying not to draw attention to themselves.

"They are the enemy, Aaron."

"The battle is over, pilot," Nomelet said reasonably.

"The battle is never over, Ship-Captain," Robinson replied, her voice strangely respectful.

"We can't always be at war," Santa said. "Now is a good time to end this one."

"You don't understand, Santa." She looked pleadingly at Aaron. "They are my *first* hate. *You* understand, Aaron. Everything I do is for this, to kill Calethar."

Nomelet said nothing. He studied the humans around him, realising his fate now rested in the hands of his captors. He had never before been so powerless. The feeling was a new one.

"Lieutenant Robinson, please put down that weapon," Captain Ardel asked, his voice polite but firm. "This is my ship, and I have extended my personal protection to all the Calethar aboard *Blenheim*."

"I am genuinely sorry, Captain, but I have my duty."

"Toma, it is not *your* duty," Santa said. "These officers have surrendered."

"It's over, Toma!" Lynch said, his voice rising. "There's no point to any of this any more!"

Robinson did not flinch or change her expression. She slowly raised the weapon and aimed it at Nomelet. The

Calethar ship-captain lifted his chin, but made no other move and showed absolutely no fear.

"If you are going to kill me, human, make it clean." He pointed to his chest. "I have some vanity. Please, not in the head. My family would be distressed."

Robinson hesitated. Nomelet's reaction was not what she had expected. She breathed hard between gritted teeth and lowered her aim. She squeezed the trigger.

There was an ear-piercing, alien scream, and Teonar hurled herself at the pilot. Robinson shifted her aim slightly and fired. At that distance she could not miss. Lynch's face was splattered with blood, and the body of the war-captain, caught by the projectile while she was in mid-air, fell heavily against him. The weight of the large female threw him down, and he hit the floor with a jarring thump. Teonar slumped against his arms, her face contorted in shock, the left side of her upper chest and lower neck a nightmare of twisted, exposed muscle and pumping blood. Her lips parted and air escaped from between them, little bubbles of spittle squeezing between her long, sharp teeth. As Lynch slowly stood up, the alien's eyes rolled back in her head and she died.

Robinson, wide-eyed and in shock, levelled the weapon at Nomelet again. He moved forward but was restrained by Makarin. "Teonar," he said weakly, his eyes darkening, his head beginning to shake. He looked up at Robinson. "Murderer!" he cried. "Murderer!"

"*No!*" Robinson screamed, and straightened her arm to shoot again. There were voices and running footsteps coming from the corridor behind them.

Lynch opened his mouth to shout, moved one leg forward to get in the way, his body reacting automatically, but Santa was faster. She lashed out with a fist. He saw Robinson's head jerk back savagely then swing forward again. She collapsed to the floor.

Endings

Thirty-five survived out of *Magpie*'s original crew of 110. Bodies were recovered and sent into a long, looping orbit that would take their remains into Maluka's sun.

Captain Ardel, sensing further profit to be made, offered the Calethar survivors a ride back to Dramorath, their dead to accompany them for no extra fee. Nomelet agreed, because he had no choice. He now also suspected his chances of returning home were small if the Federation got hold of him. At least he would return to Dramorath a hero. The information about the border worlds he had been able to transmit before the battle with *Magpie* would guarantee his hold over the right to succeed Enilka as clan head. But with Teonar gone, it would be the hollowest of victories.

A Federation destroyer arrived within four days of the battle. Her captain, a young martinet named Balzac who had never seen one day of action, demanded Nomelet and his crew be handed over to him, together with what remained of both *Magpie* and *Canar Calethari*.

The freighter captains who had claimed salvage on the stricken vessels surrendered them reluctantly, but Ardel refused to hand over his Calethar guests. With his salvage claim lost they now represented his only chance of profit from the whole affair. It had also now become a matter of honour: the Calethar were under his protection.

"They have surrendered to *me*," he lied to Balzac. "I will not release them to you."

Balzac threatened all kinds of bureaucratic retribution, but Ardel believed the Navy had no legal case.

In frustration Balzac called on Lieutenant Patha for assistance. They met on *Magpie*'s bridge.

Santa had not been on the bridge since the day of the battle, and when she arrived she looked around curiously. The basic controls were operating again, the main screen had been repaired, the blood had been cleaned away. But there was no Kidron, no Kazin, no Danui. It no longer felt like it belonged to *Magpie*, but rather some other ship.

Her eyes rested on Balzac. He was lounging in the captain's couch. He was a thin man, dressed in officer's whites. He regarded her distastefully.

"Is that what passes for a uniform amongst pirates?" he asked.

Santa looked down at her loose trousers with six pockets, the sleeveless top that gave her maximum movement and comfort, the functional boots. Then she looked at the starched popinjay in front of her.

"That's Captain Kidron's chair," she said quietly.

"Kidron is dead," he replied lightly. "I don't think he has any further use for it."

"That is Captain Kidron's chair," she repeated darkly. She took a step towards him and he quickly stood up.

"I asked you here so we could work with each other on certain issues," he said hurriedly. "I was hoping together we could convince this Ardel fellow to hand his prisoners over to me."

"They are not his prisoners," said Santa. "They are his guests."

"This is semantics," Balzac said dismissively.

"The distinction is vital, Captain. Life in the frontier sector is basic, and there are few customs. But hospitality to strangers, even those who have been your enemy, is the oldest and strongest of them. While Nomelet and his people are Ardel's guests they are under his protection."

"I want you to argue my case for me," Balzac said.

"There is nothing I can do."

"I want you to *try* –"

"There is nothing I can do."

"This is getting us nowhere!" Balzac snapped.

"I agree. If we have finished I will get back to my duties." Santa turned to leave.

"I gave you no permission to go."

Santa stopped. She turned on her heel and glared at Balzac. "Say that again."

Balzac was not intimidated. He pulled a piece of paper from a jacket pocket and handed it to her.

"That is a copy of an agreement signed between your dead captain and the Federation. As you can see, it stipulates quite clearly that until *Magpie* returns those items and weapons obtained from Diarmaid she is registered as a Federation naval vessel, and her crew are Federation naval personnel." Balzac sneered. "Do you recognise your captain's signature, *Lieutenant* Patha?"

He gave her time to read the document then snatched it back.

"By the way, I have a report on my desk which mentions you struck a fellow officer – a fellow *naval* officer – Lieutenant Toma Robinson."

"I was stopping her from murdering a defenceless prisoner –"

"I am not interested in the details. In fact, I'm not greatly interested in the report. I'd even be willing to 'lose' it in exchange for co-operation between you and me on certain matters . . ."

He let the sentence hang.

Santa was thinking furiously. She realised she had to make a decision, and quickly, about what to do next.

"By the way, where is Lieutenant Robinson? I haven't met her yet. Perhaps she would be more willing to assist me in my pursuit of my duties."

"On Maluka," Santa said tightly. "It was decided it was best for all concerned she not be on *Magpie* or *Blenheim*."

"I may pay her a visit, then," he said cheerily.

Santa shook her head. *Enough is enough.* She turned to leave.

"Lieutenant!" Balzac cried. "I still haven't given you permission to –"

She was gone before he could finish.

Santa found Lynch and without explaining anything told him they had to get to *Blenheim* as fast as possible. Lynch could tell from her tone she was in no mood to argue. Five minutes later they were in *Lark* and heading for the freighter.

Captain Ardel greeted them in his cabin.

"To what do I owe this unexpected visit?"

"Captain Balzac hasn't given up trying to get his hands on your guests," Santa said. "The longer you stay the more likely he is to get what he wants."

"How?"

"Nomelet officially surrendered to *Magpie*."

Ardel shrugged. "That makes no difference. Captain Kidron is –"

"Balzac showed me an agreement Kidron must have signed with the Federation just before we started on our last voyage. Briefly, *Magpie* is a naval vessel. In effect, Nomelet surrendered to the Navy."

Ardel and Lynch were dumbfounded.

"One effect of this agreement was to make *Magpie*'s crew naval personnel." She smiled grimly at Lynch. "We're both naval officers, Aaron. How's that for a turn?"

"Then you must co-operate with Balzac –" Ardel began.

Santa shook her head. "I'm mutinying. Have you a spare berth?"

Ardel laughed. "Wouldn't that put Balzac's nose out of joint! I would be honoured to have you on board *Blenheim*!"

Lynch said nothing. Santa turned to him. "Aaron?"

"I can't join you, Santa." He shrugged. "I don't know yet where my future lies. It isn't with the Navy, it isn't working for my uncle, but I don't want to be an outlaw, either."

Santa nodded.

"We'll leave now," Ardel said. He shook Lynch's hand. "Live well, Lieutenant Lynch, and don't forget my offer to come and work for me. *Blenheim* can always use a good pilot."

Santa walked back with Lynch to the loading bay and *Lark*. They reached the cutter's gangladder when someone cried out: "Aaron Lynch!"

Lynch looked up, saw Nomelet and Makarin near the loading bay hatch. Makarin hurried forward. "Captain Ardel has just explained the situation to us," he said. "Thank you both for what you have done."

He grasped Lynch's hands between his claws. "I hope your gods look after you, Aaron Lynch," Makarin said. "Your courage and intelligence deserve reward."

"May your gods look after you, Helm-Captain. I'm sorry you're not returning home on the bridge of your own ship. It cannot be easy for you."

"I am still breathing, and there will be other ships."

Lynch turned to Santa. There were so many things he wanted to say, but they simply smiled at each other.

Lynch started up the gangladder, stopped to look across at Nomelet. The proud Calethar nodded gently, then left. Lynch stared after him, wondering if they would ever meet again.

"You must hurry, Aaron," Santa said softly at the bottom of the gangladder.

Lynch looked down. "Goodbye, my friend."

He climbed into *Lark* and closed the hatch behind him.

As Lynch piloted *Lark* back to *Magpie* it tore at his heart to see her so badly wounded. Large sections of her were still open to space, and where the hull was intact the signs of battle had gouged and scarred her skin.

It was at that moment he knew with a fierce certainty his future lay with the battered privateer.

He promised himself that someday, somehow, he would bring her back to the frontier.

Magpie would fly again.